Amalie Berlin lives with her family and her critters in Southern Ohio, and writes quirky and independent characters for Mills & Boon Medical Romance. She likes to buck expectations with unusual settings and situations, and believes humour can be used powerfully to illuminate the truth—especially when juxtaposed against intense emotions. Love is stronger and more satisfying when your partner can make you laugh through the times when you don't have the luxury of tears.

Born and raised just outside Toronto, Ontario, **Amy Ruttan** fled the big city to settle down with the country boy of her dreams. After the birth of her second child Amy was lucky enough to realise her lifelong dream of becoming a romance author. When she's not furiously typing away at her computer she's mum to three wonderful children, who use her as a personal taxi and chef.

BACK IN
DR XENAKIS' ARMS

AMALIE BERLIN

A DATE WITH
DR MOUSTAKAS

AMY RUTTAN

MILLS & BOON

First Published in Great Britain 2018
by Mills & Boon, an imprint of HarperCollins*Publishers*
1 London Bridge Street, London, SE1 9GF

Back in Dr Xenakis' Arms © 2018 by Amalie Berlin

A Date with Dr Moustakas © 2018 by Amy Ruttan

ISBN: 978-0-263-93360-4

MIX
Paper from
responsible sources
FSC® C007454

This book is produced from independently certified FSC™ paper
to ensure responsible forest management.
For more information visit www.harpercollins.co.uk/green.

Printed and bound in Spain
by CPI, Barcelona

BACK IN
DR XENAKIS' ARMS

AMALIE BERLIN

MILLS & BOON

To Robin Gianna, who dropped everything
and drove for over an hour to spend a day
at Panera with me when Ares and Erianthe were
refusing to take shape. Without her, this book
would've been 'Less Than'. Love you, lady.

To Annie O'Neil, Tina Beckett and Amy Ruttan.
You three can make any project fun, and I'm always
a better writer for having worked with you. <3

PROLOGUE

Ten years ago...

ARES'S TIRES SPUN gravel as he tore from the access road into the parking lot at Mythelios's only airport, but they couldn't compete with the churning of his stomach.

At the edge of the tarmac, he slammed into Park and launched himself from the car.

Please don't let me be too late.

His heart, still beating hard enough to bruise, hadn't slowed for a single second since his best friend, Theo, had called him twenty minutes earlier in a blind panic—Theo's parents were sending his little sister away. Today. Right now. Or maybe a few minutes ago if time wasn't on his side.

He'd thought he would have more time to spend with her before they took that step—the step he now couldn't even imagine why he'd agreed to. Her father had said nothing about Erianthe leaving the next morning...

He burst through the chain-link gate along the back of the hangar where all the partners of Mopaxeni Shipping kept their private planes. Gravel became tarmac as he pounded through the baking waves rising from black pavement. Even as fast as he could move, he might as well have been running through quicksand; every yard of effort seemed to return an inch of sluggish distance.

The same threat had been lobbed at Erianthe by her parents when they'd reacted just to the myriad ways she had rebelled. The new millennium might be well underway, but they were still firmly rooted in the past—strict, traditional, image-obsessed Greek Orthodox billionaires, who'd decided that the best place to hide the shameful pregnancy of their teenage daughter was in a convent.

Theo had never believed they'd actually send her away, but Ares had known for nearly eighteen hours. He'd just thought there would be more time before she left. She wasn't even showing yet.

It was something else Theo didn't know about—like the yearlong secret relationship they'd carried out to protect the dynamic of their group, their *real* family—the neglected children of Mopaxeni. A fail-safe in case things went haywire between them.

Theo didn't know it was Ares's fault his little sister was basically being exiled to another country, hidden away, with the adoption of her child forced on her by their "loving" parents. He thought his parents were sending Eri away to boarding school, so she would avoid distractions and concentrate on her studies.

He rounded the hangar and saw the plane already pulled out, door open, stairs still attached. The long black sedan her father often drove sat between him and the plane, but the darkened windows on the car blocked him from seeing whether they were still inside or already onboard.

How had Dimitri Nikolaides talked him into agreeing to give her up? To give up his child?

It had seemed like the responsible decision when Ares had gone to her father, but now all he could feel was panic.

He pushed harder, his lungs burning, unable to keep up with the demands he was putting on them in the already sweltering morning sunshine.

"You're both too young to be parents."

"You'll hurt her worse if you're married by the time you get bored with her."

"She's only sixteen."

Now, seeing it all so rapidly come to pass, it couldn't be clearer that he'd been wrong. *So* wrong...so many mistakes. He was losing her—he was losing them both. And then he'd lose the rest of them too.

The door stood open—there was still time. He'd tell her father he wouldn't give up his rights to his own child. And if that didn't work, he'd knock Dimitri out and they'd run. They'd run away, just like she'd begged him to. There had to be *somewhere* they could go.

Rounding the sedan, he'd reached out for the stair rails when a blur of movement in his peripheral vision caused him to slow down. Something impacted on him before he could turn to look back, and sent him sprawling onto the sizzling pavement. Weight and heat.

The air blasted from his burning lungs. Large hands—more than one set—grabbed his upper arms and hauled him up before he could get enough air sucked in to say anything, to do anything. To shout for her.

Guards. Dimitri had brought guards.

Digging in his heels, Ares tried to twist free, but air was still an issue. They began dragging him roughly back around the car, away from her. She must be on the plane.

So close. He was so close.

The adrenaline that had kept him going could hold up for only so long. Eventually all he had left to keep fighting, to let the girl he loved know he was there, was his voice.

"Erianthe!" he shouted, over and over, his eyes locked on the darkened portal into the private jet.

They didn't stop dragging him toward the rear of the

car. They pulled, and he staggered backward still, toward the hangar.

He shouted again. He screamed for her. His vision wobbled from the forced locomotion, but it always returned to the only place of hope he could fixate on.

His heart stopped, then surged into the stratosphere as he finally saw her, there in the doorway. She'd heard him.

Shrugging out of her father's hands, she launched herself down the stairs and ran straight for him. The shining curtain of her dark hair flew out behind her, and as she got closer he could see how pale she was but for the redness around her midnight eyes.

Closer.

The men stopped dragging him.

Closer.

They let go.

With newfound strength he lunged forward, running to meet her, arms outstretched. If he could just hold her…

With all these people, even the hope he'd clung to couldn't convince him now that there was any chance they could get away today.

If he could apologize, he'd have that to hold in his heart until he could find a way to get to her.

As he neared, ready to grab her, her face contorted. The tears he'd guessed would be there became rivers down her cheeks and she skidded to a stop, drawing her right arm back in a full swing.

A sharp blast of pain radiated from his left cheek and his head snapped to the side, sending him back a step to maintain his balance.

She'd *hit* him?

It took a few seconds for the situation to make sense through the expanding hollow filling his chest.

"Eri…" He said her name, the words he'd practiced in the car evaporating in the heat of her stare.

"I trusted you!" She half sobbed, half screamed, smacking away his hand as he instinctively reached for her. "I thought you were different, but you're just like *him*."

"No…" The word came out because it was the only one he could wrestle through his closing throat. He *wasn't* like Dimitri Nikolaides, but he'd been tricked by him, his fears twisted, his weakness exposed. Made to doubt. "We can go—"

Her short, broken laugh stopped his words dead and ripped at his insides.

"I hate you." The words, almost a whisper, hit him in the chest like a cannon blast.

She *hated* him.

Dimitri reached his daughter and began hauling her back toward the plane and onto the flight to a country Ares couldn't name because they hadn't told him. Somewhere far enough away that no one here would know about the baby—that was all he knew.

No hands grabbed him this time, but his feet still stayed glued to the ground.

"I will never forgive you for this!"

He wanted to say he loved her, but how could he say that now? Why would she believe him?

"I'm sorry." He said the words, the only words he could find, and repeated them again and again.

I will come for you.

The words swam up—the words he meant to utter but couldn't say to her. Not now, when the eyes that had always looked upon him with sweetness boiled over with such rage he could barely breathe.

The men who had been dragging him away now joined

their boss in wrestling a struggling Erianthe back up the stairs.

The last words she screamed at him would still ring in his ears long after the plane departed. Because she was right.

This was all his fault.

CHAPTER ONE

THE LAST TIME Dr. Erianthe Nikolaides had set foot on the island of her birth she'd been barely sixteen, pregnant and betrayed by the boy she'd loved. Ten years on it had taken the earth actually moving and the request of her adoptive brother to pull her back.

Weeks before, Mythelios had been struck by a strong earthquake and Theo had sent up the beacon to call them home to staff the only medical facility on the island, which they were all tied to. But Theo had urged her to stay and finish her medical degree before she answered the call, so her arrival had been regrettably postponed.

The heat of the July sun baked her dark hair like coals on the back of her neck, sucking the strength from her so that every step toward the lovely three-story stucco building housing the Mythelios Free Clinic became a marathon. That was why her knees wobbled and she barely had her suitcases under control. Nothing else. Not the weight of her past and her secrets. Not the rock in her middle that came from knowing Theo Nikolaides wasn't the only man she'd be seeing today.

Ares Xenakis had received the same call to come home that she had. Theo had summoned home the whole merry band of the pampered children of Mopaxeni Shipping, forgotten until they messed up—the men who funded and regularly staffed the clinic and Erianthe, who had nothing to offer but her skills. She'd cut all contact with her parents years ago, and that had included her trust fund.

Her training had been officially completed only last week, and she was late arriving to the disaster. She was that final piece of the family they'd forged when they'd still been counting their ages in single digits. The family that would be broken forever if the others ever found out how her seventeenth year had ended.

She clanged her way through the main entrance, her resolve to take her position at her brother's side stronger than her ability to control the four-wheeled storage system erratically rolling behind her. One wheel caught at the door frame and her suitcase snagged just as the door swung closed on it. *Perfection.* It would be really great if one part of this journey could go smoothly.

She put some weight into a tug and the case snapped free, making her stagger backward into the clinic, an expletive bouncing off the teeth she'd clenched shut. By the time she turned around, every eye in the packed reception area had fixed on her with the kind of wariness that said they expected calamity to accompany such cacophony.

If the heat had left any extra air in her lungs, she would've laughed. The only harm she'd ever caused on Mythelios had been to herself, by trusting the wrong boy and not running away the first time her father had uttered the word *convent.*

The urge to laugh evaporated like water in the summer sun, but Erianthe tried to cover it with a smile, hoping to make a better impression on her future patients than that.

She'd had a week to prepare to see Ares again, to prepare for the first run-in with her treacherous parents, but she no longer had that wellspring of rage that had fueled her daydreams of vengeance in the first couple years. Now she had no idea what she should say to any of them, or even how she should feel. Ten years was a long time.

Focus on today.

The door swung shut, clamping off the blast furnace her years in England had made her weak to, and taking away the light her sun-blinded eyes needed to see.

She pinched the bridge of her nose and breathed slowly out.

No, today was too big. She had to focus on this minute, this second. Not one of her three betrayers was presently there. She didn't have to know how to deal with them right at this second.

It wasn't so much that she saw someone in front of her—her eyes were still closed and obstructed by her hand—but she felt a presence in her personal bubble and opened her eyes.

"Dr. Nikolaides."

The woman standing before her smiled, not waiting for any answer, just relieving her of her cases with one hand and using the other to steer the visibly travel-bedraggled doctor somewhere that *wouldn't* affect the clinic's image.

"Your brother is with a patient, so just have a seat in here and I'll send him shortly."

She clicked on a light, allowing Erianthe to see the small office she'd been ushered to—and the woman herself. Friendly, but firm, with a touch of something motherly about her—not that Erianthe had much experience with what *that* was like—and just enough silver hair threaded through her ebony curls to give her gravitas. To make her somehow emanate comfort as she carried on speaking in a calm tone.

Maybe it was just that Erianthe was no longer a spectacle, disrupting the waiting room, but she felt a little better. Less as if the sky was trying to press her into the rocky dirt.

The woman added something about coffee and departed, leaving Erianthe to fold into the closest chair—which happened to be one that spun.

Petra. She'd said her name was Petra.

Goodness, she had to get it together. What kind of doctor took half a minute to process something simple like a person's name? A name she'd expected to hear, no less. The wonder woman Theo often raved about. *Petra.* Who had gone to fetch the magical elixir that would sharpen her buzzing senses and keep her from appearing like a bigger catastrophe than the quake had been.

The cool, supple leather of the chair reached through her light linen trousers, giving another tactile wink of comfort, soothing against the heat she'd absorbed, enough for her to notice that her head ached in a way that said it had probably been throbbing for a while.

The office door stood open and she swiveled the chair to watch through the aperture, silently counting breaths until the roar of memories she'd been trying to ignore since Theo's call faded back a little.

The will that had carried her through those first months after her banishment forced it into something closer to a buzz. No, not a buzz—though it was just as discordant. Like her head was a radio receiver.

She stood as if at the edge of the signal for two overlapping stations—oldies and current hits. Annoying. Distorting. Confusing. Impossible to ignore. Because she knew the old song better, and it broke through the new one just enough that she wasn't quite sure which song she was actually listening to. She could walk around in the present— she'd learned the lyrics—but the old song she knew by heart.

During the first two years after she'd been gone, the balance had been different. Her days had been filled with the oldies station, but now and then something new had broken through. Eventually she'd forced herself to learn the new words, to sing the song of today, and the balance had gradually shifted. She'd studied harder, because a mind full of calculus and physics had less room to wallow in the terrible injustice and loss of what had happened to her.

A corridor of bright light opened across the floor of the reception area, broken by a lumbering, misshapen shadow as the door swung closed, followed by the sounds of exertion. A call for help came from a rusty voice, and those she could see sitting in Reception turned worried eyes to her through the office door.

No one was out there to help. And they *did* see her as a doctor, no matter her clumsy, inept, socially awkward arrival.

Strength she'd been faking the whole day appeared, and Erianthe launched herself from the chair and out of the office. A man crouched on the floor beside a pregnant woman who leaned heavily on her left hip as she pressed at the right side of her swollen belly with her other hand. Six months? Seven? Less if it was multiples.

She'd made her occupation treating and helping pregnant women in distress, but when childbirth came unnaturally there was another feeling—something that twisted her insides and made her second-guess her career choice. Just for a second.

Erianthe knelt beside her, introducing herself and asking the man, "Did she fall onto the floor?"

"No. I put her down. You're the baby doctor?" the man asked, reaching for her arm as if touching her made her more real to him, more of a comfort, and that conveyed all the trust and hope he was putting into her by giving this woman into her care.

The baby doctor. Theo must have told them she was coming.

"Yes. I'm an obstetrician. Tell me what happened."

Just then Petra came out of somewhere with a mug of something steamy and a plate in her hand—but, seeing Erianthe kneeling beside a patient, she put them down on her reception desk and ran to get a wheelchair.

God bless her, the woman really was the dynamo Theo had promised. How had she forgotten about Petra?

The three of them got the patient transferred to the chair and Petra took control, steering them all toward the office Erianthe had just vacated and leaving them there to get files and supplies.

"You're having pain?" Erianthe asked the woman, who nodded and pressed on her right side.

"Tell me about the pain. How did it start? Can you describe how it hurts?"

Though it was difficult for the woman to talk, within a couple short sentences Erianthe was able to determine that she was likely not dealing with a normal—if premature—birth situation.

"You were shifted to your left hip on the floor, so does it hurt more when you lie on your right?"

She took the woman's wrist to track her pulse rate, while listening to the patient describe symptoms she had already expected: increased nausea, but only after the onset of pain, which had coincided with the sudden onset of bowel issues…

Petra returned with a familiar face in tow.

"Cailey!"

Erianthe hadn't seen her onetime good friend since leaving the island, back when they'd become close because her mother had worked in the Nikolaides household. Cailey was someone Erianthe had always missed but had lost because she hadn't been able to think of a way to talk to anyone *and* maintain her secrets back then.

Still couldn't—not really. The first thing she wanted to do upon seeing her was confess, clear the air, but that kind of confession would only throw more debris around. They'd all choke on it.

It was hardly the time for even a proper greeting, let alone a confession, so Erianthe grabbed Cailey by the shoulders for a quick hug—she'd offer to help with the wedding when they had a few minutes to catch up. Then she got on with it, because that was what the moment demanded.

"I need temperature and blood pressure. She's presenting with symptoms of appendicitis. Do we have a proper examination room? What about imaging equipment? I'd like to do some tests. There's a lab, right?"

"Appendicitis?" the man asked, the wobble in his words conveying the worry of a husband and father, not just a friend. Which she should have expected if she'd given it a moment of thought. Mythelios was still quite traditional, even beyond the standards of the rest of Greek culture. And he was a good husband, if the deep furrow of his brows and the amount of lip sweat meant anything.

"That means there is an inflammation in her appendix. We're going to check it out very well. Then we'll know more about what we need to do to treat her. How long has the pain been going on?"

Over the next few minutes Cailey confirmed the low-grade fever that spoke of infection, and the husband spoke of having worn his wife down and made her come to the clinic after a night of increasingly unbearable pain.

"Who is our surgeon?" Erianthe would be happy when

she got up to speed well enough to keep from alarming her patients by questioning the treatment options available here.

"Dr. Xenakis has the most experience," Cailey answered.

As hard as Erianthe had worked to know as little as possible about Ares, she did at least know his specialty was emergency medicine, not surgery.

She leaned in to speak quietly to Cailey. "No general surgeon on the staff right now?"

"Ares has a great deal of experience. He got it in the field, with that unit he's with. The one that travels to isolated areas to help people."

Something she hadn't been aware of. Ares was with an outreach charity? That didn't strike her as fitting his always larger-than-life personality.

"Is he here?"

As if she didn't know...

"He is. Let's get Jacinda into a room," Petra interjected, once again taking charge. "I'll send him in. Dr. Nikolaides, do you want to change your clothes? We have extra scrubs in the corner cabinet there. Just close the door after us and change. We'll be in the rear examination room."

Not exactly the way she'd pictured her first day back. She had planned to say hello and tell her brother that because she felt weird about interrupting his new love nest with Cailey she was going to stay elsewhere, all the while carefully avoiding seeing Ares with the ninja-like sneaking skills she possessed only in her delusional imagination.

Now she was going into surgery with him. Another perfect point to her first day.

"You're going to get her into CT?" she asked, snapping back into motion before Cailey could escape.

Cailey paused, the expression on her face reticent, regretful. "We don't have a working CT scanner at the moment. Ours is on the fritz after the earthquake. I figured you'd want a CBC to check for infection?"

She waited for Erianthe to answer, but Petra kept going with Jacinda.

The CT scan wasn't absolutely necessary—doctors had been correctly diagnosing appendicitis decades before imaging became available—but it was like a safety net. And today they would be working without a net.

"Yes to the blood panel," she answered, weighing her options.

Flying in and out of the island was still difficult, and time was of the essence with appendicitis. She'd consult with Ares, then make the call.

Ares.

She didn't need the warning flares her body was sending up to remind her how emotionally loaded his name was. She couldn't even think it without those feelings of outrage and heartbreak rushing into her mouth, metallic and bitter.

Dr. Xenakis was safer. Easier on her fraying nerves.

Having something to do would help her, as it had always helped her. And helping her first patient on Mythelios would be even better. Filling up the hole that had opened in her chest with honorable duty.

The cabinet's supply of extra scrubs needed restocking, and she made a mental note to see if an order had been made. They'd probably been hit hard in the days after the quake, when patient clothing had been ruined either in accidents or during emergency treatment and scrubs had been given out to wear instead.

She found a set of bottoms she could wear, due to the horrors of a drawstring waist, paired it with a tentlike top, then hit her suitcase for better shoes, a hairband and a stethoscope. Scrubs weren't *meant* to flatter a person, and she hadn't come home to win some kind of fashion award.

Later she'd let herself feel guilty for being glad someone needed her help. Having any kind of focus would let her meet Ares on a professional front, put all that personal stuff away—or at least make it clear to her brain what was important to the Erianthe of today: work. Personal emotional wounds, no matter how grievous, couldn't bleed out or cause sepsis.

She'd worked cordially and professionally with both lukewarm ex-boyfriends and jerks she'd rather kick in the face than speak to, and she had *never* lost her cool with them. Even when there had been good reason to lose her cool. This would be no different. He was no different from any other colleague.

Closing the office door, she headed the way she'd been directed, grabbing her coffee and snack in transit, and practically inhaling half before she arrived at the patient's room.

She reached for the knob of the exam room door, but before her hand closed on it Theo appeared at her side and immediately grabbed her in a quick hug that required she hold her arms out in a wide V to avoid dousing him in coffee.

Ever affectionate, even after the years of absence and neglect she'd forced on them both by staying so far away that his only choice in seeing her had been to come to *her*, this small display of affection when she was already worked up caused her throat to constrict. There was nothing she'd have liked better than to take shelter in the arms of someone she knew would always have her back. If she ever let herself ask.

It galled her how close to the surface those old feelings had risen since she'd gotten off the boat.

Turning her head, she kissed his cheek—something she *could* do—then stepped abruptly back. "Careful—you'll end up with coffee down your back."

"Glad you're here," he said, in that laughing way of his.

"We'll catch up after, shall we? Are you up to seeing her? Do you need anything from me?"

He was worried about her—and probably the patient too. Theo *always* worried about her, and one thing she hoped to accomplish by coming home was relieving that worry without burdening him with the secrets she'd hidden from everyone. Seeing this first patient to the best possible outcome would be a good start.

She smiled, but then it wasn't hard to smile at her almost inhumanly good-natured brother. "I didn't walk here, or cross loads of time zones. I'm completely fine. I'm waiting for the blood work to get back to call it officially, but I'd be very shocked if there are no signs of infection. If she needs surgery, then I'm assisting."

He considered her for the swiftest second, then nodded. "Whatever you say. You're the only obstetrician on the island since last spring, so you're automatically picking up a full load of patients. We stay pretty busy, and we're always looking for more people, but you're going to need to hire a midwife and nurses. We'll talk about that later."

More bits of information to file away for later. Good. All good things. Fill her head with work—best thing for her.

Work had always saved her—or had done since the convent. The shock to her system from being sent away from everything and everyone she knew had helped kill the rebellious bent of her teenage years, but it had been the desire to provide for her child that had turned her life and her attitude around. And afterward study had been the only thing she'd had to cling to. She'd developed steady hands, a steady voice and eventually steady thoughts.

But seeing Ares again would hurt, and even walking into a room he might already be in felt like reaching into an oven without gloves on—stupid, dangerous, damaging...

She knocked and entered. Her eyes sought every corner

of the room, and when they failed to find Ares anywhere, they found their focus instead.

Cailey had peeled the paper backing off a bandage and applied it to the crook of Jacinda's arm; the blood was already drawn.

The husband hovered, tears in his eyes.

Her patient, now in a hospital gown, lay curled on her left side. When she moved, and another pang hit her, her face crumpled in a way that drew attention to how young she was—just on the other side of twenty. But she didn't cry out. She was not giving an inch to her pain, with the will of someone who'd already survived more than this could amount to in her life.

Five minutes later Erianthe had double-checked for signs of early labor, gotten up to speed on her patient's medical history, and was gingerly palpating her right side in the waist region when Ares burst in.

She'd almost started to relax, but that ended the second he arrived. He said nothing, and she didn't look over at him, but she felt him there—like the tingle of power in the air after a lightning strike.

Out of the corner of her eye she could see his height, knew him to be taller than he'd been before, but couldn't bring herself to look at him directly yet.

"I'm Dr. Xenakis."

A pang vibrated in her belly, like a gong calling every cell in her body to attention.

That voice wasn't the voice that had whispered in her ear, murmured the sweet, artless words of a lust-drunk teenager, it was deeper and more resonant. Different. But the way he spoke…

She'd never have mistaken his voice for another. There was a sort of roundness to his speech, an almost magical way of making simple words luxurious, like things you wanted to touch, to wrap yourself up in.

It took her aback, and if she was going to function at all, she had to stay in the present, not go back to when she'd believed him to be the very essence of warmth, love and safety. Better to stay here, where she knew his promises had been knit with strands of bitter lies and had shattered under the weight of a few firm words.

No protection. No safety. No love.

It was different, because she knew better now.

The others—Theo, Chris, Deakin and all the professional organizations who had licensed him—trusted Ares with patients, and so would she. Because she had no choice. And it wasn't as if she had to count on him tomorrow. Just today. She wouldn't fall into that well of longing if she looked at him.

That little reminder made it possible, even a little easy, to finally look at him.

"Dr. Nikolaides said we had a—" His words came to a sudden, jarring halt when he focused on her.

Different, her mind reminded her simplistically. *Hairy* was the next descriptor. He'd always been polished, with his dark hair cut every three weeks to keep the curls from taking over. Now his hair was long. Long enough to wear in a ponytail at the back of his head. But it was the beard that really brought the difference into focus. She'd never seen a doctor, let alone a surgeon, with such thick facial hair.

The air around him still said Ares, and his eyes—those vibrant green eyes that made her hate the first leaves of spring—were the same. But nothing else matched the Wildman in Scrubs she saw now.

Still, her hands shook. Her breath shook. Her heart and belly and all parts in the middle... For a second she even thought it might be a late aftershock hitting the island, but no one else looked alarmed or off-kilter. Just her. And him—staring at her with cavernous silence.

"Appendicitis." Erianthe forced the word out, then took Jacinda's hand, turning her attention back to her patient.

He's just another doctor. Just another colleague. Pretend he's Dr. Stevenson, the brilliant jerk from your last hospital.

What would she say to Stevenson?

She'd be bold. Certain. She *was* certain.

"It'll take another ten minutes for the leukocyte count to come back, but it's a formality. We should start prepping the surgical suite."

Another glance confirmed he'd gotten stuck in…what? The past? A desire to run? Dealing with the juxtaposition of seeing her again over a heavily pregnant belly when the last time he'd seen her she'd been carrying his own child?

"Dr. Nikolaides?" Jacinda's voice contained enough alarm to reclaim all Eri's focus. "Your hand is shaking."

Damn. She smiled at Jacinda, even if it was a dodge in order to keep from talking about the fact that her focus was split. It *shouldn't* be split. And it wouldn't be. This event would pass—she'd force it down and contain it.

"It's just a need for coffee."

"Not because you're worried for the baby?"

That she could be truthful about. "You're far enough along that anesthesia is safe for both of you, and we're going to take the very best care of you and your baby. I don't want you to worry."

She let go of Jacinda's hand and got her coffee again, tipped it to take a big drink with a hand she willed steady by mentally playing through the steps of the coming procedure. Force of will and work always saved her.

Ares finally started moving and stepped around the table to the right of Erianthe. She eased higher up, to keep plenty of space between them, but despite that she still felt him enter her personal bubble, as distinctly as the whiff of ozone in the first minutes of a hard summer rain.

"Where is the pain?" he asked Jacinda, and then followed that up with all the other questions he needed to ask in order to make his own assessment.

Not a criticism, she reminded herself. Any good doctor would do the same. And Dr. Stevenson would've handled it far more condescendingly.

She stayed largely silent and focused on Jacinda. If she wanted to stay with her patient during the surgery, she and Dr. Xenakis needed to get over this. Be completely professional and in the present. *Be strangers.*

The way he looked, she could almost believe it. Ten years was a long time—they practically *were* strangers. Or at least she was a stranger to him. Even the strongest woman couldn't go through all that and come out unchanged.

"It's hurting too far up," he said, somewhat quietly. "It's not appendicitis."

No accusation—just a statement. But it was an incorrect diagnosis on his part.

"In the third trimester," she said, surprising herself by how level her voice stayed, "the appendix gets shoved out of the pelvic cradle by the growing baby."

Both patient and husband turned their gaze to Ares, and his silence forced her to look once more at him.

She ignored the pang that turned to a swirling in her insides when she looked into his beautiful eyes.

Now he'd got past that brick wall his words had run into upon seeing her, the set of his mouth in that Wildman beard proved he felt the strain of their reunion as well.

"I assure you that I've seen this condition several times, Dr. Xenakis."

He didn't simply watch her now, and his frowning stare

could mean lots of things—but none of them were good. Most likely his frown meant he was questioning her diagnosis.

Shoving his hand roughly to the back of his neck, he rubbed like it was on fire. "Would you come with me to brief our anesthesiologist, Dr. Nikolaides?"

No.

Her body shrieked the word along every nerve ending, and she knew she'd gone pale by the funny looks she was receiving. So much for trying to remain calm and appear as though there was no liquid panic rushing through her veins.

She nodded—an act of will—and once that domino fell, others followed.

Everything was fine. She should be happy they had an anesthesiologist. Relief was the only acceptable emotion right now. Forget the rest.

"I'd like Cailey to stay with them," she managed to say, and waited for Ares to fetch her soon-to-be sister-in-law, giving her a moment to reassure her patient again and project the confidence she would surely start to feel any second now.

Cailey brought the lab results with her, and Erianthe peeked at three numbers before giving a couple of quick instructions, then following Ares.

Just another room. Just another doctor. Everything was normal. This walk *didn't* lead to a gas chamber. Just to a conference with another colleague.

Having never come to the clinic before, there was nothing for her to do but follow Ares to the anesthesiologist's office.

At the end of a short corridor, he opened a door and held it for her.

Polite. Common courtesy. *Normal.*

She stepped in.

Tension in her shoulders spread to her chest as she scanned the unlit room. No desk. No people. Two bunk beds.

Not an office.

This must be the on-call room for the doctors. Her thought train derailed there. Rounding on him, she reached for the doorknob, her body registering her unease before she thought of a rational response.

"Erianthe?"

"There's no anesthesiologist," she blurted out.

He stood in her way, and that was enough to make her draw back from the door and her only escape route.

"I've never done an appendectomy on a pregnant woman. You want me to go with your diagnosis—I get it. She's in a lot of pain, and her appendix could rupture before we get her to Athens. But—"

"Where is the anesthesiologist?" she interrupted, cutting her hand through the air to make him focus, because knowing he wasn't about to attack her didn't make being alone with him feel any less dangerous.

"Not here. They called him in already. He's on his way. Before he gets here, tell me exactly how many of these surgeries you've been involved in. I've performed emergency appendectomies, but none where the appendix wasn't in the lower right quadrant. We don't have a CT scan to work from, so we don't have a lot of options, but if your diagnosis is incorrect, this is unnecessary surgery. It puts her and the baby at risk. And the weight of that call is on *me*."

There it was—the elephant in the room, its neon hide impossible to ignore. Words flew out of her. "Do you really think that I, of all people, would put a baby in needless danger?"

The color drained from his cheeks, confirming that her words had struck right where she'd intended. He stepped

back from her, opening up a space that had suddenly become tight and toxic.

"No." It took him several seconds to make that one-word
answer, and in this small room she couldn't help but look
at him, watch him, try to read him—not that she'd done
so well in reading him when she'd been young and foolish
enough to trust him.

CHAPTER TWO

THE SATISFACTION OF seeing Ares blanch came and went in a single sluggish heartbeat. Fighting about the past wouldn't do anything to help this situation, and Jacinda and her baby deserved one hundred percent of their focus and attention. Now wasn't the time to talk about their own child.

Erianthe tried again. "I've assisted before in this type of surgery twice. I've observed another couple times. I'm not a surgeon, but I perform C-sections and I've done surgery rotations. If we had any other option, then I'd say send her off the island, but you saw the level of her white cell count. It's possible the damned thing has already ruptured. It has to come out as soon as possible. We cannot wait."

He held out his hand for the results and she handed them over. It wasn't so much that she wanted to look at him, but there was nowhere else to look in order to divine what he was thinking.

Resignation was clearly written in the grim set of his lips, the furrow of his brow. "Tell me where the appendix tends to get shoved. Is the surgery usually performed with an ultrasound to guide?"

She shook her head, then waved a hand. "Imaging *is* used, but not usually ultrasound. I think we could do that, though, if you wanted to get a look at it."

He nodded. "Have you ever assisted in this surgery without the patient being pregnant? Can you tell me what differences occur between the two surgeries?"

He was going to do it. Thank goodness. "I can tell you what I know, but it's been years since I saw a run-of-the-mill appendectomy."

"When?"

"My first year in residency."

"How are you with an ultrasound?"

That she could give him confidence with. "Excellent."

"That's your other job—assisting and maneuvering the wand so we can get and keep a visual on the appendix until I understand what I need to do."

"I can do that."

"I'm trusting you," he said—which shouldn't have made cold shoot through her, but did.

She couldn't bring herself to say anything, to pretend the sentiment was reciprocated. It wasn't—except probably medically. Whatever might have been said or done between them, she didn't trust him personally. She was just taking the only available exit from a burning building right now, and that was what made her stomach pitch and roll like a dinghy on the front edge of a tsunami.

"The anesthesiologist—do we know if he's put under a pregnant woman before? It's not as deep a sleep. And there are frequent issues with reflux, so we need a good proton pump inhibitor."

He opened the door and stepped out, one curt hand motion beckoning her to follow after him.

Inside thirty minutes they had Jacinda in the surgical suite, were both scrubbed in and had her under. Erianthe kept the anesthesiologist busier than normal, demanding that the heart rate for both mother and baby be announced at any change of more than three beats per minute.

In her head, when she'd pictured how this surgery would

go, she'd been standing on the opposite side of the table from Ares, with the patient—and *space*—between them. But with the introduction of the ultrasound she not only had to stand beside him, she had to be close enough that the fabrics of their surgical gowns brushed and rustled against each other.

Something else to ignore.

She focused on the ultrasound wand in hand and maneuvered the cart holding the unit with her foot, so that Ares could best see the screen.

"Here—that's the cross section of the appendix."

"Enlarged…" he murmured, confirming the diagnosis in that second.

Why hadn't she thought about ultrasound to image the appendix before? Because she wasn't a surgeon. Because she was used to modern, fully equipped hospital situations. Because she didn't even know what equipment was located at this facility—which had to change immediately.

Moving on, she slid the wand to another position and pressed, showing the path usually taken in such a procedure. He had her move the wand a few more times, until he was satisfied with the visual and knew that he'd have room to move.

As soon as he'd made his incision the ultrasound was abandoned, and her job shifted to handing over the instruments as he asked, holding back tissue with forceps, controlling the flow of blood.

"How's the baby's heartbeat?" she asked the anesthesiologist yet again, probably ensuring that he'd never want to be on the same surgical team with her ever again, prompting him for readouts even if he'd only just given them.

The pattern they fell into was surprisingly easy. Ares's hands, always elegant in their masculine way, moved with a certainty and grace his current appearance contradicted.

She'd gotten by on having faith in her coping mechanisms for so long, but she found that faith shaken before they scrubbed in. Chatter and keeping her mind occupied held the line between being shaken up and on the floor, but she couldn't dismiss her doubts about how long she could keep it up.

However, unlike what she'd expected, he was professional. And extremely skilled.

And *different*.

But then so was she.

"I see it," he said, and leaned over a bit, letting her visualize the swollen, enflamed organ.

"Goodness, it's big. But it looks clean."

"Doesn't look like it's ruptured either. I'll extract—you examine it."

She passed over instruments, one at a time, allowing him to clamp the organ off from the ascending colon, then repeat the maneuver from the colon side so he could make a clean extraction.

Once he had placed the faulty organ into the surgical tray, she maneuvered it around to look for any openings.

"Intact," she announced after pressing and examining for longer than she would probably have done under normal circumstances. She needed an extra layer of assurance that her powers of observation and attention were still functioning at a high level, even with the chaos going on in her head.

Finally satisfied, she returned to his side to help flush the area with saline before closing up.

"We'll have to check our antibiotic inventory. If there's one you prefer but we don't have in stock, we can have it by the evening. I'm starting her on whatever's the best we have in the meanwhile. Eri… Dr. Nikolaides…"

Even with the face mask he wore, she saw his silent correction in the squint of his eyes. But she didn't know what it meant. She didn't know what any of this meant to him. He'd frozen, briefly, upon seeing her. And again when she'd reminded him what the health of her patients meant to her, but she still didn't know what it meant to him.

He could just be reacting to the worry that she was going to lose it in front of everyone and he'd have to answer difficult questions. Or he might not care at all about her, or the events that had rewired her brain to expect betrayal from those she loved.

But she told herself she didn't care about how affected or unaffected he was. She cared about Theo, Chris and Deakin. She had to figure out how to be around Ares without losing her senses, or all those years of keeping secrets from the rest would come undone, and that would mean she'd gone through all that alone for no reason.

Theo, the quintessential protective older brother? She didn't even have to wonder how *he'd* react. And, no matter what Chris and Deakin might think, knowing what had happened between Ares and her would divide the four close friends, probably forever.

Even if the clinic didn't rely on them all getting along and maintaining their long, loving, sibling-like relationship, she didn't want to be the cause of their pain. Every single one of them had gone through enough pain in their lives without her adding to it now, when it could change nothing about the past.

And she'd lost enough. She didn't deserve to lose Chris or Deakin, even if they were more forgiving than her superprotective brother would be.

"Dr. Nikolaides?" He said her name as if he'd said it before, and she finally realized what he'd said about the antibiotics. She hadn't answered him.

"I'll look as soon as we're done," she said, clicking back to the present. What was the next step? "Does anyone in the lab stay around the clock? I'd like labs drawn tonight and in the morning, to track her blood count. And I want the bacteria in the appendix cultured to check for resistance."

"We can arrange it. If not, I'll stay and do it. I've done them before."

"Do you do *every* job with your charity outfit?" He'd clearly learned pretty adept surgical skills there.

"We all do whatever we have to, to keep things going. They're even worse off for personnel than we are here."

He tied off the last suture and she clipped it, then took over swabbing the incision site and applying a good dressing. That was the next step. The anesthesia was out, and she grabbed a stethoscope to listen to the baby's heart and then the mother's.

"And I'm good at what I set my mind to," he added.

Hearts were steady—both of them. Jacinda's rate was a little higher than she'd like, but that happened with infection.

"Do we have a recovery room? I'm guessing not…?" Erianthe asked, pulling the earbuds out.

He'd removed his mask and gloves but stood watching her in that same way he had in the patient's room, looking too long, too intently. It made the back of her neck prickle, and she felt that tension return. What did it even mean? She had no way to know what he was thinking and never had—even when she'd thought she couldn't know anyone better than she knew him.

"She's coming up," the anesthesiologist interrupted.

Erianthe removed her mask to stand over her patient's head. "Jacinda? Open your eyes for me."

When she complied, Erianthe delivered the good news and Ares backed her up.

"We're going to take you back to a room and look after you there."

His voice changed when he spoke to Jacinda, becoming

imbued with a gentleness that made her own throat thicken. It reminded her of the way he'd held and comforted her after the pregnancy test that had changed everything. When she'd been terrified of the way Dimitri and Hera would react to it, wondering if they could run away to be safe.

"Where are you going?" he asked her now, the voice change denoting the shift from comforting his patient to addressing Erianthe.

"Nowhere…" she croaked, then cleared her throat.

"You're backing up."

He did seem farther away.

A shake of her head and she gestured to the door. "I'll go with her to monitor vitals."

"Was the baby's heart rate still good?"

"Yes," she confirmed, still wanting to talk about the patient as it kept her from thinking about the way he was looking at her. "Can we bring the ultrasound to her room?"

Ares pulled his surgical cap off and tossed it into the bin, tired all the way to his bones suddenly. Too tired for gentleness, or for this weird circling around one another that they were doing.

"You take her up and I'll bring it in a moment," he said.

She had always bristled when told what to do, but who knew if she still had something to prove? It was a long time ago, and they'd both had to grow up in that time.

All he knew was that he needed air at this precise second, so he might as well go home. If he stayed, as was his usual custom, he'd only be stuck in a room with her and nothing to do. Judging by her actions and words so far, there was no way she'd leave a pregnant mother and child in possible jeopardy.

Besides, his own island was very close to Mythelios proper, and his boat was fast. He'd rather stagger out of bed in the middle of the night and rush here without pants on than stay in a room with Erianthe for hours, when every time she looked at him her expression seemed stuck somewhere between *someone just vomited on me* and *why is that spider carrying a machete?*

"Who is going to show me where that is and help get her settled?"

The fact that even now, when they weren't focused on their patient, she still didn't want to look at him said enough about her state of mind on the matter. She probably still hated him—and Ares couldn't blame her. There was no undoing what had happened. He'd keep paying for that mistake, just as she would. But he didn't want that heartache to spread.

He'd known it would be hard to see her again. What he hadn't expected was the tightness in his chest that just kept on increasing. Every look at her had him cataloging the changes over the last decade. The small line between her brows said she frowned a lot. There were no faint matching brackets at the corners of her mouth to evidence smiles and laughter.

He couldn't change that. He still didn't know what he was supposed to have done back then—what might have made it work out for all three of them. If he hadn't come up with the answer in ten years, he wasn't going to now. All he knew was that she'd borne the brunt of that mistake alone—without him, without anyone.

His suffering paled in comparison to hers.

He didn't expect her to forgive him and wouldn't ask her to. Couldn't even picture what kind of heart could even offer him that kind of absolution.

"I'll get Petra to organize everyone," he said, then pulled off his gown to fish a pen and notepad out of his pocket.

A quick scribble of his number and he laid the sheet of paper on one of the machines, waiting for her to stop counting beats for the baby's heart and remove the buds she'd replaced in her ears before he carried on speaking.

"If you need me to run the labs, or if she shows signs that there's a leak or that we missed something, call me first. Don't go through someone else—call me. I can be here in ten minutes."

She lifted one hand but didn't immediately reach for the paper. The way her fingers curled, then stretched too hard, was like watching someone warm up before arduous exercise. Like picking up this single sheet of paper was heavy lifting and she didn't want to sprain her thumb.

In that second he regretted his decision to leave. The way she looked at him right now, would she call him for *any* reason?

"What time did you get up this morning? It was a travel day for you…" Ares said, ignoring the irritated sigh he got in answer.

She could sleep there. He didn't care. But it would be stupid, and she would probably remain at the bedside of their patient all night long rather than count on the night nurse to wake her if something did go wrong.

He wouldn't let any of his colleagues do that in her situation, he told himself; this wasn't specifically about *her*.

"Erianthe."

"Huh?"

The sound came out like a space filler—a tone loosed purely to give her time to think of what the right thing to say would be. A liar's sound, a way to avoid conflict, a monotone prayer that the speaker would give up on the question.

"You traveled today. You must be tired. I'll stay. You go home with Theo."

"I'm not…" She started to say something but then looked past him toward the door. "I'm not going to stay with Theo. I need to tell him that."

He knew enough to know that her staying with Theo was the plan. Even if Theo hadn't already told him that, he knew neither of the Nikolaideses would want to stay with their parents. Hell, *none* of them would want to stay with their parents. He'd bunked down at Deakin's upon first arriving on Mythelios, until he'd found out his own father currently lived in another country.

"Why aren't you staying with Theo?"

"He and Cailey should have some privacy. Chris arrived a couple of days ago, so I'll see if I can stay with him."

"They can keep it down, I'm sure," he muttered, his friend's cozy domestic bliss suddenly irritating him. "Whatever. Chris's, then. But Theo's is closer, should I need to call you in."

"I'm going to Chris's."

His teeth clenched hard enough to make his head ache. Obviously she had no idea that she was seconds away from being pushed out of the room.

"Fine—go to Chris's. I'll stay."

He could only stay if she went. If anyone overheard them bickering, or—God forbid—saw the way she looked at him… Well, it was good that their patient was unconscious again.

"I'm being kind to you, Erianthe. We don't need to both stay, and *I'm* staying."

"I'm the obstetrician."

"I'm the surgeon."

"So?"

"If labor starts, I will call you. Do you *want* to stay here and spend more time with me, pretending every second in my presence isn't like navigating a swarm of bees? I'm already tired of it. I don't *want* you here."

What he wanted was to forget about their past—and that couldn't happen if he had to look at her and see pain on her face. He'd been in some truly terrible places during his service, so he knew what pain looked like in all forms. Physical pain he could deal with, but this sort of quiet, chronic emotional suffering ate at him. And on her it was worse. It made him want to drag her to the airport and shove her onto a plane himself…make her go where everything wasn't so loaded. Somewhere he *wasn't*.

She didn't move.

He gave her a few seconds and then his control snapped, and he prowled forward to stand over her chair. Their patient was oblivious still, from the lingering effects of general anesthesia, and would not witness him about to yank Erianthe out of the seat and march her to the door.

"Swarm of bees?" she said finally, shaking her head, her cheeks growing pink as her gaze swiveled up to him. A second of eye contact was all it took. "That beard must have made you poetic, Ares."

Then, jumping to her feet, she rounded on him and jabbed a finger into his chest, her cheeks blazing now.

"I'd have to be in a coma to miss how badly you want me gone—which is fine, as I'm not all that eager to spend time with you either. I'm leaving the clinic, but I'm done running from my home."

As soon as the words flew out his hand twitched, and it was only at the last second that he shut down the urge to grab her before she got away. As much as he wanted her gone, he also wanted to sort things out with her. It was a ridiculous and undoubtedly destructive instinct.

He could do nothing about the heat rolling over his face. "I never asked you to do that." He'd never asked her for anything—not even explanations. And he had no idea if he should…if she'd want him to. Directly acknowledging the past would probably make this tension between them that much worse.

She fumbled the paper with his number from her pocket, flipped it and scribbled a number on the other side, then handed it back to him. "No, you were just part of what made it uninhabitable for me."

He snatched the paper, half tearing it with the rough handling. "You were the one who never wanted to see me again. It was your decision to stay gone—just as it was mine to stay gone too. Until now."

"That's right. I make my own decisions now."

"Make them at Chris's house," he muttered, and stepped purposefully back from her. "And don't come back here before tomorrow unless I call you."

"Have you been listening at all? I told you I make my *own* decisions, Dr. Xenakis. You have reached your lifetime limit of making *one* for me. I'm leaving now because I'm tired, and looking at you makes me want to scream. How about you take some time to look for a drop of civility before tomorrow? The others aren't stupid. The only reason they haven't figured anything out is because they haven't seen us together yet."

With that, she turned on her heel and walked out.

That was the first thing she'd said that he couldn't argue with. They really *had* to get it together. But not tonight.

He sat down and listened for the door to swing closed behind her. A week hadn't been long enough to prepare to see her again. Maybe he should've tried to call her before she arrived, to see if they could find some neutral ground.

The shock of it was that he'd spent a decade picturing the same girl he'd known. She'd stopped aging in his mind—which was right in line with how old he felt when he thought of her. Still eighteen...still stupid. Still desperate for a solution that would work out.

Happiness hadn't even been on his radar as something that could be possible long-term—he'd learned from his parents' string of broken nuptials how infrequently marriage led to happiness. But safety? That might have been possible. Temporary happiness. Until he'd botched everything up with her and made her leave, with their child, before he could screw them up with his own ineptness when it came to family. That was right where Dimitri Nikolaides had struck too—in his weakest spot.

It hadn't worked out between them a decade ago, and now that girl was gone forever. She'd been the queen of mascara and makeup, which had made her look older and harder. Using eyeliner he'd seen her melt with a cigarette lighter before applying it, just so she could get the absolute blackest smudge possible. The reddest lipstick. The shortest skirts. Whatever would annoy her parents the most.

Brazen. Fearless. Strong.

Now she was fresh-faced, and somehow she looked younger to his eyes. Anytime her gaze fell on him her dark eyes were a string of long, empty nights and full of something even darker. Disappointment. Anger. Hatred...

Something bruised and broken dimmed the sparkle in those midnight eyes. How other people wouldn't see it, he couldn't imagine. Anyone with vision and human emotion would see right through her.

He checked Jacinda's vitals, then the baby's, and sat down.

If the three weeks he'd planned on staying was too long—and it was, even though the first week had already flown by—the three *months* he'd actually agreed to when Theo had called him was dramatically beyond the limits of what he was willing to subject himself or her to.

The second he'd seen Erianthe again—when no one had thought to warn him she'd arrived and was treating a patient—he'd seen her face and had only been able to imagine how he'd looked. God help them both if he'd looked half as distraught as she had.

When Theo had called him home, the need to be there for the friends he considered his family had made him agree to the three months requested of him.

Then his survival instincts had kicked in when he'd spoken with his boss. When he'd been asked when they could call him for his next assignment, he'd said three *weeks*. He'd even heard the word leave his mouth, known it was wrong and hadn't corrected it. The word *choice* had been an accident, but letting it stand had been a conscious decision.

Three weeks, and now he had to keep it together only until the final two were finished, then find a way to bow out quietly when his office called him for reassignment.

A lot could go wrong in two weeks.

The door opened behind him.

Dammit, Erianthe.

He surged to his feet and spun around, readying himself for another argument, but instead saw Deakin standing there, his brows halfway up his forehead.

"Do you greet *everyone* that way, or did I do something?"

"I thought you were Erianthe," Ares muttered, sitting back down. "I made her leave to get some sleep. She wasn't best pleased with me."

Back when they'd been together, hiding their relationship, pretending to pick at one another had actually been fun. Now lying to the men he considered his brothers stood out as the lesser of two evils. Hiding the ugly truth from people he loved was better than being the one who delivered the information that would burn everything down.

No sooner had the fire reference occurred to him than his conscience pinged as he recalled Deakin's extensive burns; he must be getting callous to forget that about his friend.

"No one ever riled Erianthe like you could. Just like old times."

Deakin rounded his chair to head for the patient monitors, doing what they all did with every patient—checking in. Ares took no offense and, considering his preoccupation, was even glad for Deakin's diligence.

"She's never been one to take orders easily. But she must've been tired, because she got a ride with Theo a few minutes ago. Either that or she just really wanted to get away from you. How did you make her leave?"

"I told her I didn't want her here," Ares answered. He could be truthful about that at least. It fit their pattern.

"Harsh." Deakin's one-word pronouncement came with a frown.

"I wanted to sleep for a year at the end of my residency, but she arrived in a crisis and was immediately drawn into emergency surgery."

Ares listed what he knew, leaning back, trying to will the tension from his frame.

"She needed to go and rest, and making her mad was the fastest way to assure she went."

"So it was for her own good?"

And *his*.

"Is there something you want to say, man?" he asked Deakin directly.

"Just trying to figure you out."

"She'll thank me tomorrow."

They both knew that was a lie, and Deakin's arched brow called him on it, but Ares ignored it.

"You're grouchy as hell." Deakin printed a short record of the EKG, dated it and went to slip it into the chart. "You sure you don't want someone else staying with the patient?"

Not sure. The only thing he was sure of was that he needed to get off the island—even if it meant going to the tiny adjacent island where his family's estate was. But that baby—let alone the mother—deserved his diligence. And it would be one less thing to quarrel about with Erianthe tomorrow if he stayed.

"I'm sure." He scrubbed his hands over his face, sloughing off some of his weariness but none of the lingering agitation. "This is a walk in the park after the Sudan."

"Unconvincing…" Deakin said.

He needed to work on his poker face as badly as Erianthe did. "Tough. I don't need you to be convi—"

Jacinda stirred, shutting down the grumbling between them. Ares stood over her, took her hand and said her name. She woke and he repeated what Erianthe had told her—anesthesia had amnesiac qualities.

"The surgery went very well. You're doing great. Both of you did really well."

"The baby's okay?" she asked, her words still a little slurred, but her confusion might be the first thing not to annoy him today.

"The baby is fine. I'm staying with you to keep an eye on you, but all I expect to see is you sleeping peacefully. Okay?"

She nodded, squeezed his hand and then was already drifting back off.

"Don't stay up all night," Deakin said more quietly at his side, reminding him of their previous conversation, "Get her past recovery from the anesthesia, then get some rest yourself. We've got a breakfast meeting at Stavros's Taverna. That's what I actually came here to tell you."

"Breakfast meeting? Why?"

"Because for some reason we want to see you there with the rest of us. Full group."

"With girlfriends?"

"No. Just us."

Staying up all night with a pregnant postsurgical patient would be a perfectly acceptable reason to skip *that* land mine. He'd met with all the guys since his return, but doing it again with Erianthe there... Bad idea—at least before they'd had a chance to work out how to be normal around one another. In fact, it was the worst idea he'd heard all day.

He couldn't even *imagine* them pretending to snipe at one another and squabble, in order to keep anyone from suspecting they had genuine painful issues and memories to be raw about.

"I'll try to make it, but I'm not making any promises."

"Barring emergencies, you'll be there." Deakin gave his head a small, affectionate shove from behind as he passed on the way for the door. "You should also think about shaving, if you don't want all of us thinking you're suffering from exhaustion. Logic says that anyone with even a small amount of extra energy would have tamed that thing as soon as they could. And it will have to be gone by the time the auction comes around or we'll be *paying* someone to take you."

"Just because you and Theo got out of being auctioned off to bored socialites, it doesn't mean Chris and I have to carry your weight."

There was a lot Ares would do for the clinic and Mythelios after the quake, but there had to be a line drawn somewhere. Perhaps he could buy himself...

Deakin's soft laughter creaked through the closing door, and he added something rude about posing for the next calendar.

That bullet he *had* dodged, by being so far removed from civilization they hadn't been able to find a photographer to come meet him. And he'd made a bit more of a donation to the clinic to make up for it. But the charity bachelor auction was still a few weeks away.

He'd be gone by then, if anything in the universe could go in his favor where Erianthe was concerned.

CHAPTER THREE

ERIANTHE DROPPED HEAVILY onto the side of a guest bed at Chris's gorgeous cliffside villa. How long had it taken her to become adept at hiding her feelings? And had it ever been this hard?

If the inevitable confrontation with Ares hadn't sucked every drop of energy from her, her time with Chris and Chris's baby afterward had consumed the last of it.

Theo had taken the news that she didn't want to stay with him pretty well and, after some initial resistance, had driven her to Chris's home. He'd refused to be convinced to go home until he'd seen that she was settled in, so they'd all sat down to share coffee as he'd snuggled with little Evangelos, Chris's seven-month-old son.

Soon Theo would be a *baba* himself, and if the way he reacted to his honorary "nephew" was any indication, he'd be a natural at it. Far better than their father had ever been. He would have been a wonderful uncle to her own child too...

And at that thought she'd begun to feel the weight of every atom in her body. Her movements had become jerky, sluggish, and even her smile had trembled when she'd tried to force it. The trembling was the worst part of this strange exhaustion.

It was probably a blessing that today had been a travel

day—she had something to blame for her exhaustion. Everyone had certainly put her oddness down to that today, and maybe they'd let that excuse carry for a couple of days if she was lucky.

It was easy to control the expression on her face, but her body was out of control. That feeling of helplessness was how she'd lived for the duration of her pregnancy, and she'd never wanted to return to it.

First seeing Ares again, then being watched by Theo and Chris, and all the while trying very hard not to think about Chris's beautiful baby son—who somehow managed to look like his stupidly handsome father even whilst hiding Chris's strong jawline under chubby cherub cheeks…

None of that was within her control. Nothing felt within her control right now—no matter what she'd all but shouted at Ares about making her own decisions.

She stared out the window at the play of light and shadow of the late-afternoon sunshine through the trees in the yard in an effort to control the trembling she felt inside. At least she'd gotten beyond the point where it showed in her face and hands, but it was still there in her belly, in her chest, deeper than anyone could see. Right where she'd always tried to keep everything hidden.

Pretending that Chris was only babysitting felt immature and cold. Plus, it didn't help. If he'd babysat for anyone, it would have been one of theirs.

Theo's future baby. Deakin's future baby.

She had no one to tell about her daughter, how she should have been a mother ten years ago. That she should be in the process of being driven mad by a willful tween who refused to listen, plastered her walls with posters of pop singers and thought her mother was an idiot.

Theo's extremely helpful big-brother thing meant she had nothing to do now but sit and stare. And think. And that was the thing that would drive her mad in the end. It broke all her rules about self-preservation. Thinking about the past and what she should have had: a daughter to love and protect and nurture. A decade of memories of bubble baths in the sink and frilly toddler bikinis, living in a world of pink.

Erianthe had rebelled against all those girlie things when she was growing up, but for her daughter... She'd have done her whole house up in shades of pink for her daughter.

She rolled to her side and stretched out across the bed. Chris would understand if she skipped dinner in favor of sleep—he'd looked at her with the same concern Theo had.

Tomorrow things would be better—because she willed them to be so. This emotional malaise was just the shock of being back after all this time, and shock always eventually passed. Seeing Ares again had brought everything to the surface and triggered her annoyingly leaky eyes, but now she knew what to expect. Anger. Missing her child more than she'd have thought possible *again*. Fresh betrayal. And being alone—because at least when she was on her own she never had to hide her emotions from people who would be alarmed by tears.

A night's rest would help. In the morning she would remember—she hoped—how happy she was for Theo, Chris and Deakin. How she only wanted happiness and a fulfilled life of love and family for each of them. And maybe once this passed she'd be able to consider if she could ever want the same for herself. If she could ever be that brave again.

A quick, light knock came at her door—the "Doctor's Knock," as she liked to think of it.

She swiped her eyes and hurried to the bureau so she could feign unfinished domestic tasks, looking at the door sideways when Chris popped his head in.

"Are you about to go to sleep?" There was an up-note

at the end of his question, the sound of need and a hint of concern in his expressive blue eyes. "I know you're tired, but if you're going to be up for a few more minutes…"

She slid the drawer shut and turned to face him fully across the room, her eyes dry enough that a faked yawn could explain the glassiness she knew he'd see there.

The false upbeat voice she needed somehow appeared. "I no longer have a set bedtime. I'm footloose and fancy-free. What can I do for you?"

"Can you watch Evan for a few minutes?" Chris stayed in the doorway and seemed to be blessedly unaware of her progressive state of unraveling. Maybe she was getting a grip on herself.

"Of course."

"I hate to ask when you're so tired, but then I remember you help bring babies into the world—so you probably love babies. He just woke up, and I *really* need a shower."

The back of her neck prickled, but she ignored it. It wouldn't be a huge ask for anyone else. He'd agreed to let her stay without a second of hesitation, after all. And she did like babies—at least in theory. She just didn't spend much time with them, and most of the time she did they were *in utero*.

"I'm happy to. Do you need me to feed him or anything?"

Happy to. Happy to. She sent the phrase around her mind like a mantra.

Happy to—but she'd be even happier if she had some kind of task…something that would occupy her mind.

A few minutes later she stood there holding Evan, who was looking up at her with that unabashedly adoring way babies had, and that maddening tremble returned to her arms.

Chris had already fed him. Already bathed him—he

had that powdery fresh scent as proof. She had nothing to *do* for him. Nothing but hold him.

He wouldn't judge her trembling arms.

Maybe she should just *sit* with him?

That seemed infinitely more reasonable—and responsible. Decision made, she gingerly placed the baby in his crib and set the mobile above spinning in the hopes of distracting him.

She shouldn't have been holding him with shaky arms anyway—she might have dropped him.

The comfortable chair beside the crib sank with her as she eased into it, careful of squeaking springs or sudden movements—as if moving quickly would make him detonate, or cry, in the baby equivalent of an explosion.

Relieved of her adoptive nephew, she felt the tremble in her arms abate. If she could get the tremble in her gut to go too, she'd feel even better.

Laying her head back, she closed her eyes, once more counting her breaths. Just a few more minutes for Chris to finish his shower, and then she could sleep.

Evan gurgled and she froze—then felt even more ridiculous. He was a baby, not a jar of nitroglycerin. And she was being selfish, self-centered. And horrible.

Tomorrow things would be better.

Breathe in.

Sleep would be like a mental and emotional reboot. Turning something off and then back on again usually fixed it. It would work with her too.

Tomorrow she would do better.

Breathe out.

The baby started to cry.

At seven the next annoyingly sunny and cheerful morning, after many unsuccessful hours during which he'd tried to convince himself it would be better if he pulled the cord on his emergency parachute and called the office, asked for redeployment instead of waiting for them to call him, Ares dragged himself into the *taverna*.

He was legitimately exhausted. And still undecided about the call.

What he *did* know was that he desperately wanted to leave, but he thought that would make him a coward or—worse—someone who abandoned his family when they needed him most.

"Who bribed you to open this early on a Thursday?" he asked Stavros, stopping at the bar where the owner stood, scowling his way through the pages on a clipboard, his glasses on his nose.

It was polite to stop and acknowledge Stavros, he told himself. It was certainly not him avoiding his friends on the first time they'd all been in one place together in ten years. No pressure there.

Stavros looked at him in stony silence for long enough that Ares almost spoke again to fill the gap, figure out what was wrong.

Just when he'd opened his mouth to ask if the owner of the *taverna* was all right, the other man finally spoke, his voice surprisingly quiet and hoarse. "Tell your friends to keep it down. My head isn't up to dealing with any nonsense from the lot of you this morning."

Something was off.

Ares looked at Stavros closer, searching for signs of hangover or injury, but his eyes weren't bloodshot, he wasn't slurring his speech at all and he didn't smell like someone who'd been on a bender. While he'd never been an effusive man, he was personable enough not to make customers wonder if they were welcome in the local *taverna*.

Focusing on Stavros while his friends waited for him

might have been something of a dodge, but now he had reason for concern, so he lingered and kept his voice low as he asked, "Are you feeling all right, Stavros?"

"Headache."

A one-word answer—and not a request for medical advice or assistance. Ares nodded slowly. "If you need anything—"

That was all he got out before Stavros cut him off. "Don't expect me to serve anything. Kitchen is closed."

"Got it," Ares answered, not asking about coffee. Or ouzo. Or anything else about the man's head. He could appreciate him wanting to be left alone.

Pushing off the bar, he finally wound his way to the large table in the center of the *taverna*.

Ares was careful not to look at anyone too long—especially Erianthe. *Brief glance. Look away. Make sure she's keeping it together. Look away. Look once more to check for obvious signs of distress.*

Her cheeks had always flashed a deep red when she got angry—yesterday's showdown included.

"There's the scarecrow!" Deakin joked, leaning back in his chair as he caught sight of Ares arriving.

He could feel all eyes on him. Except hers. That wasn't suspicious at all, was it?

"No, he's a fur model," Theo corrected. "He grows a mean beard. Really, man. It growled at me yesterday. And the other day I think I saw it eat a bird."

The two of them were entirely too jovial for seven in the morning.

"I usually feed it the souls of my enemies." He tried to joke, but it came out flat and bored.

He dropped into the chair across the table from Erianthe and to the left, so he wouldn't be staring at her anytime he looked up, or accidentally touching her when he moved his limbs.

"Stavros said to keep the noise down."

They all looked toward the *taverna* owner behind the bar, and Theo got a serious look on his face, lowered his voice. "He's been grouchy for a while now."

"Maybe he and Maria are quarreling?" Deakin offered, as if that was the only reason for a headache—fighting with your wife.

Regardless, they all went with the low-volume request and leaned in to keep their chatter lower.

Despite Ares's best efforts, Erianthe's gaze pulled his like a magnet. No red cheeks or smiles. No talking that he'd witnessed yet either. She didn't look away, for once, and the light shadows under her eyes said she'd had about as much sleep last night as he had.

"No coffee. No breakfast. We should've met at Theo's instead." Deakin stretched and yawned, then settled into a comfortable lean.

"Why are we meeting at all?" Ares asked grumpily, hoping to move things along.

"Breakfast." Chris finally said something. "But now Stavros has said the kitchen is closed."

"And because most of us have been back at one time or another, but we've not all met in one place in years." Deakin kicked his foot under the table, giving Ares a look that said: *This again? Really?*

Ten years. It was ten years. Almost exactly. But Ares didn't correct him. It would make him seem… He didn't even know what. Pathetic. Like someone who forgot everyone's birthday—sometimes even his own—but who passed the sad anniversary of the last time he saw Erianthe by drinking anything that would blur the edges.

"You stayed up all night anyway." Deakin shook his head. "So I suppose you're worthless today."

"You suppose right," Ares confirmed. "I need to go home and get some sleep. Someone's going to have to fill the gap if you have some kind of surgical emergency."

"Takes a bit of time to get here from your island," Theo said, backing Deakin up.

"Not that long in my boat." They were on a small island, and his even more tiny island was visible from the main island if you knew where to look. "Or call Chris if it's really urgent. He can do more than carve brains."

Chris snorted. "Impossible to get a babysitter on short notice. I had to ask Erianthe to watch Evan just so I could have a shower last night."

Ares looked at Eri, and as if on cue her cheeks paled and she immediately dropped her gaze. *Yeah, I bet she enjoyed that.*

A quick glance around the table confirmed that no one else was watching her, so no one had noticed her discomfort yet, and he felt a need to keep it that way. Take their attention.

"I'll go to sleep in the on-call room, then. That's as close as I can get without actually bunking down in the OR."

"How are Jacinda and the baby?"

Erianthe broke in with a new subject, but her words were so soft he seemed to be the only one who'd heard her—the others had gone off on a tangent about staffing logistics.

"Both fine," he answered, and that did get their attention. Speaking about something important quieted them down. "I did a CBC in the night, and her white cells were already dropping. Did another blood draw before coming—it's at the lab now. Her pain is better. Baby's heartbeat is steady. Baby's still not moving around a lot, but the general anesthesia takes a while with them. Or so I read last night."

"It does," she confirmed. "Dodged a bullet there, I hope."

"Things certainly seem to have changed since yesterday."

Deakin lifted a pointed brow and Ares resisted the urge to shove him off his chair.

"Keep it up and maybe you two won't scare off the patients with your bickering after all."

Deakin was *really* going to get on his nerves today—which was the wrong reaction for him to have to that kind of brotherly ribbing. He always gave as good as he got—they all did. But Ares had always acted like the world was a joke back then. Before everything had stopped being funny. Today, he couldn't tell the difference between being amusingly sarcastic and a bitter smart-aleck.

"We only argue in front of anesthetized patients who are unaware of what's going on and wouldn't remember later on even if they did hear us," he said.

"We also argue when Ares is acting like he's the boss of me." She countered his statement with words she'd used so many times when they were children that it read playfully, like a joke.

They all laughed.

Just like that, the conversation eased a little, and so did he. Erianthe even seemed to relax a touch too. Maybe this would be all right.

After ten years of never being in one place together, that old feeling of camaraderie and a sense of belonging settled over him. This was something he'd miss when he was gone.

The conversation, which had originally been touted as a meeting, continued to be more about catching up. They shared crazy cases they'd worked on, compared what they'd seen at the clinic with different facilities.

Theo explained how during the first forty-eight hours after the quake—when the clinic had become a hub for the injured and those looking for a place to go—he'd struggled to understand what had driven Ares into emergency medicine. Theo handled emergencies sometimes, but he liked being a GP—it suited him much better than emergency specialist.

"It's not for everyone." Ares didn't try to explain the draw it held for him. Or why he chose the most extreme version of that practice—going to places with minimal hospital equipment and the worst need. Truthfully, he wasn't even sure himself why he chose the mission hospitals.

"All I know is if we have something else like that happen, I don't want my baby sister to be overwhelmed by what we might see," Theo said, and then grinned at her and teased, "This is your first big-girl job!"

She thumped her brother square in the chest, making him laugh and then lightly rub at the spot. Growing up the only girl among four boys, she'd learned how to communicate in boy language early and keep up with them. She hit harder than it seemed she would, and often harder than they ever hit one another in the few times things had ever gotten heated in their youth. But she'd only ever hit Ares that one time…

"Seriously, I know you've been working at that fancy birthing center where you qualified as an obstetrician, but I'd feel better if you spent some time getting used to the emergency aspects of serving in the clinic."

The hair on the back of Ares's neck stood up. *Emergency aspects.*

"Might not be a great idea if we don't want the two of them fighting in front of the patients," Deakin said, and for once Ares didn't comment.

Erianthe didn't either. Instead she turned toward Theo. "I've already done a stint in emergency—it was part of my residency, which wasn't all that long ago."

"It was a few *years* ago."

"I still remember how things went."

She'd never liked being told to do anything—even indirectly. Or maybe she didn't like being told by men. He hadn't ever seen a woman try to manage Erianthe, even when her behavior had screamed for some management.

After yesterday's fight, the only question in Ares's mind was whether she'd respond to orders from Theo differently than to orders from anyone else.

"Are you two really incapable of getting along in front of patients?" Theo asked it as a serious question, but his laughing tone lightened what could have turned heated.

Erianthe scowled her answer. Ares kept his face carefully blank. If they both strenuously objected, it would raise more suspicions.

"I just don't understand why I need to, when there are certainly enough women on the island to keep me busy every minute of the day between preventative tests and a myriad of other women's health needs—not to mention prenatal monitoring and actual births. Speaking of which—how frequent are they here? On an island of about ten thousand? Should be one to two per week?"

"About that," Theo confirmed. "It will take a few days for word to get out and for you to get busy, and we all handle overflow cases in emergency situations. You can shadow Ares for a few days until patients begin lining up to see you."

The deep breath she took made Ares look at her face for signs of attack. Was this the breath before the tirade?

There was a touch of pink in her cheeks, but she expelled the breath and leaned back without shouting. "Fine. If I'm not otherwise needed for women's health issues, I will shadow Ares."

He didn't need to wonder if she would have backed down

for *him*—he'd practically had to throw her out the window to make her leave yesterday. Maybe he just brought out her quarrelsome instincts. Or maybe they would forever be at loggerheads with each other.

Didn't matter. All he had to do was make a call, that emergency parachute would be deployed and he'd get out before things got too bad.

"Well, I'm about to fall over. Maybe she can start shadowing me tomorrow."

"And you'll be at the wedding on Saturday?"

He was on his feet, but his stomach fell to the floor anyway. He hadn't gotten out soon enough. "Who's getting married?"

His father was currently married—last time he'd checked—and his mother had taken herself off the market after her sixth divorce a while ago. Besides, neither of them were residing on Mythelios, so they couldn't be the usual reason he had to go to yet another wedding.

"Me and Cailey!" Theo looked at him like he'd told him this twenty times and he was losing his mind.

Scanning back, Ares looked for any landmarks that had made him zone out, like he always did when people talked weddings.

Theo and Cailey were living together—that might have been enough reason for him to check out of the conversation.

"I must be more tired than I thought. Of course I'll be there. Where?"

He was stuck until Saturday. He'd have to wait until Monday to pull that cord.

Midday Friday, and despite Theo's instruction that Erianthe shadow him, Ares had to go looking for her to let her know there was a pregnant woman to see her.

They'd had a reprieve from each other on Thursday.

He'd slept in the on-call room until the afternoon, then gone home. Today he'd been happy to see she had patients every time he found himself between cases, as it gave him an ideal excuse not to bother her.

Only now he had to take it the other way and go find her.

Dr. Lea Risi, a psychiatrist who had been on holiday on the island when the earthquake had struck, and in staying on to help had subsequently turned his buddy Deakin into a love-struck jokester, had caught Ares asking Petra if she'd seen the newest Dr. Nikolaides and had directed him to the clinic's Serenity Gardens, with a somberness in her green eyes hinting that something might be amiss.

When he found Erianthe in the garden, he understood. She sat on a bench beside the fountain, staring unmoving into the water. She looked so deep in thought he stopped a good ten feet away, dread rising on the back of his neck.

He didn't have to say anything. Without even looking at him, she asked, "Do you need me?"

He skipped right over the jolt of something he'd rather not examine in favor of answering her question in the most mundane, emotionless way possible. "There's a patient for you. Pregnant."

Whatever she'd been sunk into, he could almost see her shove it aside mentally. Decision made to bounce back, she stood, smoothed her scrubs and headed toward the door.

"Just a checkup, or do we have a problem?"

Ignore the *we*. This was not a *we* situation. Take her to the patient, drop her off, return to his corner.

He took the lead, guiding her to the appropriate exam room, not far away. "She said she wanted to have a checkup. But she's worried, and she said she'd heard the baby doctor was here."

He knocked, opened the door and led Erianthe inside.

"Nyla Sarantos, this is our resident obstetrician, Dr.

Nikolaides." Ares introduced them and then filled Erianthe in on basically what he'd already told her, which was all he really knew. "Miss Sarantos is seven months in and worried about her baby."

Erianthe turned her attention to Nyla, the patient, making it clear she no longer considered him to be needed.

He'd told himself he'd leave after the introductions were made, but as Eri stepped forward and began going through a string of questions to get her bearings, he found himself staying, leaning against the counter.

He worried about pregnant women to the point where he actually often passed their treatment to other doctors, even when it was something simple, like a cut that needed stitching. It was something he'd shoved aside during Jacinda's surgery because he'd had to. And because Erianthe had needed him to.

Truthfully, he didn't like thinking about pregnant women at all—and treating them was worse.

"Okay, Nyla, tell me what you're worried about," Erianthe said, taking her patient's hand and leaving no room for doubt that her attention was focused entirely upon the person she was treating. The bedside manner of a doctor who really cared.

Medicine hadn't been an interest in her teenage years—at least not one she'd shared with him. If he'd had to guess then, he'd have placed her in an academic field, or maybe the arts, but she suited medicine.

"I'm afraid the baby is sick. He's not moving much."

The gentle smile Eri had worn faltered, and she let go of Nyla's hand to don her stethoscope immediately. Using the bell, she listened to the woman's belly, then began moving the instrument around, the furrow of her brow deepening with every move.

The third time her hand lifted, it shook. Ares found

himself back at the table, his eyes fixed on Erianthe's face. Over the following seconds her honeyed complexion turned ashen.

Grabbing his own stethoscope, he joined in listening for the baby's heart from the other side of the woman's belly.

Nyla's heart was racing—beating hard enough to make him concerned. And the baby's…? He couldn't hear the baby's heart for the power and speed of the mother's.

Cold hit his chest and his own heart rate kicked up.

He tried a lower quadrant. Still nothing.

Erianthe moved the bell of her stethoscope again, and so did he. But the second hers made contact with Nyla's stomach, her hand came over his—a touch that made his whole body flame with awareness. He searched her face, not moving, not even breathing.

The brows that had been pinched and worried had relaxed. He saw softness there, and a tiny smile starting in her eyes. *Relief.* The relief he saw on her face was absorbed right into him through the petite, delicate hand over his.

"Is he gone?" Nyla's voice broke, and he shook his head immediately as Erianthe started to speak.

"He's there."

Her voice creaked with emotion, and she listened to the tiny heart beating a moment longer, then seemed to realize she still had hold of his hand, and removed hers from on top of it.

The buds in her ears came next, and she explained, "Your heart is beating very fast, so I want you to lie down here for a while and we'll see if we can get it slowed down. That's all I was able to hear at first, and that's not good for him. So, we'll just do some deep breathing exercises and see if we can slow it down."

Despite her no longer touching him, he still took a moment to recover his senses enough to make it back to the counter and give them some room.

Together Erianthe and Nyla breathed through the pattern Erianthe set—slowly in, hold, slowly out… After a full minute she listened to Nyla's heart again and nodded. "That's better."

She let the mother listen too, and things began to settle down. But his own heart rate refused to slow. He hadn't even asked the patient what she was worried about—had taken time to find Erianthe and hand her off. What if the baby had been in trouble and had needed something in those minutes?

Quietly, he practiced the breathing technique Erianthe had established, but it didn't help.

He should leave. A proper examination was the next step.

For once, despite the wave of weakness he couldn't think about, his feet listened to his orders. He walked toward the door, excusing himself. "I'll get Cailey."

A minute later Cailey slipped into the examination room and Ares waited outside, where he could still see the door.

As he waited, his heart finally began to normalize. Heat flooded him. The look on Eri's face, the shake of her hands, how she'd paled… All of it ran on repeat through his head. He should still be feeling guilty for not having placed the welfare of a patient above his own need to get away from Erianthe, but he was too busy being angry that she had gone to the opposite extreme.

This was the second time he'd seen her with a pregnant patient—and he knew the whole point of her specialty was helping pregnant women and delivering babies—but she had absolutely no barrier between how it made her feel and the face she presented the world. Even the expectant mother had grown concerned, watching her new doctor's face drain of color.

Was she punishing herself?

There went his heart rate again.

A short time later Cailey led Nyla out and he went straight back inside, having lost none of his concern.

Erianthe stood at the counter, her back to him, making notes in the file.

He didn't wait for her to turn around. "Why do you do this when it so obviously hurts you?"

"You mean...?"

Feigning ignorance? *Oh, hell, no.*

He crossed the counter and took her elbow, making her look at him, letting him see her face. A quick scan almost convinced him he'd imagined her reaction, but he hadn't. The patient had seen it too.

"Why obstetrics? Are you some kind of glutton for punishment?"

He'd expected to see anger at his words, but the grief he saw in her eyes set him back on his heels.

"It doesn't always hurt me," she whispered, and extracted her elbow from his grasp so she could look back at the file, though clearly she wasn't reading it. "But that particular symptom, especially today, was worse. Maybe it's just because I'm here. I don't know..."

That particular symptom.

He gripped the edge of the counter to keep himself from reaching for her again. He didn't know what to say to her. He hadn't actually thought she'd answer him—he'd become used to her pushing him away.

She gathered her things and turned to leave, making him catch her by the hand again to stop her. Skin to skin, the feel of her lit him up. But the flash of pain on her face made him let her go almost immediately.

"Wait."

"What? Why?" She backed up a little, clutching the file to her chest with folded arms.

He didn't want to ask, but he couldn't stop himself. "Is that how it happened?"

"Is that how I lost my baby?" she clarified.

Our baby.

He wanted to correct her, but he nodded instead. "My mother never gave me any details. Just said that it…it was late in the pregnancy…when it happened. Hard for you…"

Tears rushed to her eyes and he felt a burning in his throat that was mirrored in hers when she rasped, "I can't do this right now. I have patients to see."

It still ate into her.

He'd asked his mother only once and later had been glad she'd refused to give him enough details for him to agonize over. He still didn't know if he'd ever be able to know and then put it out of his mind and get on with things. But he needed to hear it, and he needed to be able to let it go. Every time he looked at her it was still right there between them, and he couldn't imagine it wasn't the same for her.

But she was right. Now was not the time.

CHAPTER FOUR

ERIANTHE STUFFED HER stethoscope and the various pens and pads from her pockets into a cubby in the office cabinet, stashing them there to keep from having to carry it all back home at the end of the day.

Well, not home. Chris's house. And while it was lovely, and a place she was made to feel welcome, it still wasn't restful. So keeping as little as she needed there appealed to her in some fashion. The clinic was to be her home for the long haul, and even with Ares lurking around the place she didn't dread going there, like she regrettably did Chris's.

The weight of Ares's stare behind her alerted her to his arrival, but she wasn't going to greet him. It had been too long a day for her to chase tigers.

"Are you leaving now?" Ares asked from behind her.

She should ask Chris about the neuroscience behind that feeling of being watched. It wasn't exactly what she felt when Ares was around, but it was the closest she could come to describing it. Knowing someone was there, feeling his eyes on you… She actually wished his gaze had that same creepy, hair-prickling quality of a stranger's. Contrarily, Ares's gaze felt warm and soothing—which was ironic, because nothing else about him was soothing in the slightest.

"Yes. Is everything all right with Jacinda?"

"Last I checked." He showed her the keys in his hand. "Can I give you a ride?"

Erianthe closed the office cabinet where she kept her bag, put the bag carefully on her shoulder and considered the keys in his hand. The creeping sense that she was being set up was too much for her to wade through right now.

The old Ares had never done anything without a plan. Showing up with keys to drive her home? Likely he was not being as gallant and kind as anyone else might be fooled into thinking.

At least she knew him that well. His mind had always worked in advance. Everyone else played the game right before them, but Ares played three moves ahead. Which was why she'd never known how to view his going to Dimitri ten years ago as anything other than getting her and the problem of her pregnancy solved. Any idiot would have been able to predict that her father's reaction to the news would be detrimental and extreme.

She should remember that when she thought about the creak in Ares's voice when he'd asked about her stillbirth. Nothing had changed on that front since this afternoon—she still didn't want to talk about it with him.

But those were boat keys, and boats were loud, which meant there was little chance he would try to talk to her. About anything. A boat would get her to Chris's villa fast, and then she could race up the path without a long walk on top of an already long day.

"Is it a hard question?" Ares interrupted her mental list of pros and cons.

"Yes," she answered immediately, then looked at him, daring him to argue it.

Until today, every time he looked at her it had been as if from behind a mask—guarded, sometimes irritated—but now the corners of his mouth actually turned downward, and he had what she could only call remorse in his eyes.

If she went with him, she could enjoy the water and let the salt spray wash away her hard day. Let him feel better about himself by giving her a lift and let that be the end of it. More important, if anyone noticed them being weird or avoiding each other, they'd ask questions, and questions were bad for everyone—at least on *that* they could agree.

If his plan was something else, she could always shove him into the Aegean—they'd be too far from the shore for anyone to see.

"Eri?"

"You've had all day to consider this. You can give me fifteen seconds to decide."

She waved a hand toward the door, indicating her decision, and started walking.

In less than five minutes she was seated on the back bench of a speedboat, and Ares had it maneuvered out from the docks. He sent it hurtling far from shore, where it was safest to speed. She closed her eyes and turned her face to the sky, letting the sun warm her as the mist rose from the boat skipping across the water.

He didn't try to talk to her. He didn't bother her at all. Two good things. She hadn't expected him to ask any questions—still didn't understand why he had. Why now? Why not when he'd first heard about it and she'd been so devastated and alone? No one to talk to. No one to grieve with. Was it simply that proximity had made the topic fresh enough to make him wonder about it again after such a long time?

She realized then how long they'd been speeding over the water. It wasn't that far to Chris's house. And shouldn't the sun be warming the other side of her face right now?

Opening her eyes, her hand placed above to shade them,

she looked toward where the shore should be—and wasn't. Her eyes twitched and she peered in the other direction. Yep. He *had* turned in the wrong direction—away from Chris's house and toward his own little sheep-infested island instead.

Wedging her bag between the bench and the boat, she grabbed the side for support and made her way to the front so she could push him in. Or hit him. Or maybe just scream until he heard her.

As soon as she appeared in his peripheral vision, he slowed the boat, and when it stopped, he killed the engine.

She didn't need to know what he was doing, and she really didn't want to think about why. She just wanted to cut this nonsense short. "I don't want to go to your island. It has been a very long day, Ares."

He took the keys out of the dash, stuck them into his pocket and gestured back to the bench. "I know you don't want to go there. I know you want nothing to do with me. I get it. Sit down and talk to me—it won't take long."

Out on the water, with the boat not moving, it was getting hot fast. Or perhaps *she* was getting hot.

Crossing her arms, she planted her feet. "It's already taken too long."

"We have some things to sort out—even if everything *was* finished between us a long time ago," he said.

Not entirely accurate. She still had questions about why he'd done what he'd done, but those answers wouldn't change what had happened. Those answers couldn't make her heart hurt less over that loss.

"We have nothing to sort out," she denied flatly.

Ares stepped around her and went to sit on the bench, ignoring her instinctive flinch away from him. He leaned back, not quite sprawling on the seat, and with his sunglasses on, he looked like a caveman who'd got lost in a Sunglass Hut, with loads of curly black hair—some of which the wind had pulled free of the band he used at the clinic in a vain attempt to keep it neat.

When the glasses were on, all she saw was hair, beard, shiny black plastic and forehead. She did not look lower than the beard. Because she didn't need to think about his body, which was probably blanketed in similar thick fur.

"The questions aren't going to stop if we don't straighten things out—or at least figure out how to be around one another."

Had it been only a day since their breakfast meeting, with Deakin pointing out the tension between them? Even if it had been a week, it still would have felt too short.

Her spine stood like a marble column between her shoulder blades, holding her unnaturally erect—which made it hard to stay on her feet in the natural sway of the boat on the waves. She spun the captain's chair and sat in it, keeping her distance.

"I know."

The fewer words on her part, the quicker their conversation—and she wanted it over with. She couldn't deny it. He might have plucked the exact same thoughts from her head earlier.

He pushed the sunglasses back into that mass of wild black curls. His spring-green eyes pinned her to the chair.

"What do you suggest we do about it?"

"Put the glasses back on."

He paused, the look on his face irritated and yet he was considering her request. "Why?"

"So I can go on pretending you're not you."

He didn't move for several seconds but eventually did as she'd asked. "What can I do to put you at ease around me?"

"Nothing. You can't make this up to me. It's not a thing that can be fixed."

"Why did you never tell Theo about it after you left?"

"I didn't leave. 'Leave' implies active participation. I was taken away." Once she'd pointed that out, she waved off the rest. "We'd all lost too much in our lives already. I wasn't going to be the instrument of anyone losing any more."

"You're under no obligation to me."

"It's not about *you*. Knowing would have hurt *him*."

"Because he loves you. I know he'd feel loss over—"

"And he would lose *you*." She cut him off. "He'd look at me and see…"

"What?"

"An explanation."

"And my guilt?"

"Theo always watched out for me. While I was away, I wrote to him all the time. I could certainly have told him a thousand times what had happened, and what was going on with me. Because he asked. He asked so many times. But I played it off as something else—something shallow. It would have hurt him to know *any piece* of it. He'd have lost you as his best friend. He'd have known he'd lost the chance to be an uncle—have you seen him with Evan?"

Her throat filled with what felt like a lifetime of hurt, and she had to swallow twice to force that emotion back into her chest so she could speak again.

"He'd probably have felt honor-bound to turn his back on Deakin and Chris too, if they didn't agree with him over cutting you out of his life. They would *all* have suffered. In your head this might be all about how soft-as-cheese Erianthe is protecting *you*, but what I'm really doing is taking care of *them*."

The bonds that tied them together had been forged by heartache and discord in their homes. They'd become a family because they'd needed each other and found solace together. Theo was her *actual* brother, by adoption, but in reality they were all her brothers. Except for Ares. She'd known very early on that he made her feel different.

They all understood what having a family break apart felt like and she'd never do that to them—not to *this* family.

"But these days we're not as close. It might not hurt them to lose me. Especially if I just leave. Out of sight, out of mind. Nothing dramatic to instigate it…"

"So you'd just go and never come back?"

He nodded.

"And I would then have to pretend not to know why they'd lost you? Your magnanimous bowing out would leave *me* to keep yet another secret."

"Or tell them later. I don't know, Eri. I don't know how to solve this problem now any more than I knew how to solve it then."

A blast of furious heat hit her face, but she gritted her teeth and forced herself to skip over the fact that he'd referred to their daughter as a "problem." She just didn't have any more room in her head or her heart for more hurt.

"I can't tell them. It would hurt Theo more to know any of it now." She swallowed past the gravel in her throat and turned her gaze out to the deep blue sea. "He and Cailey are expecting their own baby. It would hurt him to know what I went through and that he wasn't there for me. I don't know the answer either. What is it you want? You had to have an objective before you kidnapped me."

"This is not kidnapping. It's the only way I could get you to stay in one place long enough to talk to me. You smile at everyone but me. You look at everyone but me. Like you're doing now, you stare off into the distance when we're talking. And *they* see it."

"I haven't smiled at *anyone* today."

She heard him sigh, even over the sound of the ocean.

"No, no smiles today… If we can't figure out some way

to be around each other, this will fall right off the cliff. And our patients will pick up on the tension too—which I know you don't want. I've seen how you connect with everyone you treat. You even reach out to those who accompany your patients. It's *suspicious* that we don't connect at all—especially when we can't explain why other than using those dumb teenage excuses. *He bugs me. She's too bossy.*"

It wasn't meant as a complaint—logically she knew that—but the subtle sound of loss in his voice pinged at her conscience.

"If I could turn this feeling off, I would."

"How do you deal with your parents?"

"I don't. I haven't spoken to either of them since I became an adult."

"At *all*?"

She shook her head. "I stayed away. Changed my number. Ignored emails. Sent back letters and deliveries. I never came back. Not even once."

"Since you left home?"

Even now she had a hard time calling Mythelios "home." Was it because she didn't ever go to her childhood home? Or to Ares's home, which she'd spent a year of her life picturing as *her* future home?

She still couldn't bring herself to look at him, but looking out at the water brought no rocking, soothing comfort as she longed for it to do. There was just the baking heat of the sun and a loss of the anger that had briefly fired her up—and the realization that she couldn't *wait* her way through this anymore.

Sliding off the captain's chair, she joined him on the bench—far enough away to keep from touching but closer than she had been. It was all the overture she had in her right now.

"You didn't come home for holidays when you were in school?" he asked.

"I came to Greece once, the summer I was seventeen, and stayed in my aunt's house in Athens for a few weeks. But mostly if school was out, I found other things to go to. Extra schooling. Volunteer work."

Why was she telling him these things? Because he sounded hurt? Because the idea of causing him pain still twisted in her belly like a blade? She should just change her name to *Brie*-anthe. She was so tired of hurting, but hating him wouldn't bring her daughter back.

"I didn't think it would still hurt so much to be here now. But if I act a little weird, they'll understand that it's weird for me to even be here."

"Home?"

She shook her head.

"Eri… *Psihi mou…*"

A jolt of agony sliced into her and she was on her feet, rounding on him before she'd even really understood what he'd said.

"Don't call me that!"

If she was his soul, he was in worse trouble than she was.

He scrubbed both hands over his face, up under his sunglasses, then let them fall back to his nose as he turned away to look out over the endless blue.

The marble that had set in her spine began to soften and she sat again, not stopping until her elbows on her knees were all that supported her. She'd have just lain down on the deck of the boat if she could. Being with him had used to energize her. Now they were done talking, she felt half-dead.

A full minute passed and then he stood up and returned to the captain's chair, sitting but not spinning away from her as if he was about to start driving again.

"What they know is that you were sent away from here because of your *rebellious activities* so you could focus on your studies. They'll imagine that being away from home was really unpleasant and lonely, but unless you tell them something traumatic happened while you were gone, then your behavior *will* seem strange and worrying."

She looked up then. "Are *you* worried about me?"

"Yes, dammit. Of course I'm worried about you. If I could do *anything* to take what happened from you, I would. All I know how to do is to try to contain it."

"*Contain* it?" The words shouted through her but came out quiet.

"Not increase your pain by having you watch it spread and wreck the rest of them, or relive it by answering a million questions."

He slid off the chair to squat before her and reached for her hand.

Sluggish and slow, she saw what he intended, but only mustered the strength to snatch her hands back when he was close enough for her to feel the energy he put out. One touch a day—more than that and the thread of hope she dangled from might snap.

She sat up straighter so he wasn't so close, so that the wind didn't part around him as if he was sheltering her.

"All this is too much for you," he said, not standing up but tucking his hands away, accepting her dramatic hints not to touch her.

He was worried this was too much for her because it *wasn't* too much for him. It had never been as real for him. How could it have been? Her stomach had still been board-flat when he last saw her. He hadn't spent months of lonely sickness, wonder and worry, watching her body grow round and her clothes grow tight. He hadn't felt *life* moving within her or heard the strange, alien sound of that little heart beating.

He might have tried to imagine it, or maybe he'd just put them both out of his head after the way it had all ended. There were times when she could even picture him being *relieved* that her baby had never been born.

It didn't leave her with much room to know how to react to him. How to *see* him, even.

There seemed to be no half measures with them in these fraught conversations. One thought led to another, and another, and it was simply too much. If he admitted to feeling relief about the baby… Well, she didn't know if she *could* continue to keep protecting the others. Or him. Even if she did worry about him too.

"I'm worried about me." Also true.

"Do you want me to leave the island? Maybe it'll be easier for you if I just go."

"You can't just go. That would just have the same effect as me acting…"

"Shell-shocked?"

The bleakness in his voice clawed at her. She might never be ready to hear how he felt about the baby, but she heard guilt scratching through his voice. Guilt over *her*.

He knew Theo, Deakin and Chris would demand answers if he left suddenly so soon after her arrival, and they'd most likely hold it against him. He'd lose the only real family he had—and they were still important to him, no matter what he'd said about the physical distance between them all. And yet he was offering.

Guilt and sacrifice—that was what he offered. For *her*. It was there in his voice, in the way his jaw clenched, as if he were chewing on nothing, or everything.

He'd do it.

But she couldn't do that to him, let alone *them*. This was

all going to come undone if she couldn't bring herself to make a better effort.

"You never answered my question about why you brought me out here to talk. What did you have in mind?"

"Exposure therapy. My idea was exposure therapy."

"I've already been exposed to you."

"But not enough to build a callus."

She wanted to poke holes in his theory, because she didn't want to commit to spending more time with him than her already fraught nerves could support. But there was a kind of logic to his suggestion. Continuing to say *It's too soon* was stupid. When was it going to be long enough if not ten years?

"Not enough to build a callus?" she repeated, bracing her elbows on her knees. Propping herself up was easier than holding herself up when her muscles were already strained to the point of exhaustion just having this conversation. "Define exposure."

"If I say it, it'll sound like a come-on."

"If you say sex, I'll push you in and turn you to mush with the propeller."

He chuckled a little. "No, I was thinking dinner."

"At your house?" So he'd come this way for a reason. "Won't your father wonder what's up with us?"

"He's currently residing in France."

She'd heard nothing about that, but then she didn't ask questions about any of the Xenakises. "Why?"

"New French wife."

"Oh." French wife—that was indeed new. "When did that happen?"

"I don't know. Must've been some time this year, since they're not divorced yet. I've lost count of his marriages, but I want to say this is the tenth. Maybe eleventh? The last wife I met in person was number eight."

"You're just numbering them now?"

He shrugged. Nothing in that shrug showed how his parents' frequent divorces had devastated him as a child. He'd definitely built a callus over that, she thought.

"What's her name?"

"It's not worth trying to make family connections with someone who won't even be around next year."

His parents hadn't been neglectful so much as absent, and his stepmothers had made more of an effort to be in his life when they were married to his father than either of his true parents had. But the inevitable divorces had come along and they'd always disappeared. She remembered that it had been another lost stepparent that had been the catalyst that had had her stealing a boat to go to him and ending up in their first kiss—once upon a time in a completely broken fairy tale.

The knot that twisted in her throat said she wasn't up for this tonight. "I think I'd like to go to Chris's house now."

Unlike earlier, he met her request with a simple nod, returned to the helm and fired the engine.

Soon they were bouncing across the water again, in the correct direction this time, and she kept her eyes open. Not because she expected another trick, but because the whole conversation had left her unsettled—emotionally dizzy. Having something solid to pin her gaze to seemed the most sensible action. Even if looking over the battered coast of her homeland brought its own kind of ache.

Soon enough they were docked, and he tied the boat up before offering his hand to steady her as she climbed off.

She almost took it, but her courage faltered at the last second and she grabbed the rope to steady herself instead. Counting on someone else to save you was the quickest way to get lost. She knew *that* lesson—had learned it over months and years of agony and heartbreak.

But she didn't have to trust him. She just had to stop flinching from him if they were going to make working together a viable option.

"Part of exposure therapy involves confronting the things that trigger your anxiety," Ares said. "What do you fear will happen if you look at me or touch me?"

With her feet on the solidity of the dock, she wanted just to keep walking. But the short conversation had eased her a little. He'd been honest, and she'd leave him with the same courtesy.

"I'm afraid I'll cry."

CHAPTER FIVE

ARES STOOD ON the steps leading up into the local registrar's office, waiting. Not for someone, but for his guts to stop swirling. The idea of his best friend marrying in this place had haunted him since he'd been reminded of it in a way he hadn't been able to ignore.

He'd tried to talk both Theo and Cailey into having a small ceremony at his villa instead, but neither of them had gone for it. The mayor was opening the building on his day off, at a late hour, as a way of saying thank you to them for their efforts after the quake. And they didn't have time to get an off-site wedding put together. Location didn't matter, they'd argued, just sentiment.

But experience told Ares differently. The one time *he'd* tried to orchestrate a registrar's wedding had turned into the biggest sin of his life.

He should've known it would end that way—just like all his parents' marriages.

Knocking Theo and Cailey out and *forcing* a change of venue wouldn't be acceptable from a guest—let alone the best man.

"Why are you standing there?"

Erianthe's sweet voice reached over his shoulder and bade him turn around. She stood at the base of the stairs, several feet away, and she had changed for the wedding too. She wore a flowing, strappy peach dress that looked made out of sunshine. Her years in England showed in the paleness of her naturally tanned skin, and that gauzy peach number left her looking like some kind of confection.

Like a dog eyeing a particularly tasty treat, he felt his mouth instantly watering. No matter how many times he reminded himself that he had no right to have that reaction to her, that she wasn't his anymore, his body kept arguing the case.

He was supposed to say something. Explain why he was loitering halfway up the stairs. And he was just too far from caring even to try to concoct a cover story. "Hate weddings."

"It's not your *baba* getting married."

Leave it to Erianthe to shoot right at the heart of it. She apparently didn't have it in her to dance around subjects she didn't like either. At least they had that in common.

"Thank all the gods," he muttered. But somehow acknowledging it—or maybe just speaking to her about something that wouldn't hurt *her*—helped the tension ebb from his shoulders. "Not my *mama* either. She gave up getting married after divorce number six."

"At least she learned. Eventually."

She walked up the stairs toward him and he knew he should step aside. A gentleman would step aside. She wasn't coming to him—he was just in the way of where she was going.

But she looked so lovely walking toward him. Her hair had been coiled up high on top of her head in a thick bun that left her slender neck bare, as well as her delicate collarbones and her shoulders in that pretty, sun-worshipping dress. But it was the hairstyle that drew his gaze up. To her ears. Her ears had always tickled him. They were smaller than average, but they stuck out from her head in a way he couldn't help finding totally adorable, which she'd always hated.

"Why are you smiling?"

"Am I?" he asked, and shrugged.

A lifted brow was all that answered him as she came to rest on the same stair as he, taller than he'd become used to seeing her due to her high-heeled footwear.

"Just thinking how cute your ears are with your hair up."

All semblance of being cool and collected evaporated with the blush that stole over her cheeks. She fumbled with one ear, as if she could mash it into her head or will it to lie flat. "Don't make fun of my ears. I'm trying to look sophisticated and ladylike."

"I'm not making fun of them," he argued, offering her his elbow.

The sleeves of the relaxed linen tunic he wore would keep them from accidental skin-to-skin contact, but she still took several seconds of pondering before she wrapped her little hand over it.

"I'll be staring at your ears during the ceremony."

"You'd better not."

They took the remaining stairs at a casual pace.

"Have you learned to wiggle them yet?"

Teasing her made it easier to enter the building.

"Shut up, Xenakis."

There it was—the first hint of amusement in her voice toward him in ten years. A smile he couldn't control split his beard.

He couldn't resist more teasing. Since he'd come home, he hadn't felt even an ounce of the warmth he felt now, playing with her.

"I think those little dangly earrings would dance delightfully if you did."

She dipped her head forward, in a way he'd have liked to

call fond or affectionate, but when she lifted her chin again, her black eyes had become wet obsidian. Sad. Tearful.

Her hand relaxed and fell away outside the building's entrance. The warmth that had infused him and given him the will to walk in evaporated with the lost touch.

He'd taken the teasing too far. Fallen back on the affectionate playfulness he'd given up all rights to when he'd gone against her wishes to talk to her father.

His knees locked up, and he would have abandoned all plans to attend his best friend's wedding if Erianthe hadn't opened the door and held it for him, not commenting on that final tease.

Their pact to act normal hung in the air, and for once she didn't look away from his gaze. She knew he saw the tears, knew he knew what they meant—she was mourning for what they had once been to one another, what they could have been.

"This isn't the start of the downfall of their relationship. Theo never gives up on anyone," she said as he reached for the door to hold it for her instead.

Theo might never have fully given up on anyone so far, but there was still the potential for it, or she wouldn't bother about telling him that. If anything could push Theo to doing it, it would be finding out about Ares's betrayal of his much-loved little sister.

In a little more than a week and a half his supervisor would call him and Ares could turn his promised three months into three weeks and fade out of her life again. Let her life normalize. Remove the danger of an explosion. If he stayed, it would only be painful for her for longer. Or, worse, he'd lose the battle with his desire and make it much worse.

Erianthe headed inside and broke away immediately, leaving him to find the guys and act normal. He could do that. He'd done this wedding thing at least a dozen times before. What was one more?

After a stop for directions, Erianthe found herself standing outside the solid wooden door to where she'd been told Cailey and Lea were getting dressed.

She took a moment to catch her breath before she knocked. It hadn't been physically arduous to traverse the hallways—it was something else that had made her breathless. Being close to Ares excited her almost as much as it hurt. Talking to him. Playing with him. Anything besides what ate at her all the time was easy. Playing with him gave her a thrill, made her feel warm. Loved.

Expelling a final centering breath, she knocked. A second later Lea peeked out and then waved her in.

Lea was dressed up, wearing a pretty gray-and-pink floral maxi dress with a bandeau neck.

"You look wonderful."

"Thank you. I haven't really got a full wardrobe yet. Luckily this was delivered yesterday and it fits right."

Did these two women understand the strange family they were being drawn into?

"Where's Cailey?"

"Back here!" Cailey answered from a small adjoining bathroom, prompting Erianthe to peek through the open door.

Cailey looked in the mirror and swiped on some pale lipstick, then turned toward Erianthe. "What do you think?"

Her sea-foam-green dress might have graced the cover of some 1940s-era *Vogue*—sleeveless chiffon, with a deep V-neck in the front and the back, and a wide band beneath that kept the flowing material close to her curves.

Erianthe hurried to her childhood friend and soon-to-be sister-in-law, giving her a tight hug and babbling, "You look amazing. Theo's head is going to explode. When did you find time to go dress-shopping? Was it before or after you decorated that room out there? All those flowers and ribbons—you'd forget this was a registrar's office."

"I didn't, and I didn't." Cailey stepped back, looking radiant and happy.

Erianthe felt a twinge of envy—she was the only true singleton in the room with these happy women. It was going to be a miracle if she managed to make it through the ceremony without turning into a blubbering basket case. The only thing in her favor was knowing her parents were still on holiday and would be absent from this impromptu ceremony.

"My mother had the dress from ages ago, and we decided it was perfect for this occasion. And the decorations? That's the mayor's people."

Cailey's voice was pure champagne—bubbly, celebratory, so happy... What did happiness that acute even *feel* like? Erianthe couldn't remember.

"They went all-in. Coming in after hours, decorating..." Lea said, looking as astounded as Cailey looked happy.

Cailey sobered. "The mayor told Theo he wanted to arrange everything as thanks from the whole island. We only did what anyone would have done after the quake, but he insisted."

Erianthe knew that the mayor was also a friend of Mopaxeni Shipping, and kissing up to that kind of wealth was still a thing—even if she'd been so far removed from that lifestyle for so long now that it felt truly bizarre to witness it from the outside.

But they had done a lot for the people in their time. Painting the mayor with a Dimitri-shaped brush did nothing good for anyone.

She swallowed and offered, "Anything I can do?"

Soon enough the bride was ready, and they all exited the tiny office—Lea and Erianthe hurrying ahead so that Cailey and her mother, Jacosta—who'd come to inform them that everything was ready—could make the traditional, escorted entrance together.

As soon as Erianthe was through the door, Ares took her arm and wordlessly pulled her back into a corner. With all eyes on the door, waiting for the bride, she couldn't do anything but let him. He didn't steer her to a seat—there were no seats, standing room only in the office—but stopped at the back edge of the crowd, his tall frame blocking her vision.

"What the hell are you doing?" She tried to whisper, but the flash of heat she felt at being cornered by Ares messed with her volume control.

"Stopping you from running into your parents without warning."

The wall was now at her back, and Ares and his intense stare wiped out her ability to see anything else. And her ability to think went with it. She heard her heart in her ears—at least a dozen beats before his words made sense.

"But they're on holiday in Switzerland."

"Looks like they returned for their son's wedding."

A rush of acidic sourness in her throat had her wondering if she was going to be sick. But it never came to that—just stopped at that stomach-churning place.

"Where are they?"

Did she have time to leave? Would anyone notice? She wasn't *ready* for them.

"Front of the crowd, where they can get the best view."

She was expected to stand in the front with Cailey, and they'd be right there, next to her.

"Look at me."

He still had hold of her arms, but it didn't make her feel

worse right then. It was his calm, confident voice and the way he'd made himself a barrier for her that gave her the spine to resist running.

She locked her gaze to his. Even with that Wildman beard, he was still the most beautiful man she'd ever seen—which was a large part of why she tried not to look at him so much. But she looked now.

"When we're up there, you look at *me*. Don't look at them during the ceremony. Keep your eyes on me."

In that moment the idea of doing exactly what he'd ordered was so appealing it brought a cascade of feelings flooding back. Good feelings. Dangerous feelings. The feelings of someone who'd been taking care of herself for so long the temptation to let him support the weight almost buckled her knees.

"*You're* not much better," she said, as much to remind herself as him.

He accepted that with a nod. "No, I'm not. But I'm not asking anything of you. Just think about what an ass I am and be less upset about *them*. I kidnapped you and took you on a boat, made fun of your ears…"

A hush fell on the crowd, denoting Theo's move to the front. Her heart stopped cold, then began hammering against her sternum.

"It's time."

Ares folded her hand over his arm and led her to the front, his purposeful locomotion enabling her to walk. But then he let go and took his place beside Theo, opposite where she waited for Cailey—they were the only two people not watching and waiting for the bride. She might see *them* if she looked away from Ares.

Not that she needed to actually *see* her parents. There was such a dark awareness shrieking its warning in her mind that it conjured their images for her.

Don't look at them. Don't make a scene.

They wouldn't make a scene.

Appearances meant everything to her father. Enough to send his daughter to a convent a thousand miles from everyone who loved her so that he could hide her shame from society.

Appearances *were* everything. He'd always kept up appearances. He'd used to try to talk to her, but she hadn't listened to a word from him since her eighteenth birthday—the day she'd counted down to since the day she'd lost the child he'd intended taking from her anyway. She hated him. And that was something else that would be ruined for Theo if he ever found out. She knew her brother would never forgive that—at least probably not before the old man died. They'd only recently started making nice officially again after their own troubles, which were bad enough without adding the death of a baby.

Ares coughed lightly, and she realized her gaze had drifted down to the floor. She pulled it back up to him.

Cailey had already walked down the "aisle," as it were. The sea of people who were watching had separated to let her through. And Erianthe had missed it. But she didn't even have enough room inside her to feel guilty about that.

She locked her gaze to Ares's beautiful green eyes, but she couldn't do anything about the mask of misery she felt her features twisted into. Not crying. There would be no crying. Not here. Not in front of everyone else. Not in front of *them*.

Ares's jaw bunched and flexed. He was gritting his teeth, she realized.

She caught the wedding in snippets. Heard the "I do's," saw the kiss, remembered to cheer. But she looked away from Ares only in short bursts and always found her way back to him like some kind of base. His grim expression was the only bastion of solidarity.

The ceremony ended and Ares stepped forward, offering his elbow to lead her out behind the newlyweds.

"They're on the right," Ares murmured to her.

As if on autopilot her eyes jerked to the right and collided with the coal-black eyes of Dimitri Nikolaides. She was aware of her mother at his side but couldn't pull her gaze from his. She stumbled and would have fallen if Ares hadn't flung his arm around her waist at the first wobble and kept propelling her forward.

"Look at *me*," he growled, but she couldn't. The only thing that saved her was his stride moving them past.

The next thing she was aware of was fresh air and early-evening sunshine—and Ares's strong hand enfolding hers.

"The *taverna*…"

"No," he said—one simple word—and turned her down the street toward where he'd parked.

Were they not going to the reception?

"I'm taking you home."

CHAPTER SIX

"NYLA?" ERIANTHE HADN'T even waited for the patient folder to be handed to her—just entered the room on Monday morning as soon as Petra informed her who was waiting. "What's wrong?"

She closed the door and crossed to the exam table, where Nyla sat rubbing her belly.

"Not moving. No movement for a long time again."

Erianthe immediately donned her stethoscope, listening past her own pounding heart while searching for the baby's heartbeat. That process might never lose its visceral slam for her. When she'd lost her daughter, there had been a lead-up of increased anxiety that she hadn't been able to explain, and now she couldn't dismiss Nyla's, even without specific symptoms to cause alarm.

Unlike last time, the heartbeat came through straight away, normal and strong.

"I hear him," she said immediately, not wanting to scare her patient again, even though she knew the fear Nyla harbored wasn't going away just because things seemed okay *now*.

When her baby had died, she'd felt something was wrong for a long time beforehand, and her concerns had been brushed off as teenage whining. Now, even if a patient's fears were unfounded—not some kind of intuition as she'd come to believe hers had been—she knew they had to be listened to, respected.

Did every obstetrician worry as she did? She'd often wondered if her innate fear made her a better, more compassionate doctor, or if it made her prone to emotional decision-making.

Even if Nyla couldn't articulate precisely *why* she was worried so, Erianthe knew through hard statistical data that different external stressors increased the likelihood of miscarriage and stillbirth. The best she could do was investigate.

"What's going on? How have you been since the quake? Did you have any injuries? Did anyone you love have injuries?"

Still rubbing her belly, still worried, Nyla answered, "Me? I wasn't hurt. My house is damaged, but still standing. Mostly."

Mostly? That word more than anything got her attention. And over the next quarter-hour she got to the bottom of Nyla's fear.

It wasn't some dodgy intuition that couldn't be helped or investigated. She had concrete problems—legitimate situations that could hurt her and her baby. Worries had stacked on worries, and now they became a medical concern.

The best way to help Nyla and her baby was to help address her problems. If someone had done that for *her*, she might not have lost the baby. Her own situation had been in line with the statistics.

She did the best she could in that moment, fetching the ultrasound machine to show Nyla her baby—her *sleeping* baby—who woke when Erianthe pressed the wand against him.

A knock interrupted the impromptu sonogram, and she called out permission to enter.

Ares popped his head in.

"Dr. Xenakis." Erianthe paused, the wand held over Nyla's belly, looking at Ares across the way. "Is everything okay?"

He stepped in, closed the door and gestured. "I heard Miss Sarantos was here, and after the last visit I wanted to check in."

"He's sleeping," Nyla interjected for Ares's benefit, and Erianthe returned to what she'd been doing.

Was he worried about Nyla and her baby, or was he worried about how *she* would react to Nyla having diagnosable problems? She couldn't take the time right now to work it out. She had to just ignore him, so her attention wouldn't be fractured.

A moment later she got her brain on the right train again and took some measurements, a couple pictures, and printed them for Nyla to take with her. It was all the meager reassurance she could offer right now.

It was the end of the day when Ares caught Erianthe in the staff room, standing over a table, notebook and pen at the ready, phone pressed to her ear. She spoke fervently about the need to locate an apartment and apparently was having no luck.

"Chris's house too stressful for you with Evan there?" he asked quietly when she hung up and they were alone.

Erianthe looked momentarily confused and then guilty. "I'm not looking for me. Not today."

"Who, then?"

"Nyla." She rubbed her head and laid the cellphone on the table. "She had a great job, doing the accounting for a small local business, but the quake seems to have killed the business and she doesn't have the funds to do any fixing of her house right now. It's damaged. She has no family. The father of her child abandoned her. She's alone—in a home unfit for a newborn *or* a pregnant woman. Do you think Mopaxeni needs any accountants?"

"Maybe... I don't know—I'm not involved there at all."

She was going above and beyond, and jumping from one problem to the next, but she still hadn't answered the question.

"So you're trying to find her a job, or somewhere to live? Since the quake, housing is limited."

"Both." She drew a line through the fifth item listed on the notepad before her. "Know anyone looking for tenants?"

Although she spoke to him, she still had her gaze fixed on the list. Ares leaned over to read it.

There was one more item on the list: Deakin's boathouse.

"He'd probably be fine with her living there short-term," he said. "But it's really not built for more than a night or two. And the stairs are really narrow and steep for a pregnant woman to safely navigate."

A quick move and she covered the list with her hand, as if he *hadn't* just read it. "Oh, I didn't realize it was that small and confined."

"Were *you* hoping to move there?" He tried again.

She glanced up at him, and the rueful sideways bob of her head said enough. "I can't. If I tell Chris I'm moving out, he's going to want to know why. I was thinking of the boathouse so Deakin and Lea could look out for her. Like...all the time."

"Did you find something to be concerned about when you checked Nyla? I mean, outside of her housing situation."

"Yes."

"Symptoms?"

"Not physical symptoms. Well, *some* physical symptoms. Her blood pressure is a little higher than I'd like—but that might just be because she's always so anxious when she comes in. But mostly her anxiety is not abating. She doesn't feel better when she comes here—she just feels relieved that the baby hasn't died already. She's worried all the time. Pregnant women without partners or any support system are at greater risk of miscarriage and stillbirth than otherwise healthy women who do have them. We don't know why, beyond suspecting that cortisol and other stress hormones play a part. But I don't want her feeling alone."

A silent warning sounded in his head. The way she said it was so very personal, giving the words a weight and meaning beyond what she'd actually said. She wasn't just talking about Nyla—he was certain of that.

There were no more patients to see, but there was a chance that one of the guys could walk in if he made her cry again. But he couldn't *not* ask.

"Like you did?"

She visibly swallowed, pulling her gaze back to her list. "It's worse for teenage mothers...the statistics. But she's still at greater risk than someone who isn't alone. She's also afraid the water line to her home is damaged and that the water's unsafe for her to drink, that it might hurt the baby. There's more to this situation than me feeling protective just because I identify with her."

But that was part of it, he knew.

"Chris doesn't want her at his house?"

"I can't ask him to do that. He has Evan, and he's still learning how to be a *baba* after the surprising way that came about. It's not right for me to play on his good nature or thrust a stranger into his home when he's got a baby there and other problems to deal with."

"Theo?"

"He and Cailey are probably naked all the time right now. And too busy to take in an expectant mother."

It was right there, hanging in the air. *His* home was the

next logical choice, but she wasn't going to ask. He glanced at the notepad she still covered, wondering if he'd missed seeing his name there.

"So, you're waiting for *me* to offer?"

The grimace twisting her lovely face confirmed it even before she sighed and nodded.

It was an opening—something he could do for her to take *one* worry away, at least. But maybe...

"She's welcome," he said, then dragged out the chair beside her and sat down so she'd look at him. "If you come too—to watch out for her."

She fidgeted with the paper, bouncing her pencil on her thumb for a long while before she looked at him.

He wasn't going to be there much longer. She needed to get out of Chris's house. He could stick them in their own wing and avoid them both, if that was what she needed.

The look on her face was a definite *no*, but for some reason she didn't say it—just alternated between looking at him and staring off into space, breathing fast, clearly at odds with his offer.

Time to go.

She needed time to think and he'd give it to her. She'd probably be more inclined to say yes if he confessed about his upcoming recall, but that would just start another fight for a different reason.

"Think it over," he said instead, standing and turning toward the door.

There, unexpectedly, he saw Cailey—and the woman had no poker face. Her brows had climbed halfway up her forehead.

"Cailey?" Erianthe finally prompted.

"I was just coming to turn the lights out and collect some stuff from the fridge," Cailey answered, but she looked guilty and suspicious.

How much had she heard?

He did a little mental rewind. Had he said anything about Chris's house and the baby? Or had he just invited her to his place in order to look after Nyla?

Dammit.

Ares motored his boat into the docks that sat below his estate, both glad and unsettled to be putting an end to another long, strange day at the clinic.

After he'd made his invitation to Erianthe and Nyla— and after they'd been caught talking relocation by Cailey— Erianthe had waited only about two hours before calling him to accept. Yesterday, she'd taken the day off work to convince Nyla to move, and to help her pack up her small house and decide what to store.

Which had given him over thirty-six hours to get used to the idea that Erianthe would be living there, and yet he still hadn't managed it.

That morning she'd come to fetch the boat Deakin had gifted the clinic in order to make the move. That had been when his stomach had started churning. And it had continued to do so every time he thought about coming home to her.

It was that phrase that kept tripping him up.

Erianthe was at home.

What would Erianthe say when he got home?

Erianthe... Home.

Home... Erianthe.

He tied the boat off and walked at a purposefully easy pace toward the villa, slowing himself down. If he could slow his step, maybe he could slow down his thoughts, slow down the urgency he felt bubbling in him like some primal instinct telling him to run or be eaten by a tiger.

He wasn't coming home *to her*. It would never be like

that—something he'd ensured, thanks to his mortal sin of going to see her father. And he didn't really want that anymore anyway—it would only make it worse when it ended. He knew that. He *knew* it. This strangeness was just some kind of mental blip.

He found Nyla asleep on a lounger in the garden and went inside in search of Erianthe. Just to make sure she'd found everything she needed.

And once again he reminded himself: she was there to babysit a patient and to avoid babysitting an actual baby at Chris's house. And to avoid causing questions at Theo's.

Only, she wasn't actually there.

He prowled the guest wing, knocking on doors and letting himself in when no answer came, but there was no Erianthe. He hit the library, the kitchen, the pool, and the knot in his gut twisted tighter and tighter with every Erianthe-free location.

Fifteen minutes later he found himself outside, staring up at the highest hill on his island.

The island was only big enough for one decent-sized estate. The villa took up the lower hill and plateau, and a much taller hill existed at the rear. Atop the hill sat a small stone cottage, built in the mid-nineteenth century for the brother of one of his ancestors—a man who'd only wanted to watch the sea and tend sheep.

Shepherd's Cottage was the last place she *should* be— which was why he knew she was there.

The cottage had been kept in good repair, having been lived in by a groundskeeper until his father had become the master of the estate, and had soon found the need for a place to sleep away from his wife—whoever she might currently be.

It also happened to be where he and Erianthe had used to steal away when they'd been keeping their relationship a secret from everyone. Where he'd first kissed her. Where they'd created life.

His legs and lungs were warm by the time he'd hiked to the top, and he found her sitting at the back of the cottage, overlooking the sea.

The sun hung low on the horizon and it lit her and the sky in an orangey-pink light that took his breath away.

"Just going to stand there?" she asked, not looking at him.

"You shouldn't be up here."

"You said to make myself at home." Boredom dripped in her tone—either with him or at the conversation.

This wasn't how he'd pictured this going. "I couldn't find you."

"I couldn't find me for a long time either."

Irritation had crept into her voice, leaving him in no doubt. She didn't want him there any more than he wanted her to be up here, torturing herself. That wasn't why he'd invited her to the island.

When had she turned so masochistic? She could just about make him understand why she wanted to help other women deliver healthy babies, but *this*? No. Just *no*.

He balled his fists and forced words out. "This is foolish. You're not going to find anything here."

"I found that it hadn't been damaged in the quake. That would've been sad."

She still didn't look at him, her gaze far out over the horizon. She didn't look at the kaleidoscope colors in the sunset sky either. Her face was raised to the light, but her eyes had drifted down to the water. Not where the sunset colors were reflected, but closer, where the Aegean had turned midnight blue.

Something dripped off her chin. His heart lurched and

then started beating hard. *She was crying.* Sitting there, staring at the water.

Her voice was level as if the tears had been falling for a long time—long enough for her to get used to it.

"Since I've been home I haven't gone to any of my old places. I thought I'd feel it at your house. Wasn't really looking forward to it."

"Why are you doing this to yourself?"

"Just because *you* feel nothing for her it doesn't mean I'm going to forget her too."

Her.

His knees buckled and he had to step backward to keep from falling.

Her.

He didn't have to ask who. He hadn't ever known the sex of the child, but he knew now, from that one word. His daughter. The daughter he'd lost. The daughter *they'd* lost.

"You're just going to *go*?"

She laughed—a short, pained, incredulous burst of sound from her throat as she mistook his movement for an exit.

Before he could think of a response, she was out of the chair, thrusting a phone in his face. "I. *Won't.* Forget. Her."

He didn't want to look. The tingling at the back of his neck told him that whatever was on the screen was dangerous, would hurt. But his eyes tracked to the small screen anyway.

A small marble stone with tiny footprints etched into one corner sat amid green grass. The name on the stone was Ariadne Xenakis.

There were bands around his chest, squeezing, squeezing, and he felt a terrible need to move. He couldn't breathe.

She'd given the child *his* name. He'd been the one who'd

gotten her sent away, and she'd still given their baby girl his name.

He grabbed the phone, unable to do anything but look. "Ares…?"

He heard her say his name, coming from the wrong direction, and he realized he had moved away from her with the phone. He stood with his back to her, facing the stone wall of the cottage, unable to take his gaze from the little screen.

"How long?" he croaked, but couldn't look back at her. "How long did you have to wait before delivering her?"

"A day. They wanted me to wait until birth started naturally, but my father intervened. It's the only thing I can say in his favor. He made them induce me and she came the next day."

This time when she spoke she didn't sound angry. She sounded *young*. And hurt. And as if she needed to tell him—or needed to tell someone and he was all she had.

She needed to talk and he needed her to get it all out at once. Rip it off like a bandage over a wound that had festered. Mechanical debridement. Tearing the flesh off so the wound could finally heal.

Hers. His. Someone's.

"You said she stopped moving…?"

"Babies sleep in the womb, so I don't know when it happened."

She spoke in a rush, her voice growing steadier instead of more distraught. It was he who was cycling down into a hell he deserved to be in.

"After a few hours of trying to convince myself it was just worry that made me afraid about her not moving, I complained. Told the nuns I wanted to go to the doctor. But I worried a lot. I worried all the time. I went to the doctor so often I was like the boy who cried wolf. The nuns sent me to bed—told me the next day would be better. But in the night my fear hit a peak and I sneaked out. They found me at dawn, hiking up the road for the town, and finally took me to the hospital. But it was already too late."

And then she'd had to fight to be able to give birth to her daughter, and how many hours had that taken? How long…?

He placed one hand on the stone wall and braced himself, unable to ask the questions that would allow her to get it all out.

Her soft hand curled over his and she removed the phone from his grip—gently, firmly, as if she might take away something that was hurting him.

Then she ducked under the arch of his arm and wrapped her arms around him, up and over his shoulders. He folded down on her, unable to hold himself upright. All he could do to keep from collapsing, crushing her all over again, was to spin them both sideways when his legs buckled.

He landed hard but held her tight, his face buried in her shoulder.

"You loved her too?" she said in his ear.

The surprise in her voice shouldn't hurt—he'd given her no reason to feel otherwise—but it did.

Her arms slid up, moving over his shoulders. Her hand found the back of his head and stroked it gently.

He was crying. The realization might have shocked him if he'd had any room left for anything but the pain of the loss of his daughter and knowing he was to blame. Still, he nodded. He owed her that truth. He owed her more than that.

If he'd been with her, he'd have listened. They'd have gone to the hospital immediately.

But Ariadne was gone, she'd never had a chance, and it was all *his* fault.

And—weak, disgraceful creature that he was—he could

only cling to the woman he didn't deserve but would love forever. Take the comfort of her soothing sounds, her soft hands and strong arms. He should be comforting *her*. Should have been there to comfort her if he couldn't have stopped the tragedy.

By the time he'd calmed down, the sky was dark and a sliver of moon had risen high in the sky. She sat sideways across his lap, where he had folded onto the ground, and rocked back and forth, side to side, pulling him with her.

God help him, he wanted to stay right there. Wait for the sun, see the end of what felt like an eternal black, moonless night. But that would be wrong.

He sighed, and she leaned back enough to look at him, but he knew she couldn't see much. He couldn't see much more than the outline of her, even right there in front of him. Which meant she couldn't see how he knew he must look.

Soft and cool, her hand pressed against his cheek, and he closed his eyes against the dark, letting his weakness carry him a little longer.

Her sweet breath feathered against his face, the tip of her nose brushed his cheek—and he turned into the kiss he'd felt coming.

He'd been so emptied by the talk there was nothing but space in his aching chest to fill with her fire.

She'd clearly felt the first pangs of being home at the cottage, and now, with her kiss, he found a homesickness so sharp he'd have done anything to banish it. Devour her or run… They felt like his only options.

Crushing her to his chest, he tilted his head and pulled at her lips with his own. Frantic, fervent, needy. Her fingers twisted in his hair and she pulled his head closer, until there was nothing artful in the kiss. It was all frantic clashing teeth and stuttering breaths, and he knew she needed him too.

The darkness hid them, letting him pretend that now was then, that this was *right*. Touching her, kissing her, breathing her in, tasting her mouth and the salt from their tears became the only truth in him.

They rolled to the grass, stretching out. Her soft body was beneath him, fitting against him, perfection in the meld of its curves.

Somewhere in the back of his mind he knew he should stop this, but the broken part of him that needed her pushed forward, rucking up her shirt so he could get closer, touch more skin. He *needed* more skin.

"Ares..." She breathed his name against his mouth, then tugged on his hair where she'd tangled her fingers, urging him back. "I'm on call."

He couldn't see her, but he did become aware of an annoying jingle playing nearby and a bright light. They both looked to the side and she reached out with one flailing hand to grab her phone off the ground. The screen lit her features in a pale blue glow. Soft, swollen mouth to match swollen eyes.

Because she'd been crying too.

Ice ran down his spine and he levered himself off her so she could sit up. He didn't stop moving until he was on his feet and fighting to breathe in something besides the headiness of her scent.

She spoke into the phone, talking to someone at the clinic—probably one of the interns from Athens he was still getting used to. "I haven't seen her yet. Is she at full gestation?"

A baby. She was going to deliver a baby.

He didn't even need to ask. He found his way to the door of the cottage, opened it and flipped on the courtyard light so she could move around safely.

"How far apart are the contractions? Any problems?"

She went through a list of questions and then announced, "I'll be right there. I just need to get down to the boat—probably ten to fifteen minutes."

She had to go down the hill in the dark when she'd been crying and, worse, crying with him.

The first night at his house and he was already a mess. He was supposed to be keeping his distance, not making things harder for her. And that was exactly what things would be when he left. Unless she got sick of him before that.

He could only pray.

CHAPTER SEVEN

STILL YAWNING, ERIANTHE turned through the large wooden gate into the courtyard of Theo's whitewashed stone cottage. It was situated on a small tree-lined street leading away from the village, and stepping through the gate was like stepping into a park. The stone walls bounced any noise away, and the verdant little garden filled the air with fresh, summery scents.

It should invigorate her, but the oxygen she sucked in through another massive yawn didn't energize her in the slightest. She stopped outside his door and shook her arms and legs, trying to get her body going, out of that space where all it wanted was more sleep.

Last night's birth had been long, going through the morning too, and she'd fallen asleep in the on-call room around one, so she was still wearing last night's scrubs. Great dinner guest. No gift. Wrinkled scrubs. Perpetually yawning...

The door opened while she was caught in the middle of her usual wake-up round of bouncing calisthenics.

"Are you having some kind of seizure?" Theo asked, grinning at her, reeking of good mood.

She held up one finger, her eyes watering as she fought another urge to yawn, then gave in and performed the most important part of her wake-up routine: scratching her arms, neck, chest and belly.

"Oh, you've been bitten…or perhaps you have fleas. I saw a cat…"

"It wakes me up better than coffee." She finally spoke, the light scratching having done its job better than coffee ever did for her.

"Scratching?"

She nodded, "Really. Scratching is something that arouses—"

He cut her off with a quick jerk of his hand and gestured her inside. "Let's *not* talk about you doing stuff to yourself to make yourself aroused in my courtyard."

Rolling her eyes, she moved past her big goofy brother and hugged Cailey. "Sorry I don't have a gift for my first visit. It's as gorgeous and warm as the pictures led me to believe. Yet I show up looking like a month-old loaf of bread."

"You look just fine—but you know you could've come to rest here. You're always welcome to take advantage of our closeness to the clinic, especially when a birth goes long."

Her new sister-in-law led them to the veranda, where appetizers had already been laid and a bottle of wine was open to breathe.

"Are both mother and baby okay now?"

"They're both great." Erianthe skipped over the kind invitation with a smile and a nod of thanks, hoping to avoid talking about her new residence entirely. "Thought we might end up with a C-section at one point, so I was going to ring Ares to come assist *me* for once, but then she went from five centimeters to fully effaced in the space of about ten minutes. Pretty amazing."

They sat at a cozy little table and, having missed eating anything substantial since yesterday, Erianthe didn't need an invitation to help herself to the stuffed grape leaves.

Theo waited until she had a mouthful before asking, "So, are you and Ares sleeping together again?"

She choked and, just behind the squeeze of her throat and chest, felt herself go cold. All-over cold. Morgue cold.

Theo knew.

Out of the corner of her eye she saw Cailey thump him in the chest. "Are you trying to kill her?"

It took a second for her to swallow the too-big, too-ravenous bite she'd taken, but even that wasn't enough time to come up with an answer. Or for the prickling down the back of her neck to sort out what she even felt about that.

If she said *no*, that would be the truth, but would imply they'd used to sleep together. Maybe that wasn't such a good thing to confirm. If she'd had half an inkling he might ask something like that, she might have had a prayer of lying her way through it without any suggestion that she was lying, but she wasn't a good liar most days. She was an even worse liar when her body was shooting off warning alarms.

All she could think to do was ask numbly, "Why would you think that?"

Answering a question with a question? Yeah, liars did that. She was pretty sure that liars did that. But the question was out there now.

Theo and Cailey shared a look, and Theo poured her a glass of wine to wash down her dangerous grape leaf. "You two have been weird since coming home. Something was going on at the wedding, with him blocking you from seeing our parents—that isn't the sort of thing you do when you dislike someone—and then you left together. Before the reception."

"You didn't warn me they were coming back early." She pointed a finger but then took the wine—because wine could only help right now, either by slowing things down or just giving her something else to do. She hadn't given a second thought to her and Ares leaving the wedding together. How had she overlooked how suspicious that had looked?

"You're dodging the point."

She took a sip of her wine and let herself focus on Theo's face. His not-angry face.

He knew—at least about their past relationship—and he clearly wasn't angry at being kept in the dark about it.

This whole business of keeping things secret—past things secret—suddenly seemed ridiculous and stupid. Theo wasn't shaking with accusation, or even concern. He sounded…teasing. Like regular ole laid-back Theo.

The thousand tiny needle pricks on her neck calmed down and she breathed slowly out. "I am not sleeping with Ares."

She had kissed him. A lot. And they probably would have ended up naked last night. But last night had been an emotional land mine and they'd both needed comfort—which had been an epiphany for her that had broken her ability to reason at the time. An unexpected birth really had been the only thing to save her. There would be no repeat performances tonight when she got home.

Got back to Ares's home. That was what she meant.

"You've moved in with him."

"Along with a patient whose house is falling in, who has no family and who has been abandoned by the father of her child. I couldn't bring her, a veritable stranger, into Chris's house with him having the baby there. That'd be wrong."

"She has a point," Cailey chimed in. "And Deakin and Lea are living in his guesthouse while the main house is renovated. That little room above the boathouse would never work for two people. Or even one for more than a day or two."

"Especially when this patient is highly aware of every

time her baby goes to sleep and stops moving and immediately worries that it's something dangerous—that her baby is sick, in need of help, or…"

She couldn't bring herself to say *dead*. That fear was the one that made this case particularly personal to Erianthe. *All* her patients were her concern, but she had an undeniable connection to Nyla.

"I saw her twice in my first few days because she regularly panics over the house and the water and all that. She's in need. I thought you'd be proud of me helping someone in need."

"Of course I am. But I know…" He paused and glanced at his wife, then back at Erianthe. "I thought you'd been sent straight to boarding school when you were young, but recently Father let it slip that before that you'd actually been in a convent for a few months. I told Cailey."

The confession didn't bring the usual prickle to the back of her neck. She even shrugged without effort. "I don't care that you told Cailey—she's your wife. I only didn't tell her myself because how do you bring something like that up when you see someone again? *Hi, how are you? Yes, Mother and Father sent me to a convent…*"

"For getting caught having sex with a boy whom they would not name," Theo finished with a glint in his eye, plucking up his own grape leaf. "Whom *I've* sleuthed out was Ares."

"How did you work that out?"

Again, questions to cover secrets.

And Theo caught her at it, laughed and shook his head. "So you're not denying it?"

She drained the wineglass. "Not denying it."

Not that she couldn't have tried, but pulling it off unrehearsed was something else entirely. Too many variables—not least of which being an inability to mask her own guilt.

"Told you." He grinned at his wife. "So you and Ares were naked and got walked in on? That must have been mildly scarring."

"Mildly..." she muttered, and shook her head.

The more this became something to tease and grin over, the more it began to bother her—as if she had a right to feel something else. It wasn't Theo apparently knowing for a while but not asking until now. It was that he didn't know how big it had been, how bad...and that she couldn't tell him there was no joke to be found in that story.

"Listen, don't tell anyone else, okay? It was something we kept secret back then because we didn't want it interfering with the group dynamic. We didn't want people feeling like they had to choose sides. Or blaming him for our father's decision back then."

She said the words, maybe even said them convincingly, but she didn't know if she truly felt that way. Two days ago she had been certain Ares fully deserved that blame. Now? She wasn't so sure.

"But you're still weird around one another."

"They've seen one another naked, Theo. Having any kind of normal relationship after that is hard." Cailey championed her.

Erianthe nodded, as if that was the whole story, then said, "Please, it's my secret. Don't tell Deakin and Chris. Ares is pretty sensitive about it too. He felt guilty for a long time after they sent me away. If he knew you knew, he'd feel even more ashamed, and it's in the past."

In the past...

She almost believed it herself. Or she could *consider* believing it, even though nothing had felt as if it was safely back in the past ever since she'd gotten back...

"As long as you're okay." Theo looked at her closely,

seriously enough to give his normal jovial manner some weight. "Otherwise I'd have to beat the beard off him."

Ares sat at the docks, waiting for Erianthe to return with his boat from dinner with the Nikolaides newlyweds.

His gut said she was going to be irritated or angry when he told her he'd relocated to Shepherd's Cottage. After last night he didn't want to risk her coming there to find him. They couldn't spend time together alone there—maybe shouldn't spend time together *anywhere*. They were hard-wired to get naked when they were alone. Especially there.

Headlights across the water, speeding toward the island, told him she was coming. The night sky was still so dark that he'd brought a lantern with him tonight. As she neared he climbed to his feet, readying himself to take the rope and help tie it off.

"What are you doing down here?"

Her words and tone seemed overly bright, forced.

"Were you afraid I'd sink your boat?"

"No." He tied it off and offered her a hand to leave the boat. She took his hand, no hesitation—just took it.

No sooner had she stepped onto the wooden planks than she turned to him, her concerned face caught in the lantern's shadows. "What's wrong?"

He let go of her hand and gestured for her to walk with him down the dock. "This isn't about Ariadne but what happened afterward…"

"Emotions were high."

She kept up with his long stride, but he slowed himself down, not wanting them to get into the house and within earshot of anyone else before the conversation was done.

"What is *this*, specifically?" she asked. "Confirmation that we can't have sex? I know that. I agree."

"This is me telling you I've relocated myself to Shepherd's Cottage."

"You're moving into your dad's breakup hut?"

The incredulity in her voice stung, stopping him from walking.

"We went from fighting to almost getting naked in a heartbeat. It's one extreme or the other with us, and it would be very easy to get confused."

"*I'm* not confused."

"Well, I am." He held out one hand for the keys to his boat. "I'm working tomorrow, so I'll give you a lift. Nothing at work is going to change. I just don't think we should be alone together right now."

"Maybe we shouldn't, but Theo's already figured out something is up." She kept hold of his keys, despite his beckoning hand. "And I don't like lying to him."

It was a warm night, but he went cold. "What has he figured out?"

"He didn't ask—he just stated it. My father has apparently told him that I was caught having sex with a boy they refused to name, and that was the reason I was sent to a convent for a while before I went on to boarding school. And he asked me specifically, 'Are you having sex with Ares *again*?'"

An unnatural urgency twisted the back of his neck and spread over his shoulders. "What did you tell him?"

"I didn't tell him about Ariadne. But I didn't tell him he was wrong about us either. I said it was you. I'm not going to gaslight my own brother. He knows there was an us. And he seemed okay with it. He was laughing."

"He always laughs things off until they get serious." Ares shook his head. "It needs to stop here."

"I know that. I didn't tell him everything, and I don't want to. I just wanted to tell you the truth. I know last night was shocking to you, and it was hard for me too, but it's better between us now, isn't it? Not good—nothing about having lost her is ever going to be good—but it was good to share the truth with someone after all this time."

He didn't feel that. All he felt right now was a certainty that all this was about to go wrong in the worst possible way.

Because of him. *His* actions. Not hers.

If any man had done that to his sister—if he'd *had* a sister—Ares would never have been able to forgive him for it. Ares wasn't even sure Theo would be all right if he found out. Nothing to do with worrying about the group dynamics.

Theo would *mourn*—it was that simple. The others would be sad too, but Erianthe was right about how much it would hurt Theo. Not just the loss of his niece, but knowing he hadn't been able to take care of his sister through her darkest days. There was very little that riled him up, but family in need… That did it. And Erianthe—in a pre-Cailey world—was Theo's closest family.

"I know I just said I don't want to tell him," she said slowly, as if she was working through some kind of thought process. "But… I don't know. Maybe he deserves to know the truth. I'm not going to suddenly tell him—not without your permission—but… We deserve to have this burden of secrecy lifted from us too."

"It'll never be lifted. No matter how many people you share it with. The best thing we can do is keep looking forward and not make any more big, stupid mistakes."

"So you consider it a mistake?"

"Of course I do."

"Which part?"

He really wasn't up for this conversation tonight.

"My brilliant plan to tell your parents was a mistake. I

wanted to marry you, and the only way to make that happen with you being just sixteen was with the permission of your parents. The only way I could see to *get* that permission was to meet Dimitri on his own ground, to be what he understood, what he was...by taking charge and being a man."

"You really thought that would work?"

Her brows pinched, and the dubious tone to her voice and the disbelieving way she considered him made him want to smash things. The lantern, maybe, then he wouldn't have to see that look on her face.

"Why else would I go to him?"

"Because you knew how he'd react and then it would all be taken out of your hands. We'd be separated without you ever having to do any leaving."

Every word bit into him, chewing, chewing...

She'd spoken softly, without any emotion at all. As if she believed that. As if she'd believed it for years.

Maybe she'd done exactly that ever since that day at the airport. After his failed attempt to explain himself to her, standing outside the plane with his head still ringing from her slap, Ares had given up the idea of it. Explaining had seemed too much like making excuses for his choices, and there *was* no excuse. But there was a truth to be told. And she claimed to want truth between them.

Maybe it would help her to know. Maybe it would make things easier. Or maybe it would make it easier for her to accept how it would go if she told Theo...how her brother would feel when confronted with something from the past—a mistake—he couldn't fix.

He spoke quietly, not out of choice, but because just above a whisper was all the volume he could give his words. It took everything he had inside him to get them out.

"I would've married you, Eri. In a registrar's office. At a church. In Deakin's boathouse. I would've given up my trust fund, worked as a dishwasher, lived simply… I'd have given everything to be with you and raise our daughter."

She was wrong. Confession *didn't* make him feel better. It didn't make her feel better either. Her brows, fiercely pinched together, etched pain on her face. Tears filled her eyes. She breathed too fast and too shallow, clearly anguished.

His words chewed into her, as hers had done to him. And that was how it would be for them—pain spreading and rippling out until neither of them were whole again.

"Ares…"

Her voice wobbled over his name, in a plea or a prayer… But it was one he couldn't answer.

He handed the lantern to her, because taking care of what was before him was all he could manage. "Be careful going up the path."

She said his name again. Only, he'd already turned to head up the other, steeper trail to the cottage. He knew the way well enough to trust his feet in the dark. She'd be safer with the light.

Ares sat in the clinic's office on Friday morning, his head on the desk, door closed. It had taken him only fifteen minutes to fill out the required paperwork and make the call to summon the air ambulance from Athens for a quick transfer of his latest patient, but he was still running on yesterday's energy reserves.

Sleeping required closing his eyes, and therein lay the problem: his closed eyes provided the perfect projection screen for his brain to replay the highlight reels of his biggest Erianthe failures.

The sound of the door opening jerked him back upright to find Deakin standing there, looking at him with challenge. A challenge Ares just wasn't up for navigating right now.

"The ambulance will be here in another fifteen minutes. Is Mr. Halkias ready?"

"We got him ready before you came down here to call," Deakin reminded him, moving to perch on the side of the desk. "What's going on with you?"

"Just had a little trouble sleeping last night, that's all. I should've asked if his wife is ready too. I remember getting his wounds dressed and setting up the morphine pump…"

"She's there, pushing the button every ten minutes," Deakin confirmed, but he still had that challenging expression, now with shades of concern for his brother-in-all-but-name.

Ares was too tired to deal with some kind of talk in which he was apparently supposed to moan about his problems. He should just lay his head back down.

"I'm onto you," Deakin said, his voice low enough not to carry through the closed door.

Right. And that could mean anything.

"I don't know what you're talking about."

"You look like hell. Even worse than usual. And, since you're taking no hints, I'm just going to say it. You should talk to someone about whatever the hell is going on."

Like *that* was so easy. "There's really nothing going on that I want to talk about."

"Fine, then shut up and listen." Deakin stood up from the desk and instead leaned over to brace his hands on the polished wood opposite him. "I get it. Something bad happened, there's no way of undoing it, so dwelling on *the bad thing* does no good, et cetera."

God, when had Theo and Deakin turned into dudes who talked such crap? Historically, this was not the kind of talking they did. They complained and commiserated with one another, with anger being their primary way to express unity in the face of whatever their friend was suffering—something he'd already told them about. It was a time-honored tradition, and even Erianthe generally respected it.

"You don't want to talk to me about it—that's fine. Don't want to talk to Theo or Chris either? Still cool. But you should find *someone* to talk to."

Ares turned behind him to the fax machine and grabbed the pages he'd faxed to the ambulance company, then the folder they needed to go in, and stood up to take care of the filing.

"Talk to Lea," Deakin said from behind him, bringing up the woman Ares had recently overheard Deakin calling *ángelos mou*.

Ares slipped the file into the appropriate drawer—which should at least earn him some points with Petra, since he seemed to be losing points with everyone else.

"She's not going to tell me about whatever you discuss. And she's good at what she does," Deakin said over the silence.

A silence that was clearly doing no damned good to create a boundary between them.

"I've seen the garden, and the patients she's been able to help, and those are great things. I don't doubt that she's *very* good at what she does, and I would definitely describe her as an excellent doctor," he said.

"But you don't want to talk to her about it," Deakin added flatly.

Talking about it was the reason Ares looked the way he did today—as if someone had blacked both his eyes and his scrubs had been crammed into a suitcase for a month.

No, that wasn't true. Talking with Erianthe hadn't created the rot inside him. It was closer to being like the first slice in to clean out a pocket of infection and becoming overwhelmed by how extensively it had festered. To the point where there might be no hope of healing. Maybe all he had left in him was disease.

He shook his head, even though it confirmed the existence of an *it* to talk about, and faced his friend. Doing battle on his feet, no matter how exhausted he was, was better than doing it on his ass.

The look he suffered went on and on—enough for dread to rumble through his guts. That look was pointed. That look said something. How *onto* him *was* Deakin?

"Is there anyone you *want* to talk to about it?"

Erianthe.

Her face rushed into the front of his mind, and he would have said her name but for the general sluggishness of the day working in his favor.

Deakin's gaze sharpened. He'd seen it—that moment where his mind had shouted the answer.

He saw too much—or Ares was getting terrible at hiding his feelings. Deakin hadn't suggested Ares talk to Erianthe about his issue. Did that mean something? Did he know already that it involved her? Or had he just not suggested her because they'd worked so hard to make it appear they'd never been that close?

"This is the last time I'll mention it, but find *someone*. Hell, you could talk to Petra. Talk to those damned sheep on your land. Write it down and throw it into the sea."

Deakin didn't look at him with the exasperation he'd heard in his friend's voice, but with a muted concern that lingered uncomfortably.

"There's really nothing to write about."

Deakin rolled his eyes, shook his head and left.

CHAPTER EIGHT

ARES SAT IN his boat, waiting for Erianthe at the end of the day. He'd finished on time, but she still hadn't come out.

After Deakin's one-on-one intervention he hadn't been able to decide what, if anything, to tell her. He suspected Deakin knew about them. Or knew *something* about them. Maybe it was common knowledge about them having been together before. Maybe he *should* be up front about that part.

But the problem was the conversation that would inevitably follow might lead to worse parts than they knew. Parts that were at the heart of his whole dilemma.

Ares prided himself on being able to handle whatever life threw at him—because life had thrown a hell of a lot at him and he was still standing. But when it came to Erianthe, no path seemed clear.

This morning on the way to the clinic she hadn't said a single word to him. Not even good morning. Every time he'd looked at her he'd seen his confession from last night in her eyes. And then she'd avoided him all day.

A glance behind him at the building confirmed he still had some time to think about that. Not there. For all he knew she'd decided not to take him up on a lift home. She might be with a patient, or she might just be avoiding him still.

Nothing in who he was wanted to cause pain to anyone, but last night he'd made himself think like a doctor. Would a little bit of pain now save a lot of pain down the road? It was a gamble he'd take.

Another glance back. No Erianthe.

But someone else was there. Two someones. A man and a woman. Loitering.

He stood up to get a better look and his stomach hit the deck. Mr. and Mrs. Nikolaides. And not the newlyweds. They'd stopped at a junction where Erianthe wouldn't see them in time to turn the other way. She'd just be rounding the corner and would stumble over them—the parents she was not yet ready to deal with. He'd given her enough to work through yesterday without *them* piling in today.

The expression on her pale face at the wedding, when she'd looked at them… She'd had to be strong to get through the past ten years, but her parents had a special power to hurt her.

And he'd be damned if he stood by while they ambushed her. *Again.*

Leaping from the boat, he made a quick jog toward them.

"Mrs. Nikolaides." He addressed her mother first but focused on her father. "Mr. Nikolaides. Tell me you're not lying in wait for Erianthe."

"She won't see us," her mother said, and to her credit she sounded forlorn enough to stir a pang of sympathy in Ares.

Except he knew how hard this was for Erianthe to deal with, and he doubted they knew what would come from seeing her deal with it.

Dimitri turned toward him, his expression hard as flint, his face turning deepening shades of red. "This has nothing to do with you. You can't keep our daughter from us, boy."

Boy? That was supposed to upset him?

Dimitri Nikolaides had always had a tendency toward

bullying—something he'd used on Ares at eighteen, to put him on the back foot, from where he had managed to trip up. Or at least had started the long, complicated exchange that had dismantled all Ares's defenses and thrown in a few metaphorical kidney punches to seal the deal.

But today's taunt sounded too schoolyard to do more than make him… Well, he'd be amused if he weren't in a hurry for them to leave.

"I'm asking you politely," Ares said, as it seemed the speediest way to get them gone. "But I can become less civil. This is where your children work. Don't sully it, or your daughter's reputation, by making her react where anyone could witness it. The wedding was hard enough on her."

"You suddenly care about her *reputation*?" Dimitri snorted, and Hera Nikolaides seemed to just fade into the background, for reasons Ares didn't have time to analyze. "She's *living* with you. Outside of marriage. Are you planning to give her *another* child to lose?"

Another attempt to dismantle him. And that was the one that got a reaction.

Ares stepped forward so quickly, so aggressively, that Dimitri stepped back to avoid being touched. He wasn't a small man, but Ares was tall enough that he tended to tower over most people.

It took some serious effort on his part, and some mental reminders of Dimitri's age, but he resisted the urge to beat the man to death.

"*You* can't take care of her. Look at you—you can't even take care of yourself," Dimitri added caustically.

Erianthe hurried down the walk to the docks, checking the time as she went. Ares would no doubt be irritated with her. Ten years ago he'd told her he loved her. It had made her happy at the time, but in hindsight it seemed too easily said to remain real after things got so hard.

Last night he hadn't used the word *love*, but all the other words he'd said, they'd been so much more real. They'd added up to love.

His sudden relocation to the cottage had left her with little confusion about how much he wanted her around, but it hadn't really surprised her. What *had* surprised her was the feeling of loss that had come at his declaration of past love. That was what still burned in her chest.

"I can take care of *you*."

A man's voice, cold and threatening, drifted to her from around the corner of the building, and a chill washed the burn right out of her—along with all sense of how to use her body.

She stumbled, and had it not been for her closeness to the building, she wouldn't have been able to keep herself from sprawling at the feet of the men in confrontation around the corner.

It wasn't until a second later that she realized the voice she'd heard was Ares's. His threatening voice. She almost hadn't recognized that low, almost sinister monotone.

Her hand still braced on the building to hold herself up, she ignored the tremble turning her bones to cartilage.

"Now you're *threatening* me?"

And that was her father.

Her bones firmed up a little, along with an increased heartbeat and the need for oxygen. It was like some kind of alternate reality—a live-action fantasy that had played in her head so many times. They were *fighting* over her. Or Ares was fighting over her. Her father just seemed to be fighting.

"Not yet. Would you like *me* to threaten *you* this time? If you think I wouldn't put your ass on the pavement to protect your daughter, you've lost your ability to size up an opponent, Dimitri. Leave before she sees you. Write her a letter—send it to my house."

Threaten you *this time*?

This time.

Ares had had threats from her father in the past? Had they fought when her world had been turned inside out ten years ago? That was not the picture painted for her by either of her parents at the time. But the knowledge fitted in a little better after last night's declaration from Ares.

"How about I just go tell your beloved business partners what scum you are?" Dimitri countered.

"Yeah, how *about* that? I thought you were concerned about her."

Ares had always had an expressive, almost musical quality to his speech. When he spoke with his patients, his words were hymnlike: comforting, inspiring. When he spoke to her…well, they swung between being discordant and off-key to something as sweet as a lullaby.

Lullaby. He'd have sung to their daughter.

That realization hit her as hard as the next: he was fighting *for* her. And she was letting him do it alone. No one should ever have to fight alone.

It took her precisely three steps to round the corner of the building, and another two to put herself between them, with Ares at her back. Her mother, whose presence she'd been entirely unaware of until that second, didn't join her father in fighting. She hung back to the side, out of the way, almost invisible.

"Erianthe, *agapiméni*, your mother wants you to come home," her father said, using his voice like a weapon now— one of fatherly adoration. Calling her his beloved. Until he focused over her shoulder at Ares and all attempts to persuade her evaporated in that one look. As if she couldn't see the visible switch from sweet smile to scowling squint.

The utter ridiculousness of the situation overwhelmed her suddenly and she started to laugh. Only, it didn't sound joyful or amused even to her own ears.

By the time she recognized it as a small step away from hysteria, Ares's arm had wrapped around her waist and he'd pulled her back against him.

"If you want to repair your relationship with your daughter, stop threatening me and send her a letter. She'll decide."

Was it kind of funny?

The rising volume and pitch of her laughter swallowed the rest of whatever else was being said. The next thing she knew, Ares had picked her up and they were moving down the docks to his boat. In the last image she had of her parents, her father's face was so red it had to be on the verge of explosion and her mother wept.

He hopped on board, set her down on the bench and directed her to lean forward, one hand rubbing her back, the other taking her own hand.

"You don't have to see them. You never have to see them again if you don't want to."

She met his eyes and the laughter faded, but behind it she gulped air like someone who'd nearly drowned.

"Slow down your breathing, Erianthe."

Doctor voice. Commanding someone to breathe in a different way than their body demanded. Such a strange thing to do to someone. But they did it. They all did it.

She tried, holding her breath, which was the only way she could think to control it: stop it cold. All or nothing.

What did she tell her patients? She made them control their breathing all the time. Laboring mothers depended on breathing techniques to focus and control pain. The technique seemed insane now.

Ares crouched before her and leaned in until his forehead was braced against hers, his warm, strong hands cupping her cheeks, holding her there.

"They're gone, Erianthitsa. Breathe, honey. Slow and deep."

She closed her eyes, following his instructions as his thumbs stroked back and forth over her cheeks.

Her chest burned. Her throat. Her eyes. She normally reacted to tense situations with fire, but this time the fire had turned inside her and it wanted to burn her alive.

"Out slowly, until you have no more air to give…" he coaxed, his voice back to tender sweetness, wrapping them both in a bubble, alone, safe… Even if they were just bobbing in a boat at the dock.

Her parents could be following right now for all she knew—as stupid as that would be. Ares would definitely push Dimitri into the harbor.

Whatever he was doing, it worked. She drew in a slower, steadier breath and wrapped her hands around his wrists to make him keep touching her. He'd fought for her. He'd *threatened* Dimitri for her.

"He threatened…you…before?" Not exactly what she'd meant to say, but she panted the words anyway. "With what?"

"Same threat—different day," he murmured, then leaned back to press his lips to her head, warm and soft, right between her brows, so that the whiskers he refused to shave off tickled her face. "But he won't say anything to the others. Theo and Chris would never forgive him, and neither would you. He might have underestimated me, but he wouldn't take that gamble with his children."

"I don't think I'm in danger of ever forgiving him for what he did."

"But he holds out hope. He and Theo are getting along okay at the moment. Why would he risk that?"

She didn't know whether Theo had told the guys he was adopted, and that his adoption had been a hushed family secret because "all men need a son." But it wasn't her secret to tell, so she didn't.

At this pace, her back would be crooked with the weight of all these secrets by the time the summer was through.

"I really don't know," she answered finally, letting go of his wrists and sitting up a little straighter. "I didn't think that I'd feel so overwhelmed when I finally had to speak to them. In my head, when I thought about how it would go, I always had the right words. I knew the exact thing to say to make him mourn for her too—his lost granddaughter. To make him understand his guilt. Back there I couldn't think. I didn't have any words, even though I've literally had years to rehearse what to say in my head."

He stayed crouched before her, close enough to touch if she needed to.

"You can't make people feel what you want them to feel. One day you might be able to give him enough information for him to generate his own feelings about what he did, but it's not on you to make him a better man. He failed *you*, not the other way around."

Gently, he brushed her cheek with the back of his hand, one side and then the other. Sneaky tears. She wasn't even with it enough to know when she was crying.

"I failed you too," he murmured, but he didn't linger there for her to start crying harder, just gestured to the lap belt on her bench, tucked her bag into a secure spot and went to the helm.

He'd failed *her*?

She'd failed Ariadne.

Erianthe widened the beam of her flashlight as she hiked up the big hill to Shepherd's Cottage. She'd lied to Nyla about why she needed to interrupt their after-dinner chat to hike to the cottage, but if she was learning anything about the woman from her brief time of knowing her, it was that she picked up on lies quickly.

Luckily they were still at that super-polite stage of friendship where they didn't call each other on their inept lying. Still, it didn't sit right. She didn't want to lie to any more people.

But she couldn't think about that right now. She was too busy hiking to the place Ares had moved to in order to avoid bumping into her, back before the events of today had happened.

"I failed you too."

Words she'd never expected anyone to say to her—least of all Ares. He'd definitely meant it. And he had also said yesterday, *"I'd have given everything to be with you and raise our daughter."*

All those words, and action too, in fending off her parents. It *meant* something. She just wasn't sure what, beyond knowing that she needed to talk to him. To know him.

She had to step carefully—it had been years since she'd navigated this hill in the dark on a regular basis, and rocks and land had a way of shifting and settling in new ways that her feet didn't know from memory.

Everything he'd said framed who he was *now*, and how different the adult version of Ares had become from the boy. She couldn't say if it was simply camouflage, a deep and desired change or just a manifestation of his regret. Not shaving or getting a haircut for a set length of time was a practice in some faiths. She wasn't certain if *he* even knew what was going on with himself. But she *wanted* to know.

She skidded and had to right herself, pay better attention to the climb. Not exactly smart to come up in the dark, but it had been late when she'd sorted through what she'd witnessed enough to know she needed to go to him. He might not be as ready to talk as she was, but she could tell him how *she* felt.

If her short time on Mythelios had proved anything to her, it was that it wasn't over between them. They had unfinished business of some kind.

Maybe it was just a need to lay the past to rest so they could move on with their separate lives. But maybe there could be a chance for them. She wouldn't still be so drawn to him, so affected by simply hearing his name, if her feelings were completely over and done with, firmly in the past.

She wanted to trust him, but that trust wasn't instinctive— it was a *choice* she had to make.

Reaching the cottage, she hurried up the short stone path to the door, flipped off her flashlight and knocked. Rushing forward when she probably should be tiptoeing.

When it came to Ares, she was still that brokenhearted sixteen-year-old girl. Waiting until morning would just mean she had a whole sleepless night to contend with beforehand. No, it was better that she do this tonight.

No answer to the knock. Her stomach tumbled—whether in fear or excitement, she couldn't tell. So she knocked again.

"I failed you too."

He'd be glad to see her. Maybe he was even regretting moving to the cottage so suddenly… He still cared for her in a tangible battle-your-dragons-and-carry-you-to-safety kind of way. If they could just get through the emotional minefield that lay between them…

Still no answer.

The surf and wind competed to make it impossible to hear any sounds of movement from within the cottage, where the lights were still on.

He didn't sleep with the lights on—couldn't if he was anything like he'd used to be.

Another knock. Nothing. *Nothing.*

Then she heard it—the faint ring of his cell phone carried on the breeze.

He was out back on the veranda.

Skirting the side of the cottage with the help of the light streaming through the decorative windows, she followed the inlaid stones and found him silhouetted against the night.

He stood closer to the edge than she liked—where it had always made her nervous and triggered her vertigo.

The casual clothes he'd changed into after work were built for comfort—she'd barely recognized him in a suit at the wedding—but he looked good to her in everything he wore. Tonight, the light, probably white T-shirt he wore fit well, and although he was thinner than she'd expected him to be, his shoulders were still broad. A warrior's frame. One she found herself wishing she could bulk out.

He was still unaware of her. She stayed quiet to keep from interrupting his precariously located conversation—in English.

English.

Not someone from the clinic calling, then. Nor someone from the island. Or his father. Or mother...

"I'm not ready yet. Still have a couple of things to sort out."

He stopped speaking to listen.

Ready for what? Was it wrong for her to stand there and listen? It wasn't as if she'd come here to eavesdrop on him, but that was a particularly suspicious-sounding thing for him to say. Who could turn away from *that*?

"Maybe in a couple more weeks."

Pause.

"I know you're always rushing to fill spots, but I told you I needed at least three weeks before you could call to see if I was ready to leave. But it's only been just over two, and I'm not done. I need a little more time. Get another doctor on temporary assignment for a couple more weeks until I can get there."

He was leaving in a *couple weeks*? Three weeks was what he'd initially promised. And she'd been told he'd be staying for several *months*.

Somehow she managed to hold her questions in until he hung up the phone and stepped back, hands on his hips, head bowed forward.

Upset? Disgusted with himself?

"You're leaving?" she asked numbly, and he turned to look at her, not answering for far too long for her liking.

"They need me," he said, but from what she'd heard, he'd always intended on leaving early.

"*We* need you."

I need you to stay.

She'd never had trouble saying what she meant in the past, but her courage abandoned her in that second. She'd overestimated how deep his current feelings were for her. His feelings were *about* her—or at least about how she made him feel about himself—and they were something he expected to be done with in a couple more weeks, apparently.

He stashed the phone in the pocket of the trousers he wore, his voice pitched loud enough to be heard without too much difficulty over the raging water. "You, of course, can still stay here with Nyla when I'm gone. I trust you. It's not a problem."

He trusted her? Right now all *she* trusted were her stinging cheeks and the strong desire to flee.

"Great. That's generous of you. Letting us stay after

you're done sorting some things out. Am I one of the things you need to *sort*?"

She could see him well enough to track his movements, to make out his general body language, but not enough to see his face. The tilt of his head and shoulders said enough: he didn't want to talk to her. Presumably about this in particular, but maybe about anything at all.

"It was a shorthand way to say I wasn't ready to leave tomorrow."

"It sounded a whole lot like *I'll be ready in two more weeks*."

"No!" he said roughly, his frustration finally cracking through the surface of his voice. Reaching a chair, he dropped into it and turned his gaze out to the black. "I need an escape hatch."

"In case I get to be too much to deal with?"

"Because *I'm* not dealing with it well. *Me*."

"We just started dealing with it together." She gripped the flashlight tighter, to keep herself from throwing it at his head.

He *knew* this. He knew they were finally making some kind of real connection over her loss and *now* he needed an escape hatch? How could she even try to argue with that?

The futility of the conversation pressed down on her, so she threw up one hand to silence any rebuttal he was formulating.

"This is my fault. Once again I assumed you felt the same way I do. I had this idea that we would move forward together, but you just want to be *gone*. Might as well call them back and tell them you'll take an assignment now. I can sort *myself* out. It might have been nice *not* to have to do it alone again, but you know what? You go. I've had years of practice coping by myself. I'll. Be. Just. Fine."

"Eri…"

She didn't stick around to listen to his excuses. It was his life. If he needed to leave Mythelios—leave her—again, it was his decision.

She stomped heedlessly back the way she'd come, but once she was at the front of the house, another thought blasted through her mind and she turned to stomp right back.

"And this? This is what it looks like when someone doesn't try to make choices for you."

He more groaned her name than spoke it.

"Shut up!" she barked, then stormed once more for the front of the cottage.

She turned the flashlight on and went back to trail down the massive hill.

Ares Xenakis might be dead set on messing everything up, but she wouldn't help him by falling down the hill in the dark and breaking her head. Her having sudden amnesia would be far too easy for him.

The ass.

CHAPTER NINE

FRIDAY NIGHT HAD ended with a fight. Saturday, Erianthe had split her time between visiting Theo and Cailey, catching up with Nyla with minimal explanation—though probably enough to give everything away—and wondering whether Ares had decided to make his great escape yet.

That was how, at eleven o'clock on Sunday morning, she once again found herself hiking up the insanely steep hill to Shepherd's Cottage.

Check in, find out when he's leaving, go back down again—that was the plan.

Don't punch him in the junk.

Also part of the plan, but placed under the *Optional* heading.

Afterward, she'd go back down to the villa, laze in the sun and read something deliciously sexy about an alpha male who wasn't hopeless and hairy, and whose issues could be solved with a bit of logic and adult decision-making.

As she cleared the top, Erianthe saw something—and stopped so abruptly she fell forward up the hill, her hands the only things saving her from a mouthful of grass and dirt.

What in the world had she just seen?

A little mental rewind as she shifted to her hip and she

stayed on the ground—even if the grass scratched her bare legs. She'd seen Ares. Shirtless. *Beardless*. Planting flowers. In front of the little cottage.

She closed her eyes and imagined it again. Then she opened them.

Yep. Still there.

Maybe she was having a psychotic episode. Hallucinating.

How to tell…?

Throw rocks at him and see if he got mad?

Probably not the best idea she'd ever had.

She levered herself off the ground and *really* looked at him this time.

"I wondered when you'd stand up," Ares said, not even looking over his shoulder.

"You saw that, huh?"

"Heard it."

He finished digging a small hole, picked up a plant—a pretty flowering sea lavender—and gingerly placed it into the hole before tumbling dirt in around it.

"But no sliding or screaming."

She'd displayed no signs of distress aside from falling, so he'd left her to it? Which was fine. She wasn't looking for a white knight to take her freedom in the form of a forced rescue. She had come to find out when he was going to leave Mythelios, and had found him flower-planting instead.

And now her plan was effectively meaningless.

She stood and walked to stand beside him, viewing his work. "You like to garden?"

"Sometimes it's nice to dig in the dirt."

"When did you start that?"

"I used to help Sofia with her flower beds. Haven't done much of it since then."

He was referring to one of his father's many ex-wives. A stepmother he'd truly grown attached to. Did that mean something?

"So you just woke up this morning and decided...*I'd really like some lavender here*?"

He paused, sweaty, with a smear of dirt across his chest and his nails caked with soil that would take an hour to scrub clean. It was the earthy, naked chest, the light whorls of hair there that he most decidedly hadn't had at eighteen, that made it hard to think. It certainly wasn't any long, lingering look from him that churned up the electrically charged butterflies in her belly—he didn't look at her at all. Just planted his flowers.

When two more plants were in the ground, he finally spoke, his voice gentle—with the sweetness she always heard there for others but never for her. "They're for Ariadne."

Her eyes immediately began to sting, the sexy tingles evaporating in a single breath.

She couldn't keep from asking. "Why sea lavender?"

His initial answer was to shrug, then after a long moment he had some words. "It's what I thought of when I'd had two shots of ouzo. I know the logic might not make sense..."

She tilted her head, the better to see what he was up to without getting distracted by the definition in his broad shoulders. "Tell me anyway."

"Because bees love sea lavender. Bees make honey. Honey makes me think of the story of Ariadne, because it's the tribute to the goddess Ariadne, Mistress of the Labyrinth. I know it's kind of convoluted."

She walked around him, watching what he was doing because she couldn't seem to sift through the words bubbling in her heart to find the right thing to say—the safe thing to say, the considerate thing to say—or even to express the gratitude that welled there. As she rounded him, she came to the corner of the cottage and saw dozens of lavender plants in clumps of dirt sitting on top of the grass, waiting to be planted.

"You've been doing this all day?"

"Yes."

And he was nowhere near done. She needed to see this done. That book by the pool and its uncomplicated hero…? Completely forgotten.

"I'll help you."

"You don't have to."

"Yes, I do. But you'll have to tell me how."

Glad she'd worn shorts, she kicked her sandals off and carried them over to the door of the cottage so they wouldn't be ruined, then returned to stand beside him.

"This line of flowers is pretty random out here. Did you have a design in mind?"

He looked up at her. The furrow stayed put, telling her he was considering sending her away. But he didn't.

He stood up, got a tape measure and marked off another straight line abutting the one he was working on. "Spade there. Let me see your hand…"

She held her hand up to him, palm first, not asking his reasoning, just letting him go at his own pace.

"From here to here." He touched the base of her palm with one finger and then the tip of her middle finger. "This far apart for the holes. And they should be deep by about this much, and big enough around to put your fist into."

He described all the measurements in terms of her hands, but only touched her briefly, more often gesturing than actually touching. Then he stopped to look at her but said nothing else, just waited for her questions.

"Why did you shave?" she asked. Probably not the question he'd expected—which was fair, seeing as she hadn't expected it either.

For a moment she didn't think he was going to answer, but then his long look turned into a few words. "I wanted to feel more like how I *was*. How I would have been when I met her."

One sharp, quick breath drew his gaze to her mouth. It was just short of a sob, and neither of them pretended it hadn't happened.

She tilted her chin to hold his gaze. She had more questions, but not about the flowers. The flowers she got. The depth of his regret she finally understood. The acute feeling of loss that had finally caught up with them both ached in every breath. But she still had questions. Although there would have to be time to ask them later, because her throat had closed so tight she couldn't have spoken even if she'd had the words.

Instead she took the spade as directed, knelt and began to dig.

He said nothing else—just gathered plants and returned to his line of holes with them, two at a time, setting them up so he could methodically place them into the holes he'd dug.

The earth was hard and she had to lean into it, mashing her palm atop the spade with all her weight behind it to get it moving.

"If your hands start to hurt, stop digging."

"Watering the ground might help," she managed to say.

She didn't know what had prompted this decision, but she knew he needed to do it. Truthfully, she needed it too. She carried around that picture of her daughter's gravestone on her phone, taking it with her wherever she went, but it wasn't the same. A memorial in this place where she'd been conceived—that felt real. Putting something living in the ground…something that had meaning to her and to them…that was real.

A watering can appeared at her side, and then Ares went back to his plants, not talking beyond the absolute bare minimum required.

The earth softened with the water, and she dug her holes as deep and far apart as he'd instructed. By the time she'd reached her last one, he stood beside her again, this time with a bottle of water for her and a hand towel.

She wiped her hands on the towel, then took the bottle and drank as he began shifting the next lot of plants to the holes she'd dug and finally knelt beside her.

"What's the design?"

"A simple labyrinth. Just a few walls…"

The lines of flowers were *walls*. She'd probably not have come up with this if she'd spent the next month trying to think of an idea…not that she would have done that.

The cool water alerted her to how hot she'd become, but everything here was an overload of sensation. If she wasn't drowning in memory, she was buoyed on a sea of scents so powerful and deep she didn't have words to describe it.

"Will you grow your beard back again?"

"I don't know. Maybe."

He carefully seated each plant in the holes she'd dug and then, holding the flower stems with one hand, began pushing the wet dirt in behind them.

The salt sea spray below, the scent of earth and flowers— she'd even swear the sunshine had a smell. And all of it smelled like *him*: sweaty, rich, covered in dirt and blanketed with grief.

She'd suffered. There had been six months of angry, bitter confinement in the convent, where she'd cried every day for him. Followed by even more months where she'd cried every day for Ariadne. Then nothing. Nothing had gotten through to her because she hadn't wanted it to get through. She'd grown so sick of feeling bereft and lonely she'd just stopped letting herself feel at all.

Instead she'd put her mind to her studies, taken her picture of the gravestone in the convent grounds, and when the next school year had begun, she'd never gone back. She'd tried never to look back ever since—only forward.

But he'd suffered too. She'd blamed him, and he'd blamed himself. She was so tired of hurting every time she looked at him, and she didn't have to ask if *he* hurt when he looked at her—he'd moved to the cottage to get away from that pain.

It was a pattern he'd learned from his father, who had put painful relationships away from him, one after another, for years, by moving there as soon as the fire between himself and his latest bride had started to die.

"We can't get her back."

She hadn't even known what words were coming before they came, or even where they came from.

He stopped planting and answered, his voice quiet. "I know."

But maybe we can get us back.

Those were the words that wanted to come out next. They bashed at her teeth and she clamped her mouth shut to keep them in. Wishful thinking. And far too dangerous. Stupid. Sentimental, probably.

She swallowed the words down and instead of further talking, or saying stupid things, she knelt back down beside him and helped bed in the last two plants as he'd been doing.

He marked off two more walls with his tape, then they watered the ground and dug, and within an hour the flowers had all been planted and she felt…*better*. Not good. But better than she had. With some semblance of peace settling over her. She wasn't alone in mourning her—*their*—daughter anymore. Until she'd come home, she'd always felt alone in that.

Where Ares was concerned, everything was just too hard to think about. Some days she didn't want to imagine him suffering, and some days she did. Some days the idea that he was alone with his pain was salt in a wound she couldn't rinse, and then there were days when she turned to anger just to stop herself crying. Anger burned bright and hot…anger got things done…anger let her pretend her broken pieces were glued back together again. But seeing the pain, seeing the regret in his eyes, in the way he held himself apart from everyone, felt almost as bad.

He crouched down at her feet, putting a bit more dirt around the base of one listing plant, then stayed there, surveying what they had done from down low, one knee on the ground, his attention focused on the empty box at the middle.

"What goes in the center of the labyrinth?" she asked, prompted by the line of his gaze.

All the flowers had been planted, but there was no headstone, nothing permanent to put there, just an empty center ringed by flowers that would bloom perennially.

"The heart of the labyrinth." He didn't rise, neither in his body, nor his voice, just stayed there, not really answering her question.

She knew that state, lost inside himself…

Pull him back.

His long, messy curls had grown tangled from the number of times he'd shoved them back from his face while working, and she reached out to comb them free. Damp with sweat, but strong and silky, unrefined…

He'd been so urbane when they were young. Haircut every three weeks. Shaving every day, even when his facial hair had only been visible to him via a magnifying mirror. Charming. Confident. Cheeky.

Now it suddenly became clear to her that this was all *his* broken pieces—which he'd never even pretended to hold together. He'd shattered, and this hollow man was what remained. How had he gotten through medical school? He was an excellent doctor, but all other areas of his life seemed empty or just missing entirely.

He swayed under her hand, letting her brush his hair back several times before he got hold of himself and surged to his feet so fast he nearly knocked her over.

"Ares?"

Since she'd come home and seen him again, every time Erianthe said his name she spat it out as fast as she could. Two syllables? She made it one and a half—which was to say fast and kind of mumbled. But now she took her time and let the sound of it linger in her mouth, savoring the feel of it. The texture. The taste…

And he heard that. He'd been busying himself picking up the garden tools they'd been using, but he went completely still as she spoke, his back to her. His head swiveled and tilted just enough to make it clear she had his full attention. That he wanted to hear whatever she had to say.

She just hadn't thought of what to say besides *Stop. Come back. Don't leave me…*

Covering the physical distance between them took only a few small steps, but could the emotional chasm that yawned between them be navigated the same way? If they could find the right steps to take to get them there…get them somewhere other than where they currently were…

She stepped around to his front, and the heartbreak and vulnerability she saw on his face almost robbed her of breath.

"Did you launch yourself away from me just then because you don't want me to touch you?"

"No." His voice rasped, choked with emotion, "Yes." Then he spoke again. "No, but we shouldn't."

"But we are."

Just because she recognized it, it didn't mean she knew how to feel about it. Some minutes she was right back there, when there had been no one in the world she trusted more, and at other moments...hours...she couldn't even think his name without a white-hot seed of rage burning through her belly.

Those moments might have been days or weeks—until Friday. Then they'd started to subside.

"It's not the plan."

She snorted a little. "To be fair, your plan was to show up long enough to get credit for helping out, then run straight back to Timbuktu. What's the new plan?"

"That wasn't the plan—that was the method," he said. "My plan hasn't changed. First, do no harm. To you. To them—my brothers. I haven't figured out yet whether I've failed at that, or if it's futile to keep going... But I just don't want to hurt *you.*"

"I don't want you to leave." Her neck began to ache from craning to look into his eyes.

"It would be better if I did."

"We won't get another shot at this." Still the words weren't easy to come by.

"At what?"

"I don't know. Healing?"

She finally got out one word that made some sense, then let her gaze drift from him to the physical manifestation of that healing that they'd begun over the course of the day—planting and building something meaningful together.

"The labyrinth needs something in the center. There has to be a reward for venturing into the danger inside a maze."

He watched her with a kind of wariness that made her chest ache. More than her chest. The need to touch him was a living thing, churning her thoughts, scouring away reason.

"Our walls can be stepped over."

"*Can* they?"

She came closer, until she was close enough that a gentle sway would bring her body into contact with his bare chest. The wind blew in off the Aegean, ruffling her T-shirt, and it billowed against his flesh. But he didn't move away. Just stood there, so much taller than he had been, so much broader, so much a man.

Slowly, as though any sudden movement might startle him, she reached for his face with one hand and didn't stop until her palm connected with his cheek. The same hand she'd slapped him with on that airstrip, the same cheek, where not a scrap of youthful plumpness remained, just an overly square jaw and sharp cheekbones. No longer hidden by hair.

This time his head didn't snap back. He said nothing. Not verbally. His eyes closed and he leaned into her like a man starved of contact, but the look on his face said he was craving something that he expected to kill him. Need and resignation. Not happiness, but yearning.

Her palm burned, and so must his cheek. The heat spread from her hand up her arm. It should feel wrong, doing something that so obviously hurt another, and it did—but that guilt was washed away in a tide of needing to be close to him.

Before she knew it, her other hand was on his face and she was up on her toes, pressing her mouth to his.

She couldn't actually remember who'd started it last

time, when the darkness had hidden them both. But she could see him now, and she wanted to see all of him. He was lean, but strength had built the breadth of his shoulders and the definition she'd spent the day trying not to ogle, which now her hands craved.

They left his face to stroke down. He groaned into her mouth and deepened the kiss, pulling her so tightly to him she had to wrap her arms around his shoulders or be pinned. He was sweaty, dirty, and she knew it wouldn't stop her kissing and licking him anywhere. Everywhere.

He bent deeper toward her, his tongue stroking into her mouth, wrapping his arms beneath her butt and lifting her up.

As she'd followed his tool-gathering trek, they'd ended up at the cottage corner. A few steps from where they were now hidden. She clung to his shoulders as he carried her, blindly staggering but never breaking their fevered kiss. In the shadow cast by the building he fell to his knees, lowering her in front of him as he did.

His hard length strained at the front of his trousers, nudging at her belly as he pulled her more tightly against him with arms that had started to shake. The shaking spread to his torso, his breath, and finally to his kisses.

Hot need twisted her insides, leaving her with parts that only wanted to get closer to him, that had grown clumsy with the fight to do so. The liquid, syrupy heat building low in her belly countered the frantic, jittery greed to get at him. She yanked at his belt, determined to free the thick, wanting length of him.

Unable to kiss him and get her fingers to obey her at the same time, she pulled back enough to catch her breath and look down. As soon as she got his belt open, the trousers were no match for even her clumsy fingers, and she slipped her hand into the front to stroke her fingers lightly along the heavy, straining flesh, base to head, then around, then more firmly.

A tortured groan ripped from his throat, sounding far too much like suffering for her not to pause. She had to look at his face, to see his eyes, but they were clamped shut. As soon as she started to release him, his hand flew over hers outside the material, then gripped her hand so that she squeezed him again. He began to rock his hips. Not a lot, just enough to stroke against the hollow of her palm.

The last time they'd been together, before the world fell apart, it had been loving and fun, *playful*. Now, touching him once made her crave him more. Like an addict falling off the wagon. Because this *hurt*.

His eyes opened, clearer than they had been, but intensity still darkened them, and she felt no less conflicted as he guided her hand to wring pleasure from him after a desert of loneliness.

"You're bigger," she said, unable to keep from saying the words as she teased the pad of her thumb over that sensitive ridge of flesh.

The smile he gave her said he remembered the same spark of playfulness and exploration that had always mingled in with the tenderness and hunger they'd shared. Then he let go of her hand. But even on his knees in the grass he swayed with the effort to stay upright.

"I think…" His words faltered as she gave him a squeeze, and the sounds became just a bunch of stuttering, strangled, gasping noises that might have started as words, but failed to form.

"What do you think?" she asked, kissing up the corded side of his neck.

Knowing she could still affect him like this was everything in that moment, when she'd been living on doubt all weekend. She'd not even asked him whether he was leaving the island. She just knew the answer. *No.* Or at least, *Not yet.*

He curled his hands over her shoulders, bracing himself as he tried for deep breaths, but couldn't slow down his panting enough to pull it off.

"I think that I'm taking advantage of you."

She stopped stroking him and waited for him to open his eyes and look at her before she answered.

"I started this."

"I know—but why? Is it part of mourning?"

Slipping her hand from his pants, she pulled her tank top off, and then her bra, then grabbed his hands and placed them on her ribs.

"It's not that. It's something bright and *needed*. I've been without moorings for too long."

"Are you sure?"

He looked so afraid to hope, but his hands had already started to move up, cupping her breasts, then giving them a warm, rolling squeeze that felt so good she almost regretted asking for his thoughts. He might be using his mouth for something besides talking right now.

"I need this," she said, and a shiver hit her as he continued exploring, tracing her curves with what she could only call wonder in his eyes. "I *need* this. With *you*."

Nothing else needed to be said. He simply pulled her with him into the grass, rolling until it bent beneath her.

Clothing was tugged and removed, one of her shoes came off, and he gripped his length to urge it through her slickness, pausing at her opening to swear.

"What?" Her legs strained wider, welcoming, begging. "What's wrong?"

"I don't have a condom." He choked out the words.

She couldn't help but laugh. "I'm an obstetrician. I'm a fan of the pill. No accidental…"

The word *pregnancy* refused to form, and they both locked gazes, the simple aborted statement bringing back into focus the differences between those kids who'd been so in love and full of hope and the people they were now. She'd never have touched him if she hadn't been incapable of conceiving. It was too much of a risk.

"Do you want to stop?"

His question, incomprehensible even to consider, came with a kind of bittersweet understanding that made her eyes sting and her throat burn.

"I don't want to stop," she rasped out, grabbing him and pulling him more fully against her so she could taste his mouth again, feel his face against hers. In truth, she couldn't even stop touching his face with her hands, gazing at the starkly masculine beauty—the wide angular jaw, cheeks that were still a bit too gaunt contrasting with such soft lips.

He filled her to the point of stretching, and Erianthe could no longer tell herself that the two lovers she'd had since Ares should have been allowed to touch her. As he started to move, time and heartbreak didn't evaporate, but they faded a little. The way he held her gaze connected them in a way her rational mind couldn't label. As if they'd long ago bonded on a subatomic level.

As her pleasure began to peak, those sharp, painful edges began to dull, and she could imagine him whittling off the carved edges of her memories with his touch, his presence. And simply knowing that her broken pieces were also *his* dulled their ability to cut into her just a little. But a little relief was enough when there had been absolutely none for so long.

Later, after he'd carried her inside and run a bath, they sat wrapped up in one another in the old claw-foot tub, her legs around his waist and that once again hard shaft inside her. Erianthe locked her arms around his shoulders and let herself fall into his beautiful eyes.

"Eri…? Eri?"

He said her name and then said it again. It must have been a long time that she'd sat staring at him, because he gave her a little jostle.

"Are you all right?"

Was she all right?

"I think so," she answered.

His hands stroked through her hair, then curled around the back of her neck to pull her against him. She rested her chin on his shoulder and held him so tight.

She wasn't all right. Not really. But how could she tell him that she wanted the chance they'd been denied? Only two days ago he'd been making plans to leave.

She couldn't say it. Couldn't bare that vulnerable part of her yet.

The truth of it was, she wasn't ready to say it yet. But when she looked into his eyes, she felt what *he* felt…or seemed to. Maybe she was imagining it. Maybe she was just thinking about her own emotional experience of a situation, expecting he would feel the same.

But maybe he would see it in her eyes…

She leaned back again and caught his gaze.

The evening's last rays of sunshine painted the bathroom warm shades of sunset and set the threads of honey in his green eyes to shimmering gold.

"I've always loved your eyes…ever since we were little. Before it could be explained by attraction," she murmured. And then images of the first time she'd realized Ares was different from the other boys rose in her mind and she amended that. "Well, *probably* before."

"They're just green."

"From far away, they are. Up close, they're the color of

a new leaf and, depending on the light, flecked with gold or amber. Mine are just black. Flat and black."

"They're not flat. They shine like obsidian and reflect everything."

His gaze drifted lower, slowly enough that she could tell it wasn't a conscious decision for him to look down and away. He went from being all hers to being at the wrong angle to connect with him.

"Where did you just go?" Unwrapping one arm, she lifted his chin and, to make it easier, gave him a soft little kiss.

"I don't know." His arms tightened, and soon she was pressed fully against him, his chin propped on her shoulder.

He did that when he thought about the past. He did that when he thought about her, or about their daughter. When he didn't want to say words. She did it too.

But she could talk about *her*.

"Her eyes weren't blue. I'd expected blue, but they were dark. Hazel, maybe."

His breathing sped up—just a touch, but enough to indicate that he was listening. "They let you see her?"

"I screamed until they let me hold her. Then I looked at everything. Her fingers were yours, so tiny and yet so long." Once more the tears came, and she squeezed him a little tighter in return. "I thought I was over losing her. It's so long ago. But since I've been home it seems like yesterday. I thought I'd already mourned her, but maybe I didn't. Maybe I couldn't do it fully on my own."

"I know."

"I don't even know whether I'm mourning her or you. Us. What we might have been."

What they still could be. She knew they could—she just didn't know whether he wanted that too.

CHAPTER TEN

"HEY." THEO APPEARED beside her at the nurses' station, his usual cheerful manner holding a different tone. A tone that carried ominous inklings.

"Why does it sound like you're about to fire me?"

"Don't be silly," he said, laughing in an entirely and obviously fake manner—a sound she was supposed to believe and yet made her feel uncomfortable.

"You actually *are* firing me?"

Sure, she didn't have access to the kind of funds they all had for providing for the clinic—that lack of money had been a part of her life since the day she'd kicked her parents and their coffers out of her life and transformed herself into a poor medical student.

The sober look that came into his eyes didn't help. "Mom's in Exam Room Two."

She turned to look around the area immediately, expecting to see her father lying in wait for her again. Dimitri was at the core of her parental problems, although her mother had certainly been an accomplice.

"He's not here."

"Oh." Still that feeling scratched at the back of her neck—the one that warned the house of cards that had somehow become her life was about to collapse. "Why?"

"She said she has a 'lady issue' and wouldn't tell me

what." Theo never used his hands, but his tone made air quotes around *lady issue*.

It sounded like their delicate flower of a mother couldn't even reference an actual anatomical part of herself with her adult doctor son.

"Who's her doctor?"

"Retired."

"Dammit, Theo. You *cannot* be asking me to treat her."

"I just want you to talk to her," he said quickly, hands up in a defensive *Whoa, there!* position.

"She's probably faking it so that I have to talk to her."

That definitely sounded like her duplicitous parents. Ambushing her was a kind of trick to force her into something she didn't want.

"She's not faking her distress, Eri."

"You don't know that."

"She was crying."

The tightness between her eyebrows began to feel like a cramp. Could foreheads charley horse? She pressed the butt of her palm there and gave it a hard enough rub to mash the thin muscle into compliance—and probably cause terrible wrinkles in the future.

"I know it sucks. And I know she was complicit in sending you away." Theo was arguing on Hera's behalf. "But she's never really stood up to Father about anything. That's her character flaw. But are you going to carry a grudge forever? They're not getting any younger."

Erianthe felt her mouth fall open in sheer incredulity, and it took several more seconds of Theo's consternation at her response for her to remember: *he didn't know.*

That was the big flaw with managing her reaction to her parents around anyone but Ares. Theo was right—they probably all thought her reaction disproportionate and petty compared to what they thought she had gone through. Theo would always think that until he knew the truth. And she'd continue feeling guilty about it until she could be honest with him. But right now she had no counterargument to make.

"I'll talk to her to see what's wrong," she muttered, and immediately headed for Room Two, glad for once that her shoulders were growing increasingly stiff. Maybe that would make her feel steady physically, if not emotionally.

Not that standing up to Hera Nikolaides required much backbone. She'd never stood up to anyone for any reason—including for the good of her own children.

Not giving herself time to get more worked up, or even to think about what to say, she walked into the room and shut the door.

Her mother, always perfectly put together, wore a flowing white blouse and trousers, gold jewelry on her arms, neck, fingers and ears, and had her perfectly smooth graying black hair swept into a chignon. Perfect and predictable.

What Erianthe *hadn't* prepared herself for—and what she'd failed to notice the last two times she'd been in the same space as her mother—was how much older she looked. Hera's mascara had smudged and settled into the lines beneath her eyes. Because time kept going. She was older.

Her mother was older. Ariadne was not.

Before she could take it all in and speak, Hera rose from the plain plastic chair placed there for patients and hurried forward, arms outstretched.

"No!" Erianthe said, probably too sharply. She couldn't go from nothing to hugging, even if her mother *had* been crying. "This isn't a reunion. Theo said you're having some trouble, so we need to focus on that. Because if you're not, I'll walk right back out that door."

"I found a lump," her mother all but whispered, still a

little distance away from her, her arms falling back to her sides.

Just like that all the air went out of the room.

Hera's mother had died from breast cancer, and Erianthe had studied enough about genetics to know she'd probably inherited one of the genes. Her mother might well have inherited both.

Not wanting to help her own mother when she was so eager to help others…? She didn't need the insistent pinging of her conscience or her stomach bottoming out to shame her. That was just a perk of being a Nikolaides.

She couldn't take her mother as a patient, but she could make an ethical exception for testing and help her understand what it meant.

"When was your last screening and when did you notice the lump?"

There were a number of other questions, and they went through them one by one, each settling into their own corner as they discussed symptoms and timelines.

In the middle, Erianthe paused to go and fetch the ultrasound equipment and leave her mother some privacy to change into the usual hideous hospital gown.

"This will say if I have cancer?" she asked, lying on the examination table and positioning herself as Erianthe directed the scan.

Cancer. Her guts churned again.

"No. This will let me see the shape and location of the lump, but simple machines can't diagnose. I'm going to find it, then use a very thin fine-gauge needle to extract a sample of the tissue. We can send that for biopsy so we know what is going on."

Hera accepted this with a silent nod.

"If it hurts… I won't mean to hurt you." How awful

even to have to say that. "Tell me, and I'll try to find a different position."

"I don't mind a little pain. You get your strength from me."

Rule number one for being a compassionate doctor: never laugh in your patient's face when they babble something outlandish under the fear and stress of a possible diagnosis.

But inside her head... Really, if she had her mother's "strength," she'd be saddled to a feckless man in a barren, loveless marriage—because that was all she would've been good for after losing her child and falling into that hole inside herself.

"I lost three babies before we adopted Theo."

And that was a bridge too far. Erianthe could be polite to an upset patient, but not if she was going to try to make her talk about things she had no right to.

"Mother..."

"It was earlier with them. But it's never easy to lose a child."

She tried to ignore the subtext—the main text was bad enough. Her vision swam and she put the wand down, spinning on her stool to try to contain it.

Don't cry.

"I can't talk about this," she croaked.

"I just want you to know..."

"See—I need to *not* be shaking or crying so I can perform the biopsy safely." Her voice had gone squeaky, and that was just unprofessional. None of this was professional. Professional was not treating a family member—especially one you'd been estranged from for a decade of your life.

"I'm sorry, *koritsi mou.*"

"I'm sorry too," she said, but she couldn't say precisely what she was apologizing for—her mother's sad miscarriages, or the fact that Erianthe blamed both her parents for the loss of her own child and all that had preceded it.

Hera didn't try to talk about anything again until after Erianthe had taken cells from the lump in the upper inner area of her mother's right breast.

"I'll put this on the transport to Athens tonight. It should take a week or so for the results. Then we can figure out what the next step is."

"You mean chemotherapy?"

"I mean most likely surgery," she corrected softly. "I'm not saying mastectomy—I mean lumpectomy. That's where they take out the mass and a little tissue around it to make sure that it comes out cleanly."

Hera absorbed this with a slow nod. "Will they send the results here to you?"

"Yes."

"Will you promise not to tell Theo until we know something? I don't want him to worry."

She and Dimitri had recently become closer to Theo, who was going to give them a grandchild in six months' time. Her mother was insulating him, which shouldn't bother Erianthe. She didn't want her mother to protect *her*.

"He's the one who told me you were ill." Erianthe labeled the collection bag and sealed it up. "All these secrets... It's like no one ever tells the truth about anything. Except Theo. And he's the one being lied to over and over again."

"Theo has his own secrets."

Erianthe snorted.

Hera stood and shed the gown in order to begin dressing herself. "He's kept a secret for me."

"That he's adopted?"

"That Ares's mother, Melisa, and I paid for your university and medical school fees in alternating months so that I could keep it hidden from your father."

Erianthe dropped her pen. "Theo said it was a collective effort by the guys."

That had always been part of why she'd intended from the beginning on coming back to practice at the clinic: she owed them a debt. Theo. Deakin. Chris. Possibly Ares. She'd never asked about his donation—hadn't ever wanted to know.

"It was the only way for me to help you when you persisted in being estranged from us," Hera said, her tone dripping with the insinuation that *she* was the wronged party in all of this.

"It wasn't the *only* way, Mother. You could've stood up to Father for once in your life. You could've come to live in England with me, helped me through the pregnancy— which was hard enough even when nothing was actually wrong. You could've taken me to the hospital when I cried out to go, when there might have been time to save—" Erianthe stopped when she realized the volume of her voice was rising to dangerous levels.

Hera didn't argue any of it. But then, how could she?

Back to the subject… "Ares's *mother* paid too?"

"Melisa loves her son, and her son loved you."

What should this secret make her feel? Angry that she'd been lied to? She wasn't. Relieved that her mother had done *something* against the wishes of Dimitri, tyrant of Clan Nikolaides? Warmed to hear her mother speak of Ares's love, which somehow legitimized it even while worsening the fact that Hera and Dimitri had been fighting it? With their questioning. Doubting. Their inability to speak of their feelings in the present tense.

Always the past. That was a safe discussion.

"What do you suggest I tell Theo?" Erianthe asked, getting on with it—which was really all she could do right now.

"Tell him I'm in menopause."

She'd have laughed under any other circumstances. "Mother, you're sixty-three. He can work out *that* math on his own."

"Some women take a long time to stop having..." She sighed, giving up her own argument. "I don't know."

"Have you told Father about the lump?"

"No."

Well, Erianthe couldn't really argue that one, but she would argue for Theo. "How about I tell Theo you had a test and will talk to him about it when you're ready?"

"That will only make him worry."

"You were crying. He's already worried," Erianthe said softly.

She was worried too, and confused about every single word and gesture that had passed between them today. Where did this leave their relationship? Could she allow her mother to be a part of her life and still keep Dimitri at a distance? Would her mother agree to that? Did she even *want* to open that door again?

"Fine, then—what you said, I suppose." Hera presented her dressed self for inspection.

Erianthe reached out to tuck a wisp of hair back into the ever-perfect twist at the nape of her mother's neck and was grabbed in a fierce hug that left her on the verge of bawling.

"When you're ready to talk to me, you call me. I'll come to the Xenakis island. I don't care what your father thinks."

All Erianthe could muster was a brief hug for Hera in return, then she pulled back into her protective bubble, talking only about medicine, which was all she could understand right now.

"I haven't worked with the oncology lab in Athens yet, but I'll try to put a rush on these results. I can probably get the wait time reduced to a few days."

She spent a couple of minutes discussing aftercare for the biopsy procedure, then excused herself.

Too much information to process for one day. All she wanted to do was find Ares and then go home. To bed. Ignore the world. Ignore the problems still unresolved. Ignore Hera's possible diagnosis. Hide out at Shepherd's Cottage and pretend it was all settled.

Pretend she knew Ares was going to stay.

Pretend she wasn't afraid to ask if he wasn't.

Ares's body thrummed, his heart beating with a vigor he'd often thought would never be repeated again. Erianthe rolled with him, naked on a naked bed, too warm and too content to worry about clothing. It was like that now.

Three days since they'd flipped that switch from unsteady allies to lovers too consumed by and for one another for clothes to be a part of their time together at the end of the day after work, and after Erianthe had spent some time catching up with Nyla. And they'd been with each other every day so far this week at work, hidden somewhere in the clinic.

His breathing started to slow and he hugged her to him a little tighter, so that he stretched on his back, her head fitting into the hollow of his shoulder, and didn't have to let go of her. Even if he *should* let go of her.

She'd be asleep soon, if he was still and quiet. Not repeating the things he'd said to her when he was inside her and the madness had taken him over.

"Say you're mine."

And she'd said it. More than once. But he knew she'd ignored the second part of his request.

"Don't mean it—just say it."

"You're freaking out about something," she murmured, breaking into his spiral of panic over whether or not he was leading her on. Over whether or not they should even be doing this.

"I was thinking it's silly for us to both be living here at the cottage." Which they were. She changed for work in the morning at the villa before they left for the clinic.

"You're thinking we should go back to the villa?"

"I don't really want to…"

No, what he wanted was for things to continue just as they were. In secret, with no pressure from outside and a naked Erianthe in his bed every minute of their off-hours.

"Me neither," she said. "It feels private here. And… nostalgic. No, that's not exactly the word. You know what I mean. It feels like it's *ours*. And the labyrinth is here. I like being where it is…seeing it when I look out the window or get some air."

She didn't want to go back to the villa because somewhere along the way she'd gone all in with him again. As he'd known she would if she ever stopped hating him. Which she seemed to have done.

He needed her to take in his next words, but every inch of him wanted to do it gently. "If the guys show up here, they'll be opening up a big bucket of worms."

"Don't call her that."

Her voice had gone quiet, and he'd heard the hurt before he tilted his head to look at her.

"I wasn't calling *her* that. I just meant…"

"The secret," she clarified. "You're talking about our secret. But *she* is our secret."

"She's *part* of the secret," he ventured, shifting onto his side so he could face her. So he could look into her eyes and she could look into his, so there would be no room for misunderstanding. "I mean the whole thing—all that we've hidden that compounds the original secret."

"The cover-up is worse than the crime?" she asked, those

shining black eyes still wary, as if she wanted to trust him but it would be an act of will.

He didn't know of anything that scared Erianthe, but she was afraid of *him* right now, of what he'd say. No matter how many years passed, no matter if she forgave him, if they got married...had a family...she'd still be waiting for him to betray her again. He wouldn't. But if the situations were reversed, *he'd* never trust himself either. Not really.

"We've been lying to them about our relationship for eleven years now. In addition to our...our sad story, our bad decisions..."

She gazed into his eyes for a long, terrible moment, clearly wavering about something. He saw the instant she decided how to face it. Her gaze sharpened and her brow took on a determined furrow. Sitting up, she folded her legs and leaned her elbows on her knees, still facing him. Uninhibited. The position let him see...*everything*. And even though they'd just come down from a sweaty tangle, the urge to take her again erupted back into life.

He could kill this conversation by attacking her and reminding her not to taunt a bull with something red—or *him* with that deep, luscious pink...

"Ares?"

"Huh?"

She squinted at him. "I said I want to tell Theo what happened. He'll understand. I know he will."

He sat up, draped the sheet over her lap, buying time and bolstering his willpower. Then he briefly considered tying the sheet around her neck to hide her breasts as well. He couldn't concentrate and have this conversation when all he could pay attention to was places he'd like to kiss or...

Focus. This was an important conversation.

"Why do you think that?"

"He'll understand about us having kept our secret for a long time."

She looked down at his body as he rearranged the sheet again on her lap, then slapped his hand away.

"Good grief—you can't be that aroused already. We just finished. Concentrate."

"Trying. Cover your breasts."

She rolled her eyes, pulled the sheet up and tucked it under her arms. "Better?"

No.

"Yes."

He worked hard to look at her face, because now that they were covered he was entirely aware of how well her nipples showed through the fine white linen sheet.

"Theo has at least two secrets. One that I just found out from my mother, that he's been keeping from me for years."

That sounded somewhat promising. Ares nodded for her to continue, his attention effectively diverted for now.

"He told me you guys were all funding my schooling. So I wouldn't have to work two jobs and take loans after I cut contact with my father and his money."

"He said *we* paid your tuition?"

She nodded. "And that he'd given me a small monthly stipend."

"Who was it really?"

"My mother and *your* mother."

"*My* mother?" he repeated.

His parents had barely got involved in *his* life, but his mother had taken a part in seeing to Erianthe's needs? He was both proud and a little annoyed.

"Why?"

"Because she lost a grandchild too. And because you loved me. And because my mother needed someone to do alternating months with her so she could hide the expenses from Dimitri. Theo lied to me about it because he knew I wouldn't have accepted the money from Mother and he was worried. He did the best he could to take care of me. He doesn't know that I know about this—at least not that I'm aware."

Ares leaned back on his palms and looked at the ceiling. It made a difference—or might have done without their daughter and the circumstances of her birth…their breakup…all that… He didn't know if he could forgive it, were he Theo. Hell, he couldn't forgive it and he was the *villain* in this story. Him and Dimitri.

"We don't know what we're doing, Eri. We haven't discussed this—whatever it is."

"Do they still think you're leaving in a week?"

Erianthe's voice rose and so did she, until she was upright, straddling him, and he was fully aware of the shock and anger conveyed in her reddening face and wide eyes. She wasn't even trying to hide it.

"I'm not leaving in a week," he said, absolutely not answering her question, and thereby confirming it.

"You haven't called them back to say *Hey, that stuff I had to sort out for a couple more weeks wants me to stay*?"

"I just haven't gotten around to it. The clinic has been busy, and we've spent a whole lot of time naked," he said, shifting her off his hips and onto the bed beside him.

His response and rearranging of her to put some space between them spoke the truth. And the heat on her cheeks erupted into an inferno.

"You miserable liar! You're just maintaining your *escape hatch*." She grunted her disgust. "And you said you wouldn't leave until I told you to go. I'm not going to tell you that."

"You *did* tell me to leave the other day."

She kicked him in the shoulder. One second her legs were crossed—the next he had the flat of her foot against his arm and the sheet fluttered down in a way that just exposed everything again.

"I gave you *permission* the other day—to be a jerk and follow your original plan to leave. That was *before*."

He jerked the sheet back to cover her and abandoned the subject. "I know."

"Answer the question."

"Fine. The answer is I *know* all this is temporary. And when it's done, I want to have the ability to become busy again, doing the work I'm used to. That's what I know."

"When *what* is done?"

"This." He gestured between them, the scowl he'd been wearing 24/7 before "this" finally returning.

Her blood pressure shot up. "Being with me, you mean?"

"You want the whole story out there. And I know what happens then."

"Say it. Say you want to be with me."

"Eri…"

"Don't say my name like I'm being unreasonable. But fine—you don't want to say it? I'll say it, then. I want to be with you *most* of the time. Because I love you. I want life and truth and a man whose stupid name makes me go weak in the knees whenever I hear it. That's you."

"I know."

Which part did he know? That she loved him? That he made her weak in the knees? *Most of the time…*

"You don't love me?"

"It's not that simple."

"Yes, it is. You either do or you don't."

"I do," he said, softer, more gently than he had spoken before. "But you know that's not the only consideration."

"Explain it to me."

* * *

His twisting guts didn't lie. Ares knew beyond provable facts that telling Theo would be a mistake.

"I'm not ready. What's the rush if you're not going to tell me we're over? I can postpone my leaving date again. We don't have to make these decisions right now."

"The *rush* is the possibility of them finding out from someone else. That would be worse."

That was a point he couldn't argue. But that was something he'd lived with for years. It had become background noise for a long time—until he'd seen her face again.

"We don't know what we're even doing. Aside from…" He almost said *a lot of sex*, but that wasn't even it. They were doing much more than that, and that was what scared him.

"Sleeping together three or four times a day?"

"Well…"

Her face crumpled, and before he could process the complete loss of color in her cheeks and the shift from mildly argumentative to tearful, she'd crawled off the bed and now was going about grabbing the clothes he'd ripped off her the second they got inside.

The monster in his gut grew teeth and started gnawing at him.

"Eri, I'm not saying that's *all* this is. I'm trying to figure out exactly *what* it is before we make any announcements."

He followed her to where she wiggled into her underthings, wanting to touch her but not sure whether he had a right to comfort her if he was the one who'd made her cry.

"I wasn't as cautious about us as I should have been last time I was with Dimitri. Let's be cautious this time."

Bra on, she grabbed her T-shirt, then turned it right side out as she spoke.

"You don't want to commit to there *being* a current *us*."

Her voice wobbled a little and tears slid down her cheeks slowly. She was resigned. As if he'd hurt her and she wasn't even a little bit shocked by that.

He caught her around the waist before she could put the shirt on, and tugged until her back touched his front.

"I'm not rejecting you. I'm not saying I don't *want* there to be a 'current us.' I didn't say it voluntarily, but I should have. I love you. That's never been an issue. *Never.*"

"Then you're just keeping *her* a secret."

The gut monster broke through, and the rush of acid into his throat would only have been worse if he'd actually vomited. He didn't let go of her—just dropped his head until his nose was buried in her dark silken tresses, breathing in the sweet, fruity scent of her shampoo and the special Erianthe kick to it.

"Not forever."

"The labyrinth…" she said, pulling out of his arms and turning to face him, holding the shirt like he'd made her hold the sheet—tucked under her arms so her chest was covered. Hiding *herself* this time. "I know you wanted to honor her in the place where love made her and let love lay her to rest…"

She croaked and whispered and damned near whimpered the words.

"I love that you even *thought* of it. But it's up here—where she's still a secret. *I'm* not ashamed of her. I was *never* ashamed of her. Or of being pregnant. Or *us.* We kept it a secret only because we were trying to protect the people we loved—and ourselves by extension. But we should've been protecting *her. That's* what I'm ashamed of."

He'd known this conversation would come. They'd danced around it since that very first day. But he had no winning hand to play—just as he'd had no winning hand then.

"What was the solution? I still don't know what the right

call would have been—what would've kept us together. I don't know what I could have done to take care of you both…to take care of *us*."

"There was one thing we didn't try," she whispered, as if her voice had given out on her.

The tears he'd felt burning his eyes finally slipped out. He knew what she meant, of course. Telling the other guys. His brothers in all but name.

"How could they have helped? How do you know they even *would* have? Theo would have done what he could to help you, that's true. Although I don't know how he could have taken you anywhere, since you were not an adult. But, no, we didn't try asking them."

"I know they would have helped me. I don't know if having someone more attentive around me would have helped Ariadne in time. But I know that when teenage mothers' pregnancies end in stillbirth, their emotional well-being is tied to the outcome. Not afterward, but before. Loneliness and isolation contribute to increased rates…"

Her voice grew a little steadier as she detached herself and moved into the world of medical facts. Enough to firm up her resolve.

"I don't know if it would have made a difference. I don't even know if we could have hung together as a unit back then, because we were so young. I can't know that—and you can't know that either. But I know the others can withstand knowing *now* and they deserve to know."

The tears kicked up again and he held out one hand, praying she'd take it. Now wasn't the time to crowd her—not until she wanted him to.

"I can't have her be a secret anymore from the people who mean the most to me," she whispered, and then took his hand. "It's eating me alive and it's eating you up too. We can't go on like this. *Please*, even if there is no future for us, I can't live like this anymore."

CHAPTER ELEVEN

This was how relationships ended.

Ares sat at the small kitchen table at the cottage, his coffee untouched before him and Erianthe keeping watch out the front window.

The one comfort he could take was knowing that he was about to blow everything up for the right reasons. For *her*. Not because he wanted out of what they had together. He didn't want out. He would never want out. If nothing else, he'd broken the Xenakis relationship mold.

Theo was on his way to Shepherd's Cottage, unknowingly to hear Ares's confession. It was what Erianthe needed, and it was time to put her well-being above his. Not every hurt was equal, but that was how he'd been treating it—hurting as few people as possible instead of causing the least amount of damage overall. This step would lead to him losing her, he was certain of it, but it was also what would finally let her heal.

"He'll understand," Erianthe said from the window, looking at him with such hope he didn't have the heart to tell her how this would play out.

There was only one way for it to play out. Theo would want to murder him. At the very least he'd never want to set eyes on Ares ever again.

"I know," he lied, then took a drink of his long-neglected coffee and grimaced.

"Cold?"

"Yep."

She *needed* this, he reminded himself again. She'd come home after a decade of loneliness and isolation. He'd give her this and then he'd go straight back to work. So it was *good* that he'd failed to reschedule his departure date until now.

"You're lying. You always say *I know* when you have no idea."

She left the window for a moment, to slide up behind his chair and wrap her arms around his shoulders from behind. Her cheek pressed to his temple and he leaned his head back, enjoying the feel of her for as long as he could.

"So all the time, then?"

"He's here!" she said, watching her brother make his way down the cobblestone path through the window.

She kissed the side of his neck—one last offer of comfort—and hurried to the door.

She'd have Theo after today. Fully. Without secrets. And Chris, and Deakin, and their families. They'd understand when things got hard for her and be there to support her. Ares wouldn't let her choose *him* over them. They'd help her get through. Find her someone worthy of her.

His stomach churned at that.

She opened the door and launched herself at Theo, who caught her in a bear hug that left her feet dangling and waddled with her into the room.

"Whoa! Much better welcome than the last time I was here." He laughed, looking over her shoulder at Ares. "You know, I think that was when we were…what? Eight? We'd knocked your dad's work computer into the pool and couldn't captain a boat, so the farthest we could run away was up here to the cottage."

One look at Ares, and at the forced smile he'd tried on in order to give their talk a positive start, and Theo let Erianthe slide to the ground, his own smile faltering.

"And that's what's happening today too—we're waiting for something bad to happen." His gaze tracked from one to the other.

"No!" Erianthe said, too quickly, stepping back and knocking into the table—it was the first crack in her determined optimism to appear. "Well, sort of. But not too bad."

Theo lifted a dubious brow, and Eri slunk to the kitchen chair opposite Ares to sit down.

"So this is about you two, not about the clinic," Theo surmised. "And not about planning a surprise baby shower for Cailey…"

"It's about us," Ares confirmed.

He might not *want* to have this conversation—might be completely certain that it would damage his relationship with them all irreparably and put Eri far beyond his reach—but he'd do it straight. For her. He'd be a man. No cowering or trying to talk his way out of it. She deserved that and so did Theo.

"And about what's been going on—before Dimitri sent her away and since we both came back to Mythelios."

Theo watched Erianthe sidelong, looking for hints on how he was supposed to feel, and although she had become nervous since Theo had actually shown up, she was still clinging to the morning's optimism.

"You two were having a fling back then. I know that. And you were the guy they caught her having sex with that prompted the whole convent thing for a few months. I realize that, man. So what's with the ominous mood?"

"That's not everything," Erianthe said, her voice soft

from where she sat between them at the small round table. "That's not really what happened. It was just *their* story."

Theo's fierce frown gave her pause, and for the first time Ares saw that optimism falter. Her brows, worried and pinched, came down over eyes that were just a little too wide.

It was only for a few seconds, but the conversation had turned decidedly when Theo said, in his most level way, "Someone better start talking."

Even as Theo crossed his arms, she flattened her hands against the tabletop. "They didn't catch us."

This was supposed to be *his* part of the conversation. Ares placed a hand over hers and gave it a squeeze so she'd know he was stepping in.

"Erianthe was pregnant," Ares said, straight to the point. "I went to Dimitri to ask permission to marry her. He convinced me that sending her to the convent and giving the baby up for adoption was the most reasonable, adult thing to do."

Convinced? Not precisely the right word. *Bullied* and *tricked* came closer, but they were words used to deflect blame, and that wasn't on the menu today.

To his credit, Theo took it well enough. After his head had snapped back as if he'd been punched, his mouth hung open, his eyes flying to Erianthe's face as he tried to figure out what he was supposed to feel about it.

There were tears in her eyes.

"He made you give the baby up?" Theo asked, and then realized Ares's part in it. "And *you* let it happen? Scratch that. You agreed it was the right thing to do? But when I called you that day to tell you they were sending her away, you acted shocked!"

"I *was* shocked," Ares said. "I thought it would be later

in the summer. As soon as you told me they'd taken her, I went to the airport. But…"

"But you didn't get there in time?" Theo filled in, shaking his head.

"No. Not…" Erianthe saw things unraveling, but Ares squeezed her hand to stop her words.

This was *his* confession to make. This was *his* fault. He'd never had any illusions about that.

"They took her. I didn't know where. Just knew it was a convent. Not even what country, initially."

"And now you have a child out there?" Theo's words died in his throat as he saw the tears leaking from Erianthe's eyes. The cogs were all beginning to click into place.

Theo stood up from the table, hands on his hips, and began to prowl the small kitchen, listening, turning red in the face and generally failing to conceal his reaction as Ares told him the story that was still too hard for Erianthe to tell. That might be too hard to hear again for years to come.

Ares didn't sugar-coat it. He made sure Theo knew what she'd gone through. It was important that all the cards were on the table. Ares was the one telling the story to save her from having to do it. The more upset she was, the more upset Theo would be and the harder it would hit him.

He could see the urge to shout on Theo's face—but he couldn't shout at her, not about this, and he didn't need to. The sense of betrayal was all over his face.

Why didn't you ask me for help? Why didn't you trust me?

"You sit there telling me what happened to her, but you don't *know*. I knew she'd changed. I knew *something* was wrong. But she would never say. Same thing since she came back. I thought it was just about our parents, but it's *you*. You're here and she's reliving it all."

"I know." This time Ares meant it.

"Theo…" Erianthe said his name, her tone pleading. She could see it now—what was coming…

"It's my fault." Ares stood up and edged around the table, ready to drag Theo out of the house if it came to it. Not that he'd ever hurt Erianthe, but from the look on her face it might already be too much. "What happened to her…what happened to our daughter… It was *my* fault."

"That's not fair. It wasn't fair of me to say that." Erianthe stood at the same time as Ares did. "*You* didn't send me away—Dimitri did."

Theo's eyes narrowed and he lifted both hands to shove Ares by the shoulders, that part of the story seeming finally to click into place and enrage him even further. "You went to *Dimitri*? What the hell is *wrong* with you?"

Ares never got a chance to finish speaking. It was as if his will to explain himself had just left, and the next thing Ares knew he was sprawled on his back, pain ringing through his head, and Erianthe was between them, shoving Theo toward the door.

He was shouting something about the clinic and Ares staying away from it if he knew what was good for him. And then something else about his sister deserving better than all that *he'd* brought her.

As if he didn't already know that.

She slammed the door and was crouching over him before the room had stopped spinning.

"Oh, gosh, I thought there would be yelling… But I really figured that we'd grown beyond punching. He'll calm down. He's just upset because it was a lot to give him at once. It was a lot for him to process. He'll calm down."

Her soft hands grabbed at his shoulders, but Ares sat up before she could try to tug him from the floor. "I'm all right."

"Your eye is really red. And already swelling."

She tried to urge him to his feet anyway, and he put up both hands to stop her.

"I'm all right, Eri. I can get up on my own." The words came out more gruffly than he meant them to, but it was as if a train had just hit him, and he had to give her the official terminal prognosis.

She looked into his eyes, then stood and took two swift steps back, wariness creeping into her sweet eyes. "Whatever you're thinking, you don't have to do it."

She did see it. She just didn't *want* to see it.

He took a moment and picked himself up, then tracked back to the nearby chair he'd abandoned and sat. As much as he'd imagined how this might go down, during the day that had passed since he'd agreed to it, he had never gotten past this point—the blowup, when it would become obvious that all hope was lost.

He hadn't prepared himself on how to wrap it up. So there were no words there in his mind to tell her that she had to accept this as his decision. He had no words to make it easier for her to accept.

"I'm going to take a position in the Central African Republic."

"No. You need to give Theo time to catch his breath— and you need to catch yours too."

"I told you he wouldn't be able to accept this." He kept his voice gentle. "But it will be better for you now."

"Better for *me*? Are you *kidding* me? You're giving up after *that*?"

"I'm not going to make you choose between me and your brother. I cost you a close and open relationship with him before, and you're not going through that again. Not with a niece or nephew on the way. Not with your mother's health test pending."

"Shut up before I hit you in your other eye!"

She went to the refrigerator, grabbed a tray of ice and began cracking the cubes into a kitchen towel.

"You *knew* this was how it was going to go. What happened—what I did to you, my part in it—is unforgivable to anyone except you because of your capacity for forgiveness," he said gently.

"Ha! Tell that to Dimitri and Hera!"

He ignored that. She knew better, but she loved him and it colored her decision-making ability. "If I were Theo, there'd have been more than a single fist flying."

"No, there wouldn't." She thrust the towel full of ice at him, still helping him even if she wanted to lash out. "He's going to calm down, and next time we talk, everything will be easier. If you jump ship now, it's because you *want* to go. Just like you *always* wanted to go. Which is why you never canceled your job—only postponed it. You didn't need an escape hatch. You needed a scheduled exit and to know exactly when you could get out. Say it to me straight. You want to leave because you don't love me."

Her fire just left her as she got to the word *love*.

He'd been operating on autopilot—it was the only way to do what he needed to do when it was exactly the opposite of what he *wanted* to do. But that soft, pained statement might as well have been another train hitting him.

"I'm doing this *because* I love you." He stood up, ready to go to her if she looked as if she'd accept his comfort. "It hurts, I know…but it's what you *need*."

It took her three swallows to choke his words down. But the way she looked at him was worse than anything. He preferred the Erianthe spitfire who'd slugged him last time he'd wrecked everything. This quiet, brokenhearted creature ripped at his guts.

"My God, you've learned *nothing* from going to Dimitri. Or you've learned how to *be* Dimitri. Making decisions about what is best for me as if I'm a child. Someone for you to be responsible for, not someone you see as an equal."

She didn't want his comfort. *For sure.*

Towel full of ice in hand, he turned around and walked to the back door—out to the patio, toward the cliffs and the sea. What could he say? It was for the best. *It was.*

Every step of the way he expected her anger to well up and words to be shouted at his back. But she closed the back door to the veranda, and the surf below was making far more noise than she was.

He sat, not wanting to hear her leave.

No slamming doors came. No sound at all, But he felt her go.

She hadn't even told him to go, just as she'd promised never to do.

"Hi, Ares."

Lea answered the door to Deakin's guesthouse, where they were both living so that renovations could begin to turn the main house into something more hospitable to people than to robots.

Her kind smile made the hair on the back of his neck tingle a warning. It was too much like the kind of gentle expression he had to paste on his face when delivering bad news to a patient or a family.

"They haven't come, have they?" he asked, not budging from the stoop until he knew.

After Erianthe had moved in with Theo and Cailey, he'd spent two days wallowing in his misery before gearing up his courage to take Deakin up on his offer of help. When a man had nothing left to lose, any decision became somewhat easier. Deakin hadn't even asked him for details about his request—he'd just agreed to assemble everyone at his house.

They probably all already knew—if he was Theo, he'd tell them all and share his rage. So his plan to confess might be like receiving the answers to a test before you'd taken it, but he still needed to do this. Repent of all his sins in one go. Afterward, they could all kick his sorry ass together.

"They're on the veranda, waiting for you."

"Theo too?"

"Theo too."

Lea touched his elbow, somehow propelling him through the door, which she closed behind him.

"Has he… Has he told everyone what a piece of sh—"

"Don't do that." Lea cut him off, then answered, "He hasn't actually said anything aside from telling us that you and he got into it."

They didn't know? For the first time in days he felt a lifting sensation in his chest. "And Erianthe?"

"Erianthe isn't here." Lea sounded mildly alarmed. "She had to accompany her mother to Athens."

Athens? He hadn't heard that. "Her mother's results?"

"Benign," Lea answered, as if she was happy to give him *some* good news today. "But the lump still needs to come out."

He nodded his thanks, then followed her in.

Lea led him to the veranda, where his three best friends sat—not talking, just drinking beer. Before he said anything, Lea stepped in closer and asked quietly, "Do you want me to stay?"

She was throwing him a lifeline. With his black eye, anyone would know something was terribly wrong, but someone with training… The look of concern she gave him was worse than the gentle smile before.

"You can stay—but you're not on the clock. I'm not keeping secrets from family anymore." She hadn't married into it yet, but she was with Deakin—that was enough.

"And I've earned whatever comes from this. More than earned it."

The wound had been opened. It was now time to clean out the disease.

Deep breath.

Erianthe had never liked waiting. Now, wandering back into the waiting room at her mother's chosen Athens hospital, it was worse. Waiting while her long-estranged mother had a granular cell tumor removed made it harder. Doing it after two nearly sleepless nights…? Just *fantastic.*

Granular cell tumors were generally benign, although rare, and, importantly, they didn't mean a patient was destined to develop breast cancer. Genetic tests—which Erianthe had talked her mother into—were still out.

Hera might have the two big breast cancer genes—and a long history of the disease on her mother's side suggested it was likely—but Erianthe was determined to be optimistic and believe she had inherited only one. That would be unnerving enough, and although it made the future scary, with an appropriate testing schedule it was survivable for a long time.

Waiting.

She drew a breath, took the nicely boxed pink stethoscope from her bag and looked at it. She'd left Nyla behind at Ares's villa, and the stethoscope would help her be less afraid for her baby for the remainder of her pregnancy. Nyla could now listen for the heartbeat herself, and Erianthe would feel less guilty over having left her new friend-patient behind.

Nyla had understood why Erianthe couldn't stay after the breakup—even without the grittier details, she knew enough about what they'd been up to. Eri didn't want to ruin Nyla's chance at steady, well-paid employment, and

Ares had actually hired her to manage the estate's books. She needed a good working relationship with her new boss, and the less she worried, the better it would be for the baby.

Other people waiting for news about a loved one alternated between standing, sitting and walking around, but Erianthe stayed stuck to her chair, not having the energy reserves for restless prowling.

After the Ares and Theo debacle, Ares's breaking point had made it clear there was no future for her with him. Some people you could love but still not be able to make things work with.

That was the new callus she had to develop.

Eventually her lower lip would stop quivering when she thought about him. She'd buy her own home and build her own place to remember her daughter, without the scent of *him* all over it. Nothing to do with lavender. Or flowers. Or labyrinths.

"Nikolaides?" a woman at the desk called, and Erianthe hurried forward to be escorted into a room with the surgeon.

Everything was as she'd expected on that front. All clear. Hera was in Recovery. Erianthe would have a little more time to sit and wait until she could move to her mother's room and continue sitting and waiting there.

She'd moved in with Theo and Cailey the day after the blowup, and they'd taken her in without hesitation. Her brother hadn't stayed mad—even at her. He hadn't even asked why she had cut him out of it all. He had just processed, accepted and made it clear she could talk to him *now*. Then he'd moved on.

Surprisingly, she wasn't ready to talk about Ariadne with anyone but Ares. Theo and Cailey knew about her, though, and they'd understand when things got hard for her. That was enough for now—having the freedom to feel whatever she felt without judgment or shame.

Losing Ares this time would be different. This time she knew the answer to the question that had plagued her for years: *Could they have survived as a couple if her father hadn't driven them apart?*

No.

Letting their secret out had changed the air, and it would be easier to lose Ares this time.

Forty-five minutes later, Erianthe stood at her mother's bedside, repeating the good news the surgeon had conveyed. The lump had been easily removed. Not very disruptive to the breast tissue due to its fortunate location. Once the swelling abated, she might not even notice the scar once it had faded.

"Will you call Dimitri and tell him I'm all right?"

Would that she could say no.

Erianthe murmured her agreement, pulled out her phone and dialed. The call was brief, and possibly more taciturn than it needed to be, but it was something.

CHAPTER TWELVE

"I KNOW IT wasn't a major surgery, but you should still be resting today rather than exerting yourself," Erianthe said, her arm around her mother's waist on one side and Cailey on the other, helping Hera back into her chair.

Upon her mother's insistence, and threats to go sailing on her own so soon after her procedure, Erianthe had been forced out onto the Aegean for an early dinner on the deck of her father's yacht and was now taking care of a stubborn woman who'd stood up too fast and nearly fainted.

"I really don't think that sitting on a boat, eating food with my daughter and my daughter-in-law counts as *exerting* myself."

Hera sighed in such dramatic fashion that Erianthe almost smiled. Her mother had ways of getting what she wanted from Dimitri, and that sigh was one of them. It sounded so long-suffering.

Then she remembered why she'd been made to come out on the boat for dinner: to take her mind off Ares.

And just like that she fell back into the pit.

Edging onto her chair, Erianthe climbed back into the medical knowledge that would raise her far enough out of that pit to say something quasi-cogent.

"General anesthesia stays in the system a long time. And that's one of the aftereffects."

"Fainting?"

"Feeling faint when you stand up. Orthostatic hypo-tension."

"Erianthe—" there was another long-suffering sigh "—I'm very proud that you know all these things, but none of that means anything to me."

"When you stand up, your blood pressure requirements are different than when you're sitting." Cailey jumped in, saving her. "And it takes a few seconds longer to adjust the blood pressure controls right now. Might be better to sit forward in your chair for a minute before you stand up. Then stand for a few seconds before you walk, just in case you feel woozy."

"Ah, yes, these are things I can do." Hera sat forward in the chair, indicating her intention to rise again.

"Mother, give yourself a minute…"

"I'm doing as you both wish, but I have a job to do today, and sitting here won't see it done."

"You have a *job*?" Erianthe repeated, then looked to Cailey, who was suddenly looking everywhere but at *her*. "Something besides Keeping Erianthe From Moping Over Ares?"

The words flew out before she could think them through, and immediately she wished she could rewind the previous handful of seconds.

"My job today is to get you to the island," Hera said, then clarified, "The Xenakis island."

The *sofrito* she'd eaten curdled in her belly and Eri-anthe gave up all pretense of keeping up appearances. She slumped in her chair and rubbed her head, because that was sure to keep it from exploding.

"You need to work this out with Ares, sweet child. You don't get a choice about who you love, and you love *him*. You have to try to work it out. Not go away again."

The swiftness and heat in Erianthe's furious stare made her mother backtrack.

"I know you didn't *want* to go away last time. That was my... I didn't mean that. But you did choose to stay away. I just got you back. I don't want to lose you again. I want you to be happy."

"I *will* be happy. It's only been a few days. Surely you can't expect me to be one hundred percent already?"

"Well, no. But you should try again," her mother insisted, one firm nod backing her words.

"Just because you love someone it doesn't mean you can live with them. Or that you can live with them without giving up big pieces of yourself." That last bit might have been pointed at her mother, but it was something Erianthe had been repeating to herself for days as well.

"You had a fight," her mother argued.

"*He's* the one doing the leaving. I left the island just before his ferry got there." Erianthe's head started to pound. "He's probably already on his way to Africa."

"He's not," Cailey said, joining them at the table again.

Erianthe felt the meaning behind Cailey's words but didn't know what that meaning was, and she looked past her new sister-in-law instead, because looking into her earnest eyes was too hard.

Just past Cailey's shoulder she saw it: the Xenakis island. They'd been anchored there eating for nearly an hour, and she'd somehow *missed* seeing an entire island.

Thirty minutes later, after both Cailey and Hera had agreed to leave her be about Ares for the rest of *forever* if she agreed to speak to him one more time, Erianthe found herself being marched around Ares's villa toward the veranda.

At least they'd dragged her in the opposite direction from Shepherd's Cottage, so she didn't have to look at that going in this direction. Small blessing, but that would've been so much harder.

The idea of even *looking* at Ares made her dinner pitch and roll in her belly as if she was still on the freaking boat. Even the ground felt uneven—or her steps were out of sync with what she saw.

She couldn't do this. How had she gotten roped into this nonsense? Even the idea was beyond ridiculous. She didn't even know what she was supposed to say to him.

Hi, I'm here to make sure you still don't want to be with me and still think that you always know best.

No. Just *no*.

He was the one who'd walked out. He'd walked first— she'd walked second. And he'd made his position clear. He was suffering through the burden of having to do the magnanimous thing that would offer her the least amount of heartache.

Absolute garbage.

Erianthe stopped and looked back at Cailey and her mother. "I changed my mind. Mother, you shouldn't be walking around so much anyway. Let's get you back to the boat."

"*There* you are! We were afraid the sun would go down before you got here."

Her father's booming voice jerked her attention back around, and the idea got worse.

There hadn't been any extra boats at the docks. If she'd seen her father's speedboat…

"She's changed her mind, Dimitri," Hera said, holding a hand out to her husband.

Which was when Erianthe noticed that her father was dirty and sweaty, and so was the T-shirt he wore—probably the most expensive T-shirt on the planet.

Erianthe could tell by the way they all looked at her how

she must look. Some levels of horrified confusion defied concealment or questioning. She wasn't even going to *ask* why he was hanging out in filthy clothes.

"Down the hill, *koritsi mou*. Next terrace."

Her father's voice was far gentler than she could ever remember hearing it, and that was what pulled her gaze back to his. That look in his eyes... On anyone else she'd call it regret. Mourning. But on Dimitri Nikolaides she couldn't trust it.

"What's on the next terrace?"

"He's waiting for you."

Ares was waiting for her?

Wasn't there somewhere else she needed to be before the sun went down?

She looked toward the sky, finally noticing how late it had gotten—pinks and purples streaked in the direction she traveled.

Whatever was going on in her chest might kill her. Her heart lurched and began to bang around like a wild songbird trying to burst out of its cage.

What did this mean? He'd brought her *father* here to make up with her? Had they fought? Was that why Dimitri looked like that?

And her mother and Cailey were with her, so was Theo here with Ares?

The lifting feeling in her chest set her feet moving even as her vision filled with water and her lungs burned.

Just off the veranda, Theo rounded the pool. Also filthy. And sweaty. And *smiling*.

"Finally! He's sweating."

All the questions bouncing around at the back of her mind refused to come out, and all she managed to say to her big brother was "So are you."

Score one for the dumbest comeback of all time.

He didn't tease, for once, just chuckled and stepped out of the way. But she wasn't ready.

"Why are you both so filthy? Did you murder Ares and bury him under the terrace?"

Theo laughed. "We've been—"

"Is that an option?" Dimitri interrupted, far too eagerly.

"Of course it's not. Be *good*," Hera scolded, in that sweet way of hers that rarely evoked obedience in anyone, but for some reason occasionally inspired her father to comply.

"It's okay," Cailey said, hugging Erianthe so suddenly her eyes began to sting and fill. "He asked us to *convince* you to come. Not force you. You don't have to go down there. But I think you'll want to."

That was the right approach. A sense of calm floated down over her and Erianthe nodded, squeezing Cailey tight for a moment before she stepped back.

Releasing Cailey, she rounded the pool and headed toward the terrace below.

A wall of trees planted at the bottom of the stairs served as a windbreak but also broke the view from where she stood.

At the bottom of the stairs she met Deakin and Chris, coming through the opening in the trees and looking exactly like Theo: filthy and smiling.

She opened her mouth to say something, but no words came.

None of them looked angry. No bruises. No cuts. And then Lea came up, looking just like the rest of them—as if she'd been rolling around in the dirt.

For all that Erianthe's heart was pounding, she still didn't feel as if she had the oxygen required to walk and talk at the same time. No questions were being allowed by the fear-tinged excitement pulsing through her veins.

And still she stopped and waited.

Deakin, who'd already ambled past her once, came up behind her and stood silently, waiting too.

The look she gave him must have said *What are you doing?* Because Deakin answered.

"Just making sure you know you don't have to go anywhere alone if you don't want to."

Her chest squeezed and she had to clear her throat, but when her voice came, it was stronger than she'd thought it would be. "Now you're just trying to make me cry."

"No. You did it once. And Ares was about to do it again. It needs to be said. To both of you." Deakin ran his hand over the back of her head, then guided her to lean toward him and kissed her temple. "We'll be right up there if you need anything."

He didn't actually walk away—just waited for her to start and motion to him to stay behind.

It was only a few steps to the opening in the trees, and from there her view of the field opened up.

Lavender shrubs. Set in curving rows. Far larger, and drastically more complicated than those they'd planted on the hill outside the cottage. A new labyrinth. And in the center stood Ares.

Unlike the others, Ares was clean and polished. His hair, still long, was perfectly tied back. And he wore something she'd not seen on him since they were kids: a suit. Lightweight, cream in color, it made his golden tan look even richer. His black eye—still desperately black and purple—stood out sharper because of it.

Not that he seemed to notice. He met her gaze across the field and held it. Maybe half a football field away, he could have called to her if he'd wanted to, but he didn't. He just looked at her, standing tall. Waiting. Then slowly he looked away from her and to his side, down to the ground where something glowed.

Lights? Fire?

When she met his gaze again, he was holding out one hand to her.

"Go on," Theo said from close behind her, and then he added, "Or I can walk with you if you're afraid you might get lost in all those twisting, unnavigable, hair-raising corridors."

Theo knew how to take a tense, intimidating situation and relieve the pressure. God, it was good to have him back in her life full-time.

"The flowers are about a foot tall." She played along with his endearing silly ways, his playing the fool to help her—to give her an out if she needed it. To give her courage or just make sure she understood that things had been worked out between the two of them.

There was no way she wasn't stepping into that labyrinth.

A few quick steps carried her to the entrance, and she turned left for all of about three steps before her patience evaporated. She looked down, considered the flowers, then stepped over the closest row of flowers, and the next.

In less than half a minute she stood at the place where the heart of the labyrinth started, but she went no farther, just sought his gaze.

"That was three days of work by five grown men and Lea—who worked rings around all of us—and you just skipped over it."

He smiled as he said it, shaking his head, but the warmth she'd missed in his eyes the last time she'd seen him sparkled there, amid the greening bruise fading around his eye.

"Did you really think I'd be able to walk back and forth while I was trying to figure out what was happening in the heart of the labyrinth?"

She didn't know for sure what was going on in *his* heart, or with the little candles arranged on the ground behind him, but her own heart was beating hard and fast enough to leave her light-headed, and so full of hope it was all she could do to remain standing.

"No. You're too..." His gaze tracked slightly to the side as he searched for words.

"Impatient?" she filled in, too energized and focused to wait for him to be eloquent.

"Inquisitive," he corrected gently, wistfully. "And you've been waiting a long time."

A few steps separated them and he crossed half of them, catching her hand midflutter, drawing attention to the fact that she was fidgeting and gesturing...flapping her hands around.

He brought it to his lips, where he held it for far longer than anything that could be called a kiss. He breathed in and out, slowly, deeply, and his shoulders actually relaxed.

"Wasn't sure you'd come."

"I got shanghaied by the dread pirates Hera and Cailey." Warmth spread up her arm and she took a tentative step closer. "They all helped you do this?"

He lowered her hand but didn't let go. His steady touch and the way he gazed into her eyes made it hard to hold on to the last shreds of her reason.

He spoke. "It was like you said."

Yes, talk more. Focus on talking.

Simply throwing her arms around his shoulders and kissing him until the relief she'd been craving finally came would be premature. He'd taken action—quite a lot of it, by the look of things—but she needed to hear it to know.

"Theo came back to you?"

"No, but he came when I asked."

He gave her hand a little tug, so she took the remaining step and came to rest closer than her willpower could stand. His unbuttoned jacket brushed her chest, and she had to crank her head back to look up at him.

"Do you know the urges I'm fighting right now?" he asked huskily.

She made a sound of agreement, her gaze falling to his mouth.

"But I need to say a few dozen things first."

"I need to *hear* at least a few dozen things first," she echoed, then made herself look him in the eye again. "And I might not want to kiss you after you're finished."

There was a frown in his eyes, but he agreed. "You might not."

She knew her words were empty. She couldn't even picture a day when she wouldn't want to kiss him. She could picture a few really good reasons why she would resist that desire, but if she was going to resist, she had to do something else. His hand in hers was invigorating, but she needed more contact.

Lifting his hand, she ducked and twirled under it so she could press her back against him and wrap that captured arm around her waist. Removing the temptation that facing him brought—or at least diminishing it.

Ares didn't argue, didn't need an explanation of her impromptu dance move, just followed and wrapped his other arm around her too, pulling her close until the solid heat of him seeped into her back.

"This doesn't mean we're sorted out." Erianthe found the strength, and some small reserve of fear, to allow her at least that much clarity.

"I know," he answered, his voice at her ear holding a hint of humor that recalled the last time he'd said those words to her and she'd called him on it. Then he added, "I owe you words."

His lips pressed to the top of her shoulder, to the scrap

of flesh bared by the scooped neck of her coral blouse. Tingles ran from his lips up over her neck, down over her chest, energizing her enough to tease. "Pay up."

"We met at Deakin's…" he began, his warm breath fanning her neck. "I didn't think it would work out, but I needed to try. If for no other reason than so I could tell myself that I'd done everything I could this time."

"How did that go?"

She'd keep asking questions because it would help ensure her focus was fixed on what he said, letting her stay in the moment without listening to her body or her heart, which wanted to hurtle much farther ahead. Her head understood that although these were good words he was saying, he had said good words before—and then later screwed them up so hard they might as well have never been said.

"It was a pretty intense conversation—which only really got going after Lea, the insightful one, got us past the stage where we were just grumbling back and forth."

The way they stood kept the candles out of her sight but let her watch the last shreds of sunlight over the rings and rows of fragrant flowers, and somehow it imparted a serenity she couldn't remember feeling—something peaceful and soothing and *whole*.

"I won't ask if you came to any conclusions because…" She nodded to the flowers. "But could you talk about this?"

The growing dark made the candles a little harder to ignore, but that was for another round of questions. She loved the labyrinth, but she loved the man more.

"I don't know how to be in a relationship if there are any bumps," he said, and then took such a deep breath she wasn't sure he was going to keep talking.

Her position had one big drawback—she couldn't look him in the eye and get any inkling of what he was thinking.

All she could do was listen, feel the way his arms tightened around her as if he were afraid she'd pull away again.

"As much as I hate the way they operate, I've been doing the same thing as my parents. Once there's a serious enough disagreement or wrongdoing, I can't figure out how it's possible to get back from there. That's how relationships end, in my experience."

As he spoke—as the subject became more serious and less about the joy of being with him—it became easier to focus and resist the urge to spin and put her arms around him.

She wanted to say his issue was silly, but she understood before he even began to explain. She'd been there to see a number of his parents' marriages flame out—to see how many times he'd been angry, or just plain devastated.

"I've watched it happen at least seven thousand times between my parents and whoever they were with." That came out quiet, but strong, and then he paused as if unsure whether to continue. When he'd taken a moment, his voice was softer. "That's how it seemed to be for us back then. I'd screwed up to the point at which there could be no forgiveness for me from you. And then it was fresh for Theo when he found out, and he reacted in a way that fit perfectly with how I'd expected it to go. Just checked the expected box."

She nodded, the kind of jangly head motion that she could only hope would increase the processing speed of her brain. She understood that he'd believed himself to be unforgivable—might still think that about himself—but not why. She'd once doubted her ability to forgive him—no, not doubted, she'd *known* she would never forgive him. And then she had, despite it all.

She squeezed his hand tighter, her heart filling her throat even if she'd *wanted* to speak.

"The only person who didn't neatly fit into one of those boxes for me was you. I'd done the unforgivable, but you forgave me anyway. It took a long time, and maybe time factored into that, but I couldn't imagine anyone else doing it. Even the men I consider my brothers."

"It surprised me too. I never expected I would forgive you, or even that I'd want to. I couldn't see past my own hurt until I saw yours. Then knowing Theo would never be able to forgive you became a certainty that he *would* with enough time. If I could, then anyone could."

"Do you think it works that way for everyone?"

"Maybe…" She *doubted* her ability to forgive Dimitri, but once she'd known for sure that she'd *never* forgive him. Which was what made her ask, "How did Dimitri end up here, helping with the labyrinth?"

"Theo," Ares answered. "I didn't witness it, but apparently he went directly from the cottage to Dimitri's door and didn't stop describing what you'd gone through to your father until he broke him. No one invited Dimitri to help with the labyrinth. He just showed up and worked."

She must have made a sound, because he turned her to face him and lifted his hands to brush the building stream of tears from her cheeks.

Her father had performed an act of contrition for *her*.

"I never thought I'd champion Dimitri," Ares murmured, "but even with all his flaws he does love you."

It was the last thing she'd expected to hear. *Ever*. It hurt to hear it, to know it and to know that her father had been too proud, or too weak, to say those things to her himself. But some pain, as she knew, ran too deep to speak of easily. Or even think about sometimes.

The tremor that rolled over her made her push her arms under Ares's jacket and around his waist so she could lean against him and absorb some of his strength. She burrowed in close, until his arms came around her and he began to rock them, there in the candlelight at the center of the labyrinth he'd built to remember their daughter.

"We all love you and we're glad to have you home." He spoke into her hair. "I want this to be *your* home, Eri. Your last home. With me."

He pulled back far enough to let her look up at him, and when he had her gaze, he held it firm.

"All I need is one more second chance."

One more second chance...

"I get it now. I see how my trust had conditions. But I want to be the kind of man who believes his family will stand by him no matter his mistakes. I still see my actions as unforgivable, but I'm selfish enough to let you decide that. As much as I don't want to become like my exploding father, I don't want to become like yours either."

All the things she'd longed to hear him say.

He brushed away her silent tears again and she inched her arms around his neck to urge his mouth toward hers. He wound his arms around her, his mouth so gentle and tender, the slow, sweet crush of his lips against hers unhurried, savoring, soul-shattering.

If he said nothing else, it would be enough.

"One more thing," he said between kisses, and then leaned back enough to pull out of her arms. He stepped to the side so they both faced the candles, unobstructed. Not another word passed his lips as he stood by her, silently watching her take it in.

At first Erianthe wasn't sure what she was looking at. The white tea lights were laid in lines, arcs and angles. Then she stepped to the right and choked on her breath as the pattern came into focus.

He'd built this for her to remember Ariadne.

It was a cradle.

Little rockers on the bottom of a wedge-shaped box.

Not the most artistic rendition ever, but it was clear, and heartfelt, and heartbreaking.

He took her hand and stayed out of her line of sight so she could gaze on the bright little lights burning and the promise that rose like vapor from a hundred or more tiny flames.

"For Ariadne and the family we were always meant to have. I'm never going to be someone who doesn't want to protect you. That's not who I am. When I went to Dimitri back then, I thought I was protecting you and our child. What I can promise now is to try to not do this protecting in a way that belittles you or leaves you out."

He went down on both knees, not just one, and a small box came from somewhere. A diamond in dark velvet glittered in the glow of the candles, but she couldn't really pay attention to any of that. She couldn't look away from his eyes. Couldn't do anything but nod.

It was enough.

He slid the sparkling ring onto her finger. The next second she hit the ground before him, unable to wait to have his arms around her and have him back in hers.

Tear-salted kisses would last long after night had finished falling. They'd said all that needed to be said. The road home had taken them both through darkness and into the light and hope of a future full of love, family and finally understanding.

Their loved ones had long ago drifted off to give them privacy, but Ares and Erianthe stole away to Shepherd's Cottage for the rest of the week.

Leaving Hera to organize a quick wedding—they'd waited ten years, and that was long enough.

EPILOGUE

Two years later...

ERIANTHE REPOSITIONED THE patio umbrellas over the veranda tables to account for the sun's movement, assuring the twins' high chairs would be in the shade when dinner was served.

"We are in *so* much trouble," Ares said from behind her, his hands falling to her hips to pull her back against him so he could wrap his arms around her and nuzzle the side of her neck.

She never got tired of this greeting. When she'd been nearing term with the girls, this back-to-front embrace was the closest they'd been able to get after her belly had become so round and heavy that even Ares's long fingers hadn't been able to span the curve.

"Where are the girls?"

"With my parents." His voice sounded equal parts rueful and amused.

She turned in his arms to slip her own around his shoulders and give the man of her dreams her undivided, now fully shaded and temporarily secluded attention. "What's the trouble, then?"

"I caught them *kissing*."

"Olivia and Ophelia?"

"Melisa and Orien." He enunciated his parents' names so dramatically he might have been teaching a phonics class to children while also holding a puppet.

Erianthe couldn't have contained her laughter if she'd been sucking lemons. "You're *kidding*! What kind of kissing are we talking about?"

"The Ares Needs Therapy kind of kissing."

"Do you think they're getting back together?"

"I have no idea what that would even *look* like."

Melisa and Orien Xenakis had divorced when Ares was four, and then—of course—had had their multi-partner-divorcing sprees for the next quarter of a century. Orien had only recently returned to the island to take up residence in Shepherd's Cottage while waiting for the divorce from his *second* French wife to go through.

"Lots of tongue?"

"Stop that," Ares grunted. "I *would* like to have sex again sometime in my life. Or, more specifically, today."

"Whose tongue did you see, specifically?"

"Stop, woman!" He spun her around again so he could bite her shoulder and growl—usually another playful favorite...

Only, her stomach was not having it today.

"Ares...don't... Don't jostle me."

She gripped the edge of the table and took a couple deep breaths, waiting for the wave of nausea to pass.

"Oh, my love... Sit. Sit down." He guided her to the nearest chair and eased her in. "Want a drink?"

"Nope...just...no talking."

"It's a boy. You didn't get sick with the girls."

"Wives' tales."

She swallowed again and then leaned back as the upheaval in her middle began to subside—which was when she caught sight of Melisa and Orien carrying the twins up the stairs from Ariadne's terrace.

"They're coming."

"We should call him Xerxes."

"We are not naming *any* baby Xerxes Xenakis. That's just cruel."

"I think you mean *cool*." He squatted down before her, holding her hand, teasing her even while his thumb stroked back and forth across the back of her hand.

"I don't want to say anything until it's been a little longer. No announcing today. I don't know how much the girls understand. If they got their hopes up for a little brother and something happened…"

Most miscarriages happened in the first trimester, and even if she'd breezed through her pregnancy last time, she couldn't bring herself to count on this one yet.

"Hey, nothing's going to happen. To Xerxes." He winked at her, then leaned up and kissed her, his mouth lingering long enough to calm her mind and ease the worry that always sprang up when it came to her family. "But we will keep this our secret a little longer. We haven't had any secrets in a while."

"I never told anyone about that sexy dance I talked you into."

The faux outrage of his squint made her smile.

"You two must be exhausted all the time." Melisa was laughing as she neared the table and tried to wrestle Olivia's wriggling frame into her high chair. "They run really well for being only a year old."

"Fifteen months," Erianthe corrected, then pulled herself up from the chair. "Every month is a milestone at this age. But they *are* worryingly mobile. It's a good thing there are two of us to chase them. Are you sure you're up to watching them this evening?"

"I'm sure," Melisa said, helping Orien get Ophelia—the even squirmier twin—into her own chair and locked in.

"You two go ahead and get ready. Orien will help me with them while you're at the party."

"We *do* have the nanny if you find you need a break. She lives in. Bethan?" Ares reminded her, even though his mother had met the nanny on at least a dozen occasions. Melisa had a knack for forgetting the name of staff.

"Oh, that's right. Well, I'm sure we'll be fine, but she can help if needed. You two go."

He didn't have to be told again—just rounded the table to dole out goodbye kisses to his squirmy princesses with Erianthe following in his wake.

When they'd made it to their suite, he closed the door and took her hand again. "If you don't feel up to this, you don't have to go."

"It's my birthing center's dedication—of *course* I have to go."

He gave her a look. She knew what it meant: the Protective Ares program was booting up. It had taken them only a few months to work out a system of groans, looks and raised brows to determine when they'd reached a subject that needed *talking about*, and likely a compromise.

"I feel all right now, but we'll leave early if I start feeling worse. I promise to tell you."

She stepped into his arms again and leaned in. The nausea wasn't the worst part—it was the creeping exhaustion. She just wanted to sleep. Maybe it *was* a boy...

Over her back, she felt him doing something with his hands.

"What're you doing?"

"Texting Theo to make sure he's coming."

"They've all got the necessary childcare covered. They're all coming. Theo and Cailey, Deakin and Lea, Chris and Naomi..."

"He needs to know you're somewhat under the weather in case he has to step in and give a speech about uteruses."

She laughed at him softly and let him fuss, pulling away to lie down for a few minutes before she needed to get dressed.

Xerxes...

It really was a strong name for Ares's first son.

* * * * *

A DATE WITH DR MOUSTAKAS

AMY RUTTAN

MILLS & BOON

This book is dedicated to my Medical Romance girls,
Tina, Annie and Amalie.

You three are an amazing inspiration to me.

PROLOGUE

Nashville, Tennessee

HE HATED HIMSELF for what he was about to do.

Don't do it, then.

Dr. Christos Moustakas stared down at the contract on his desk—the one he'd just signed for a job that would take him away from Nashville and away from Naomi.

He was angry at himself for getting involved with her. When he'd first seen her—when they'd been placed on the same surgical resident rotation last year—he'd known that he shouldn't even pursue her. Naomi was the type of woman who wanted far more than he could give.

He never wanted to get married. He never wanted to settle down. He had told her that in the beginning, but now... despite his warnings...he knew that she wanted more from him and he just couldn't give it to her.

Why not?

Chris cursed under his breath and walked away from the contract. He looked about his apartment, which was full of memories of him and Naomi together. She was in his blood...she was all he ever thought about.

And he couldn't have that.

Work was more important.

He had to end it now.

There was a knock at the door and his heart skipped a beat. His jaw clenched and his stomach churned, because he knew that he was going to break her heart.

But it was for the best.

He didn't want to marry her and lock her into an unhappy marriage—just like what had happened to his parents.

He *never* wanted that.

Naomi beamed at him when he opened the door, and leaned in to kiss him on the cheek as she came into his apartment.

"There you are! What's up? You've been a bit distant recently…" She trailed off as she saw the boxes in the apartment. "Oh."

Chris shut the door. "Yeah, sorry I haven't been returning your calls, but something came up."

"I see that," she said quietly, and then turned around. "Where are you going?"

"New York City. I've been offered a fellowship with Dr. Heffernan in neurosurgery, and then I'll take over his practice when he retires later next year. I'll be the head of neurosurgery."

"Wow, that's amazing. Congratulations… When do you leave?"

"Tonight."

Her face fell and he knew that it had hit her. "You were going to leave without telling me?"

"No, that's why I asked you over."

You're a monster. You're just awful.

"I thought…" She shook her head. "I don't know *what* I thought."

"Tell me." He could take it, and he deserved her wrath. He deserved it all.

For one brief moment he wished he was a different person—but he wasn't, and he couldn't see how to change.

He knew what it was like to grow up with an absent mother who hated and loathed your very existence and a father who couldn't look at you because you were a disappointment.

Families were complicated and messy.

He wanted none of it.

"I thought we would talk about our offers together," she said. "I mean, I turned down Mayo because I thought you wanted to be with me."

Her eyes were full of tears and he fought the urge to take her in his arms and comfort her.

"Why didn't you take the job at Mayo?" he asked.

"I should've, apparently."

"Yes, you should've, Naomi. This is your career. It's important."

"I didn't want to leave you. I wanted to give us a chance!"

He closed his eyes, pain washing over him, but he hardened his heart. He shouldn't have gotten involved with her to begin with. He should've walked away after that first stolen kiss that had electrified his world.

Naomi Hudson was dangerous, and he'd known that all along—but he'd still pursued her.

"You should've taken the job, Naomi. There *is* no long-term future for us. I told you this at the start."

A tear slipped down her cheek. "I remember, but I thought—"

"You thought what?" he interrupted. "That I would change my mind? My goal has always been to make it to head of neurosurgery. You *knew* this."

"And *you* knew, deep down, that I wanted more from our relationship and yet you kept me dangling. You kept pursuing me. You didn't let me go either!" she shouted.

"I'm letting you go now," he said stonily, his heart breaking because he didn't want to let her go, but it was for the best.

"I thought I meant more to you," she said, her voice shaking.

"Look, we both knew this had to end sometime."

"I *didn't* know that. Or I guess I just didn't want to believe it."

"Well, then, that's *your* problem."

And he hated himself for saying those words, but they needed to be said. He had to put an end to it. She'd given up a job for him, but he'd never asked her to do that. She had to move on from him.

The sting of her slap on his cheek didn't catch him off guard. He was expecting it.

"Enjoy New York, you bastard! I hope to God I never see you again!"

She pushed past him, and he didn't turn around as the door opened and then slammed shut behind her.

Instead he sighed, felt a tear almost slipping from his eye. He wandered to the window, watching her get into her car and drive away.

When had he become such a coldhearted monster like his father?

He was selfish, greedy. He'd wanted her so badly, and for a year it had been bliss. Then she'd started to creep her way in through his carefully constructed walls. She'd started to plan for a future that he had never wanted.

It was time to let her go—even if his heart really didn't want to.

She would find someone better than him. Someone who deserved her. He was not the man for her.

He didn't deserve her, but he would never forget her. There would never be a woman like her for him again—he'd make sure of it—and he was also sure that he would never love another woman the way he'd loved her.

There would only ever be one Dr. Naomi Hudson in his

life, and he'd just thrown her away. She'd be happier without him, and he'd be miserable without her, but it served him right.

He picked up the contract for the job in Manhattan again. This was what his life was all about—saving lives. In some ways, at least, if he excelled at his job, it might make up for the hurt he'd caused her.

At least he could do something good with his time... even though his life and his heart were beyond saving and always would be.

CHAPTER ONE

Three years later, Mythelios, Greek Islands

ANOTHER SLEEPLESS NIGHT.

The heat wasn't helping. Even though he'd been back in Greece since the middle of July—two months after the earthquake—Chris still wasn't quite used to the temperature. His body was firmly set to Manhattan mode and Manhattan temperatures. It also didn't help that the island of Mythelios was still recovering from that earthquake.

His late grandmother's home didn't have air-conditioning either. And, since the island still remained in repair mode, renovations that weren't crucial to the infrastructure and safety of the citizens had been put on hold.

Air-conditioning would have to wait.

He yawned as he opened the doors to the small terrace of his grandmother's beautiful villa. He leaned over the balcony, watching the sun rise over the Aegean Sea.

It had been a long time since he'd watched the sun rise bright and beautiful over the turquoise sea of his youth. It had been years since he'd picked olives in his grandmother's garden or swum in the sea. The garden was overgrown now, but up on the top level of the house he had an unobstructed view of the horizon.

His grandmother's home was the oldest and the highest

of the old homes that had been built into the cliffs of My-thelios. It had thankfully fared pretty well during the earth-quake, only suffering slight damage, while newer homes had suffered and crumbled.

It was funny how it had managed to stay intact through the powerful quake.

It was funny how nothing really seemed to have changed here since he was a young man.

He'd been in America for so long, pursuing women and his career, that he'd forgotten to stop and smell the roses—or in this case the orange blossoms that wafted up from his late grandmother's garden.

His life for the last three years in New York City had been endless parties, women and work. Work had been his priority. He'd let nothing get in the way of becoming the top neurosurgeon on the eastern seaboard.

Well, that wasn't quite accurate. One thing *had* gotten in the way—and that was the reason for his sleepless nights and why he'd returned to Greece.

An ill-fated one-night stand in a long string of the one-night stands he'd had in order to get over losing the woman he truly loved had led to him having a baby dropped off on his doorstep. Well, not so much on his doorstep. He'd paid a lot of money to the mother so he could keep his son.

Baby Evangelos was his world now, and even though Chris could afford a nanny, and had one for his infant son, she was entitled to take a night off—as she had last night. He was on feeding and diapering duty whenever that happened.

Chris scrubbed a hand over his face.

Why had he let his life go completely sideways like this?

When had it gotten to be so hard?

Right—he knew exactly when *that* had happened: when he'd walked away from Naomi and put his career before love. That was when it had all gone to heck. He'd left behind the only woman who had ever broken down the careful walls he'd created to keep people out. She'd started to come even before his work, and that had annoyed him.

He'd sworn he would never settle down—not after watching his parents' disastrous marriage crash and burn.

So he'd left her. Frozen her out and left her behind in Nashville while he pursued his high-flying career in New York City. And even worse, she'd loved him and he'd held her back. He hadn't been able to give her what she'd wanted, and yet she'd turned down an excellent job for him. That guilt still ate away at him.

He hadn't been able to forget about her. So he'd tried moving on by bedding a series of different women. And that was how he'd ended up with Evangelos.

And there was no question that he loved his son. He loved being a father—something he'd never thought that he'd ever want—but this was not how he had pictured his return to his home village.

"Nice abs!"

Chris frowned and then looked down to see Ares walking through the square in the tiny village. His long curls were hidden under a baseball cap—one that Chris had sent him when he first went to America.

Ares had been one of his best friends since he was a child. He was one of the four founders of the Mythelios Free Clinic and he worked in emergency medicine. All his friends were back on Mythelios now, since the earthquake, when one of their number—Theo—had put out a call for their help.

Ares had boyish good looks, and the silly hat that Chris had sent him as a joke looked so out of place on him, but it made Chris smile nonetheless. He was glad to be back with Theo, Deakin and Ares, even though they were working in the clinic and he wasn't.

Of course none of *them* had a baby yet.

"Put a shirt on!" Ares teased again, laughing.

"Where are you off to?" Chris called down, ignoring the teasing.

"The clinic. Actually, I was going to come see you. There's a case I'd like your opinion on."

"I'm not here to practice medicine. I came back just to lend a hand and deal with my grandmother's death."

"Come on," Ares begged. "I need your expert opinion. Besides, it's high time you got your hands dirty at the clinic *you* helped found."

Ares had a point—and he did miss working. He missed neurosurgery.

Chris nodded. "Okay. I'll come by when Lisa comes back."

Ares raised his eyebrows. "Who's Lisa?"

"Evan's nanny."

"Ah, and here I thought the infamous Greek Valentino of Manhattan was up to his old tricks."

Chris snorted. "And since when do I have time for that?"

"Well, you must've had *some* time," Ares teased. "You're the only one with a kid."

Not for long, since Cailey Nikolaides was four and a half months pregnant now. Cailey was a nurse at the clinic, and Theo's wife.

"Look, either come into the house or get to work. You're going to wake the neighbors with your incessant shouting in the streets!" Chris called.

Ares winked. "See you in a couple hours."

Chris watched him jog away through the narrow alleyways of the old part of the island, where other villas like his grandmother's clung to the side of a cliff by the sea.

The homes were brightly colored and connected by narrow cobblestone streets that eventually wound their way down to a large square dominated by a church, and then there was a small path to the docks and to the clinic.

The bell at the church rang out the time, waking up this sleepy island that was only an hour's ride by ferry to Athens, a city much more modern in comparison to the simple way of life that still dominated Mythelios.

He yawned, stretched and looked down.

Dammit.

He wasn't wearing anything at all. Good thing the balcony was solid, and not an open terrace like they had in the larger cities, because he'd fallen asleep naked.

He had to get some clothes on fast, before Lisa came back.

He didn't want to give her the wrong idea.

That had been his problem his whole adult life—he seemed to give all the women he met the wrong idea. Even Naomi had gotten the wrong idea about him in the end.

"I thought I meant more to you," she'd said, her voice shaking.

"Look, we both knew this had to end sometime."

"I didn't know that. Or I guess I just didn't want to believe it."

"Well, then, that's your *problem."*

His stomach clenched as he recalled some of the last words he'd said to her. It cut him to the quick how badly he'd hurt her, but he'd told her from the start he didn't want anything serious.

And it still killed him that she'd given up that job at Mayo for him. He'd held her back and that would haunt him forever, but there was no way he was ever going to settle down with one woman for the rest of his life.

He'd watched his parents.

Once marriage came into play, everything went south. His mother had left, and no matter what Chris had done, he'd never been able to please his father.

He shuddered. He was *never* going to get married.

Chris reluctantly walked away from the balcony and headed back inside. He pulled on a robe and checked on his son, who was sleeping peacefully in his crib. The only fan in the entire house was in the nursery, but even that just pushed around the hot air.

You never wanted to be a father either, a little voice reminded him.

And yet here was Evangelos.

He smiled at his son, so like him, sleeping peacefully. He was sucking the chubby fist in his mouth in his sleep. His dark curls were plastered to his face from the heat.

This island was his world now. He'd do right by Evangelos. His son would never want for anything and would never feel like a stranger to his father—a toy that would be played with only when it suited his parents. Chris was going to make sure his son had everything he could possibly need.

Except he won't have a mother.

Chris shook that thought from his mind.

Evan didn't need a mother. *He'd* made do without a mother's love, and he'd give his son enough love for both parents.

He closed the door to the nursery and headed back to his room, where he had a quick shower and then pulled out the scrubs and lab coat that Theo had given him when he'd returned to Mythelios a few weeks ago.

"What are these for?" Chris had asked as he'd stared down at the scrubs that Theo had handed him.

"They're scrubs."

"I know that," Chris had said, "but what are they for?"

"Look, I know that your *yia-yia* just died, but when you feel the need to come back and work, we could really use you at the clinic."

"Thanks. I'll think about it. If you need me for an emergency, I'll be there, Theo, but I can't commit right now."

"I know," Theo had said gently. "But these are yours for when you need them."

It might not be the glitzy Manhattan hospital where he'd been working, but at least he'd still be working. He would still be doing what he loved and he would be giving something other than money back to his home. His time and his skills.

Ever since he'd headed to America, he'd had a financial hand in the clinic that Theo ran, using his trust fund from Mopaxeni Shipping to help fund it year after year the same way his friends did, but he'd never done more than that.

It was time to do more now, and he'd still be able to devote enough time to Evangelos, and to fixing up his grandmother's home, and to raising his son in a place that was safe and quiet. A place where he'd always been happy when he was young.

Chris was mad at himself for staying away for so long, but he'd thought life would be better in America.

He'd slipped on his clothes and was tying his shoes when the front door opened.

Lisa blushed when she saw him. "Sorry, Dr. Moustakas. I meant to come back sooner, but my cousin from America arrived in Greece a month ago, and she was visiting my family last night in Athens."

"It's okay, Lisa. I gave you the day and the night off. You deserve a break."

Lisa ducked her head and brushed back one of the errant strands of her dark brown hair behind her ear. If he'd been a younger man, and not a father, he would have flirted with her. Only, he wasn't that playboy anymore, and Lisa was from a respectable Athens family. A family that would be expecting a proposal of marriage from any man she became involved with.

"I'm headed down to the clinic. I can be reached there," Chris said as he opened the door, and then he turned back. "How long is your cousin in Athens for?"

"For a while. She's working there," Lisa said eagerly. "My father's brother fell in love with an American girl and settled over there. No one has seen my uncle or my cousin since she was a small girl. It's the first time I've gotten to meet her!"

"Well, perhaps you can spend the weekend with your family in Athens next week. Get to know your cousin a bit better."

Lisa brightened. "I would like that, Dr. Moustakas."

He nodded and shut the door. As he walked through the cobbled streets, he saw the little village at the edge of the sea where his *yia-yia* had lived was coming alive, and that the ferry boat from the mainland sat at the docks as people boarded it for the hour's jaunt to the mainland and the docks at Piraeus.

It wasn't too much farther to the clinic, and there was a bit of a spring in his step as he headed there. It felt good to be working again and helping out Ares, Theo and Deakin, his best friends, as well as their significant others—he was still having a hard time wrapping his mind around that.

All his friends were matched up. They'd finally found love. He was the only single one left among them. And that wasn't going to change anytime soon. No way.

There had been only one woman he'd come even close to *thinking* about marrying, but he'd bungled that so badly that he'd broken her heart. He deserved to be alone. That was his punishment for the pain he'd caused her. One he'd bear gladly.

Chris sighed and opened the door to the clinic. No one was at the front desk, but the door had been unlocked.

"Ares?" he shouted. There was no answer. "Ares, where are you? Hello?"

"Good gravy, what is with all the *shouting*? I'm coming!" a soft Tennessee accent answered back. One that he knew so well.

His heart skipped a beat as the owner of the voice came charging out of the back of the clinic, dressed to the nines in business attire—the high heels that he'd always thought were ridiculous and a pristine white lab coat.

Her thick strawberry blond hair was swept up off her neck in a tight bun, which didn't suit her, and her soft hazel eyes widened in shock as she froze to the spot.

"Naomi?" he said in a daze as he found his voice. "What're you doing here?"

Oh, my good Lord, what is he doing here?

She knew that Dr. Christos Moustakas was Greek, but she'd had no idea that he was here in Mythelios. She'd thought he was still in Manhattan, playing all-knowing neurosurgical God and playboy.

She'd thought when she left him behind and started working for an international relief effort as a surgeon that she would never have to lay eyes on him again, and that had been good enough for her.

She'd given up so much to take a chance on love and she'd been rejected. He'd shattered her heart and soul three years ago, and she'd never wanted to see him again. *Ever.*

That's not completely true.

She had longed to see him, but she just hadn't been able to risk him hurting her again. Not when it had taken her so long to put her heart back together after he'd so coldly dismissed her—and then she'd lost their baby. The baby she hadn't even known about until after he'd left for New York.

She'd tried to tell him, but he hadn't returned her calls.

So she'd borne that pain alone.

She hated him. He was the reason she didn't date anyone—ever. She'd put her career first because she was never going to make that mistake again.

Her heart was hardened.

You don't hate him. Not really.

Yet here he was. Standing in front of her in clinic scrubs and looking just as good as the day he'd left her all those years ago. His thick dark hair still perfect. Those dark eyes still with that twinkle in them. And even though he wasn't smiling, just seeing his chiseled handsome face made her go weak in the knees all over again.

No. Don't let him have any power over you.

It had taken her a long time to get over Christos after he'd put his career over her. She'd made her peace with that, and even though she'd blown her chance with Mayo, she'd never blown another one.

And now she was one of the attending surgeons with International Relief. She had a lot of responsibility. Maybe she had him to thank for that—for focusing her mind on her career instead of on him.

Still, she was not happy he was here. Of all the places in the world, why did he have to be here in Mythelios?

Good gravy, why did he have to be here?

She'd been assigned to work between Athens and Mythelios as a surgeon for the next couple of months. When she'd come to Athens in July, she'd gone to the clinic a couple of times, and Chris hadn't been there. Of course, during the first part of her assignment in Greece, she hadn't spent a lot of time in Mythelios, since most of the seriously wounded from the earthquake had been sent to Athens.

And now that she was going to be spending more of her time lending a hand at the clinic, rather than working in the city, he was here—and he was in scrubs as if he belonged here.

You haven't said one word since he asked you what you're doing here. Speak!

"What're *you* doing here?" she asked.

Oh, my Lord in heaven, that was the most pathetic...

She cringed inwardly, because she really didn't know what else to say.

"This is where I'm from. I've come back here because my grandmother died and I inherited her home. Also, this is the clinic I helped found with a few friends of mine. I thought since I was here I would spend some time working here."

"I've been in Greece since last month and I haven't seen you here at the clinic before—and you haven't been mentioned by anyone," she said.

"I've been busy dealing with the passing of my grandmother."

"I had no idea you were from here."

"We didn't do much talking when we were together." There was a twinkle in his eye as he said that.

She groaned. *Of course...* She quickly jogged through all those memories—which were mostly of hot, passion-filled nights. He had once mentioned coming from a small Greek island and helping to found a charitable clinic, but of all the charitable clinics in all of Greece why did she have to walk into *this* one?

It's simple. You're cursed.

That was what her father's mother had said, the one and only time she'd met her when she was fourteen. She'd told her that she was cursed by the gods because she had forsaken her father's heritage and was doomed.

Naomi hadn't given it much credence then, but after meeting Dr. Christos Moustakas four years ago, and having her heart completely trampled on a bare year later, she was beginning to believe her grandmother's words.

She was cursed.

And this just proved it.

"I work with International Relief. I'm here to help on the island after the earthquake. Mythelios and Athens is my assignment for the next couple of months. I'm a general surgeon, and I also raise funds to cover the cost of surgeries for those who can't afford it. The earthquake's damage is wreaking havoc on people."

A smug grin spread across his face. "Is that so? I hadn't heard that."

"Yes," she said firmly, annoyed with him. She clutched the file she was holding tight to her chest. "Dr. Nikolaides did mention to me that a new surgeon would be coming today, but he didn't mention it was you."

"Would that have made a difference?" he asked.

"Yes, of course it would! I'm not happy about this, Dr. Moustakas."

You're supposed to be in New York.

Out of sight and out of mind. Except that was easier said than done. He'd completely crushed her heart. She didn't trust men anymore, thanks to him.

She'd been head over heels in love with Chris. He'd even gotten her pregnant. But he'd made it clear that his career was more important to him than she could ever be. He'd broken things off, and although she'd tried to contact him to tell him about the baby, she'd lost it only a few short weeks after he'd left for New York.

It had destroyed her.

She'd been alone, heartbroken and mad at herself for getting involved with Chris in the first place when she'd known that he'd never wanted anything serious. She'd fallen for his charms. She'd been a fool.

It had taken her this long to pick herself up. To put herself back together. Seeing him again was the very last thing she needed, but it was clear that he was going to stay here and she was just going to have to suck it up and work in the same physical space with him. But that didn't mean they had to work together.

This island was big enough for the both of them.

Oh, who are you kidding?

"Well," Chris said, breaking the tense silence and running a hand through his hair, "I'm sorry that you're not happy about this, Naomi…"

"Dr. Hudson."

"What?" he asked, dazed, and for the first time she noticed the dark circles under his eyes, as if he hadn't been sleeping.

"Dr. Hudson is how I wish to be referred to by you. We're not on a first-name basis. Not anymore."

His eyes narrowed and he frowned, crossing his arms.

He was annoyed by that.

Good.

"Fine. Dr. Hudson, do you think we can work together and remain professional?"

"Of course we can, Dr. Moustakas."

She was relieved—or she should be relieved. Except that she wasn't. Not really.

This is what you want, remember?

"Good, because I really am exhausted and I don't have the energy for games. I've had enough games to last a lifetime."

Her blood boiled and she could feel a flush rise in her

cheeks. "I'm very aware of your *games*, Dr. Moustakas. Trust me."

"I don't have time for this," he snapped. He pushed past her and headed to the back where the staff room was. "I need coffee."

She turned and followed him, feeling bad. He was in the back lounge, pouring himself a cup of coffee. He rolled his eyes and groaned when he saw that she'd followed him.

"I'm sorry," she said tentatively.

He eyed her cautiously and took a sip of coffee.

"Why are you so tired?" she asked.

"No reason. Late night," he said quickly, not looking at her.

She knew he was hiding something. This was how he'd acted with her when he'd been given that job offer in Manhattan for an attending position. He would get self-protective—surly, even—and would feign exhaustion as he closed up tight.

She had no time to deal with this. So much was on her plate—including a bachelor auction she had to organize. Originally it had been planned by the clinic as a small affair on Mythelios, to raise funds for the clinic. But when Theo had realized the extent of the damage done by the earthquake to the entire island, he'd suggested to Naomi on her arrival that with her fund-raising background she should take the project on, on behalf of International Relief, and expand it to a much bigger event for maximum exposure and funds.

Having witnessed the desperate need for funds firsthand, Naomi had had no choice but to agree. The auction was now happening in Athens, in a little less than two weeks' time, so she couldn't afford to play Chris's games.

"Well, I'll let you get on with it, then," she said as she

backed out of the lounge and made her way to a small office where she could do her paperwork in relative peace.

Maybe she should cancel lunch with her cousin Lisa, who was working on the island as a nanny, and catch an earlier ferry back to Athens. Then at least she'd have the sea to separate herself from Christos Moustakas.

Only, deep down, she knew the sea wasn't enough to keep him at bay. She closed her eyes and tried not to think about Chris and their lost baby, but it all came rushing back to her regardless.

Work was the only thing that kept the pain at bay, but she wasn't sure even that would be enough now, because Chris was here in Mythelios—and he clearly still had the ability to invade both her dreams and her heart.

CHAPTER TWO

CHRIS MANAGED TO avoid Naomi for most of the morning by retreating into one of the offices to go over the file that Ares wanted an opinion on.

He leaned over the computer and frowned as the scans from the Athens MRI came up. The scans were of a local Mythelios bartender whom they all knew and loved.

He'd heard that since the earthquake in May Stavros had been experiencing debilitating headaches, but he'd always brushed them off until finally, the other day, he'd collapsed.

Now Chris knew why Stavros had been having such a hard time, because he was staring down at one of the biggest anaplastic oligodendrogliomas that he'd ever seen.

Dammit.

He knew men like Stavros; the older generation of men from the island were stubborn and brushed off what they thought were minor symptoms, like a headache, as nothing. "Minor symptoms" that might be warning them of something far more sinister. Like Stavros's headaches.

Chris leaned back in the swivel chair and scrubbed a hand over his face in frustration. This surgery would be intricate and costly.

It was too expensive to have the clinic cover the cost—especially since the clinic was still trying to recover financially from the consequences of the earthquake. And even though Stavros had a successful *taverna*, Chris was pretty sure that he didn't have enough money to pay for this surgery.

Yet Chris couldn't let him die. He had to try to find a way to help Stavros. He had to get a surgical team together. He needed an operating room and post-anesthesia care. The list was endless.

He hated cases like this, but he also loved cases like this. It was a challenge, and he hadn't had a challenge like this in so long.

"That's one nasty-looking tumor," Naomi said, interrupting his thoughts.

Chris turned to see Naomi leaning in the doorway, her eyes fixed on the screen. She was so close to him he could smell the sweet scent of her perfume. Jasmine and magnolia. It reminded him of his time in Nashville. The flowers from the trees there had bloomed and filled the air with their sweet fragrance, and every time he'd taken Naomi in his arms he'd thought of those flowers. The blooms so soft, so delicate and so beautiful...

Get a hold of yourself.

"Yes. It is. A local patient who hasn't got time to wait for a place on a state-provided health care surgery list. To pay privately it's going to be costly, and I don't think he'll be able to afford it, sadly. If he wants to live, I'm going to have to get him to Athens and do it myself."

Which made him think about how he'd have to uproot Evangelos and take him to Athens too. He would have to find a big enough rental unit so that he, Lisa and Evangelos all had their privacy. It was going to be a nightmare, but Chris couldn't sit back and do nothing. Stavros would die.

"Well, you know the International Relief effort might be willing to help this patient out."

"I thought those funds could only be used to help out earthquake victims. He might have been a victim of the earthquake, but this tumor has been growing for several years."

"Funds are to help those in need," she said. "If he needs help—"

"I have to talk to the patient first and give him all the details," Chris interrupted. "He may say no."

"Yes, but you're saying he needs the surgery. Correct?" she asked.

"Yes. He does."

"Do you know him? Do you think he'll agree to the surgery?"

"Only if he gets to pay his way. He's stubborn—like most men from this island."

He couldn't help but grin at her, and for a brief moment he thought he saw a flicker of humor in her eyes and a small twitch of a smile on her lips.

"Well, I'll try to find out more information. I would like to help in any way that I can. I used to…"

She trailed off and the pink flush of a blush bloomed in her cheeks. He knew what she was going to say, because he was thinking it too.

"You used to assist me in surgery. You were a brilliant neurosurgical resident. Please tell me you didn't give up neurosurgery."

"Oh, you mean *after* you got the fellowship and then the position in Manhattan?"

Chris sighed. "I didn't take that position to hurt you, Naomi."

She frowned. "I know that—and, yes, I'm still a neuro-surgeon, as well as a more than competent general surgeon, which was what was particularly needed in the aftermath of the earthquake."

"I'm glad."

And he was. Naomi was far too talented to be wasted.

He had been so relieved when he'd gotten that position in New York. Naomi had been getting way too close to him for comfort. She'd become part of his life in a way he'd never wanted a woman to be. The Manhattan job had been an escape and he'd jumped at the chance.

He'd completed his fellowship and then become an attending all within three years, and he didn't regret it. The only thing he regretted was losing her along the way. Being so scared of committing to one woman for the rest of his life that he'd run away rather than face up to his fears.

And he regretted hurting her career. He wanted to ask her about whether she'd ever got into Mayo. He wanted to know what she'd done after they'd parted. But he couldn't find the words. He was still far too ashamed.

He glanced at his watch.

It was noon, and he had to head back to relieve Lisa for lunch. Besides, he wouldn't mind having a light lunch at home and a quick nap. The coffee, though strong, had not woken him up. He needed sleep.

"Well, I'd better get some lunch." He stood. "Are you eating here?"

"No, I have plans. A lunch date," she said.

A lunch date? With who?

He was surprised by the sharp burst of jealousy that reared its ugly head deep inside him.

You don't have any claim on her now.

"Oh...?"

"Yes," she said noncommittally, not taking the bait and elaborating. "So, I'll see you later, back at the clinic?"

"Yeah. Enjoy your lunch date."

"Oh, I will," she chirped.

Follow her. Find out who he is.

Only, he wasn't going to do that. He wasn't going to let that jealous, foolish part of him take over. It had been way too many years since he'd gotten into any kind of a brawl over a girl, and he couldn't afford to have his hands out of commission now. Not when he had to get Stavros over to Athens as soon as possible and get that tumor out of him.

Theo was in the hall, waiting for the computer when he left.

"You done?" Theo asked.

"Yeah."

"You okay?"

No. But he didn't say that out loud. He'd never told his friends about Naomi and he wasn't going to elaborate on that secret shame now.

"I just need a nap. Babies are bad for sleep," Chris teased. "You'll see soon enough."

"Great. I can't wait." Theo grinned.

"Hey, is Stavros coming in again today?" Chris asked.

"No, he's working." Theo frowned. "Is this about those scans?"

"He has a very aggressive brain tumor. I have to get him to Athens and do a *very* expensive surgery."

"He's not going to like that," Theo commented. "He never leaves his *taverna*. He's not going to agree to surgery unless it can be done here on the island and he can be back to work in an hour or less."

Chris laughed at that. "Well, none of that's going to happen."

"The surgery could happen here if necessary."

"Theo, I'd need a surgical team that's used to operating on grade three anaplastic oligodendrogliomas. I also think he's going to need some chemotherapy afterward. And I'll need more scans to see if the cancer has progressed."

"I can tell you now—Stavros won't leave Mythelios.

You're going to have to work a miracle," Theo announced, ducking into the office and leaving Chris cursing under his breath.

Why did the men on this island feel they needed to be pigheaded and stubborn to the point at which it cost them everything? Stavros with his brain cancer…his father driving his mother away…and him doing exactly the same thing to Naomi because he'd taken the New York job without consulting her. He'd just upped and left.

Maybe he was cursed?

On days like today it didn't feel as if he had any kind of blessing from the gods smiling down on him. Not that the patron saint of Mythelios had smiled on him in a long time.

What about Evangelos?

Chris's bad attitude melted away.

Yeah, there was Evan. Chris might not have the love of a woman, but he had his son to brighten his life.

And that was all he needed.

"I'm headed for lunch, Theo," Chris called over his shoulder.

"See you," Theo called back.

Chris ducked out the back door and headed along the faster route, through the winding streets to his *yia-yia's* home. He'd just slipped off his shoes when there was a knock at the front door.

Lisa came down the stairs. "That's my cousin. I'm meeting her for lunch. I'm just finishing feeding Evan and then I'll be there."

Chris nodded. "Take your time. I'll let her know."

Lisa nodded and headed back upstairs to where Evangelos was hollering for strained peas—quite loudly.

Chris opened the door.

"Sorry I'm late, I got lost," the woman outside began breathlessly. "I— *Chris?*"

"Hi, Naomi. So you're Lisa's cousin."

He mentally rolled his eyes at the gods, who were surely laughing at him now.

Just. Great. What's he doing here? Can't I get away from him?

"This is where my cousin works. I thought you were..." Then she trailed off as she realized. "This is your home?"

He nodded. "It is. You'd better come in."

Naomi stepped over the threshold and he shut the wooden door to help keep the heat out of the house. She'd seen this house when she'd first arrived on Mythelios. It was on the topmost part of the hill and it overlooked the sea. It was brilliant white, surrounded by the bright colors of the other houses. It had a huge balcony, and she'd imagined what it would be like to live there. To always see the sea.

She'd wondered about the family who lived there. Her cousin hadn't said much about the people she worked for. Only that it was a family with money and that her charge was a young baby.

Baby? But Chris lives here.

Of course he'd found someone else. Of course he was married now. *His* heart hadn't been broken when things had ended between them.

She remembered hearing about all the women he'd been with. He was a playboy in Manhattan, regularly seen out and about with a variety of famous women. And he had money, so of course he would be married.

"My cousin is a nanny," she stated, feeling foolish.

"Yes. I'm aware of that," he said, and his mouth quirked up in a half smile—the one that had always made her melt in the past. "It's my son she cares for when I'm working."

"*Your* son?"

"Yes," he said. "My son, Evangelos. He's eight months old now."

"What about his mother?" Naomi asked.

"My, you're full of questions today," he teased.

"I'm sorry. I just… You were always very clear that you never wanted a wife or kids. You didn't want a family."

"I don't understand. Why can't I come to New York with you?"

"You don't have a position there."

"So? I want to be with you."

His muscles had tensed and she'd seen a look that had made her stomach churn.

"You knew this wasn't long-term. I don't want marriage. I don't want a wife or kids. Don't follow me, Naomi. Don't waste your life pursuing me when I can't give you what you want."

"Circumstances changed," he said now.

Yes, because I wasn't the right woman for you.

And her heart ached as she thought about the baby— *their* baby—the one she had lost. She would have loved that child. She'd always wanted children.

So Chris had got that too.

"Well, I'm happy for you and your wife."

"I'm not married, Naomi. Not much has changed on that score. I have a son, yes, but no wife. Evan was the result of a one-night stand with a woman who just wanted me for the money. She was going to get rid of the child unless I paid her quite a lot of money to have him. I didn't want her to get rid of him, so…here I am. A single father."

Lisa came down the stairs and in her arms was a baby.

Naomi was struck by how much the little boy looked like Chris. Same dark eyes and hair, but the little boy had the biggest cheeks she'd ever seen, and a gummy smile that completely lit up his face when he saw Chris.

"Sorry," Lisa said, handing the baby over to Chris. "He got up late and then his whole schedule was thrown off."

"It's okay," Chris said. "Enjoy lunch with your cousin. I'll see you back here in an hour."

Chris then turned his entire focus onto his son as he carried him up the stairs away from the hallway. The baby gurgled and laughed, and all Naomi could do was stand there in stunned silence.

Her heart was melting as she watched how loving he was with his son.

And thought how completely heartbroken it made her feel.

CHAPTER THREE

SHE COULDN'T GET the picture of Chris carrying his son up the stairs out of her mind. How he'd held the baby so close and just how much he'd doted on him.

Would he have doted on *their* baby just as much?

She wanted to think he would, but she couldn't be sure, and the fact that they would never know made her sad. Made her ache.

It had been a long time since she'd let herself think about her baby and the miscarriage. She never let her mind go there…it was too painful.

Work usually took care of that, but now she was working with Chris and he constantly reminded her of what might have been. What she might have had.

"You're awfully quiet, Naomi," Lisa said, interrupting Naomi's thoughts.

"What?"

"I said you're quiet," Lisa teased. "I thought you were a chatterbox when we first met."

"Sorry. I've got a lot on my mind." Naomi fidgeted with her napkin and tried to put Chris and his son out of her mind—but she couldn't.

She just saw him again and again in her mind's eye, kissing that baby who was the spitting image of him.

"I noticed. You've completely missed those handsome

men over there who have been trying to get your attention for some time."

Naomi turned and glanced over at the men in question. They were young—around Lisa's age, which was about eight years her junior. They were definitely flirting with them, but Naomi wasn't interested.

"Did you know your father's mother? Our *yia-yia*?"

Lisa frowned. "Not really. She died when I was about seven years old. She lived outside of Athens and we rarely went to see her. She hated my mother. And *Yia-yia* travelled a lot. She died shortly after she came back from America."

"She used to say I was cursed." Naomi laughed half-heartedly.

Lisa looked confused. "Cursed? What? You were like… what…? Fourteen when you met her?"

Naomi nodded. "Yep—and she called me cursed or the cursed one the entire time she was visiting. Really annoyed my mother and father."

"Well, my father said that *Yia-yia* had that effect on people. I don't think you're cursed, and I definitely don't believe in curses, but people around here do take religion seriously. When they bring out the Saint for his yearly airing, people are really into seeing his mummified remains being carted around in a gold sarcophagus. They say it brings good luck, but I don't know…"

"I could use some good luck," Naomi said, and groaned. "This bachelor auction is coming up fast at the end of the month. It's being held in Athens now, rather than on Mythelios, so we can get more exposure and hopefully more funds for the wider community as well as the clinic. Theo thought I was the perfect person to take it on, and it's a great idea, but now I have to find some bachelors from Mythelios to auction off. Bachelors who are willing to give a romantic fantasy type of date. I was hoping to coerce some of the male doctors here into it, but they all *have* someone."

Lisa took a sip of her iced tea. "There's always my boss. He's single. He has a baby, but it's just a date for charity. It's not like you're selling off husbands or something. I'm sure if he knew what it was for he'd say yes. He's quite generous."

I'm sure.

"I'm sure he has enough women on his hands that he doesn't need to be auctioned off."

Lisa frowned. "Actually, no, I've never seen him on a date. He's totally devoted to his son and his work. Mind you, I've only known him since I was hired to care for Evan. I don't remember him from when my family would visit the island when I was a child."

"Do you know anything about the baby's mother?"

Lisa frowned. "Nothing. I just know that she's not in the picture and that Chris has full custody of his son. Which is why he hired me shortly after he returned to Greece a few weeks ago. The only woman who lived with him before I came was Dr. Erianthe Nikolaides, but not for long. She's married to Dr. Xenakis now."

Naomi worried at her bottom lip, because she couldn't help but wonder what kind of woman Evan's mother was. Why didn't she want her baby?

Naomi would've given anything to keep *her* baby.

One thing she knew: she felt really sorry for that sweet little boy, growing up without a mother.

"I can't ask Dr. Moustakas to take part in the bachelor auction," she said, steering the subject back to the auction because she didn't want to think about Chris and his baby. How it had made her completely weak in the knees to see them together.

She'd never seen him like that before. So gentle, so loving. It made her long for what had been taken from her. For what she'd never got to have.

"You *can* ask Dr. Moustakas. He'll probably say yes— and, honestly, he needs a night away," Lisa said. "He really has no life."

Lisa continued to chat about different things, but Naomi was only half listening. It surprised her to hear that Chris had become something of a hermit when he'd been the quintessential playboy in Manhattan—or so all the tabloids had said, when she was doing her fellowship in Nashville.

The church bell in the center of the old town chimed the hour.

"I'd better get back. Evangelos is due for a walk and Dr. Moustakas has to get back to work." Lisa picked up her shawl and purse. "Are you heading back to Athens tonight?"

Naomi nodded. "There's no place to stay on the island after the earthquake—though Dr. Nikolaides did offer a boathouse. But a place like that is more suited to a bachelor. Are you headed back to Athens too?"

"No, I'm on for three nights and then off for two. I have a small room close to Evangelos. I suppose when the boy gets older I'll be making the commute daily, but it's really not that long."

"No, but it would be easier to stay here. Isn't there a ferry that goes to Spritos?"

Lisa frowned. "Spritos? What do you need to do there?"

"There's another small clinic there, and I was told Spritos could be accessed by ferry from Mythelios."

"On the other side of the island. The ferry only runs twice a day. Once in the morning and once in the evening. Pray you don't get stuck there, because they really have nothing—but it's a beautiful place."

Naomi walked Lisa back to Chris's house.

"I hope we can visit more," Lisa said as she unlocked

the old wooden door to Chris's home. "It's nice that you're here, and if *Yia-yia* did put a curse on you, perhaps we can lift it, eh?"

Naomi laughed. "I would like that."

She turned and began walking back to the clinic. She made slow progress and was annoyed with herself for wearing completely impractical heels—especially when walking on cobbled streets. Then her heel broke, and she swore out loud and leaned precariously against a wall to inspect the damage.

Yep. Definitely cursed.

There was the beep of a horn behind her, and she looked over her shoulder to see a little scooter being driven by none other than Chris, who was grinning from ear to ear as he leaned over the front.

"I told you those heels would be your downfall one day."

She snorted. "I wasn't thinking. In Athens it's no big deal."

"Here, especially on the cobbled streets of the old part of town, flats are your friend. How badly is it broken?"

"Bad—but I do have a pair of flip-flops in my bag back at the clinic. I was planning on getting a pedicure in Athens when I returned tonight."

"Well, you won't make it hobbling like that. Do you want a ride to the clinic?"

She eyed the scooter speculatively. "I thought you walked."

"In the morning, yes, but I'm running late and I thought I'd take this for a spin. It was my *yia-yia's* and is proving handy."

"Your *yia-yia's*?" Naomi tried to picture a tiny little grandmother, dressed in black, motoring around Mythelios on this little turquoise scooter.

"Why not?"

"A scooter's not very practical for a man with a baby."

"I have a car on the mainland. The ferry's not a far walk and neither is the clinic. Do you want a ride or do you want to spend all day holding up that wall?"

"Thanks."

Naomi hobbled over to him and climbed precariously onto the back of the scooter, sitting sidesaddle behind him because she was wearing a tight pencil skirt. She crossed her legs at the ankles.

He glanced over his shoulder at her. "Uh…you do have to hold on."

"There's nothing to hold on to."

"Sure there is. Me. You have to hold on to *me*."

Definitely cursed.

"Fine," she murmured as she slipped her arms around his waist.

Under his loose scrubs she could feel every single one of his abdominal muscles, and when she closed her eyes, she could see him without his shirt on and it made her heart beat just a little bit faster.

She'd never really forgotten the electric effect he'd had on her, and being so close to him now, with her body pressed against his, it all came rushing back, making her blood heat and her palms sweat.

She hated that he still had this effect on her. Why *did* he still have this effect on her? Why was she letting him get to her?

Because you're weak. Because you've never really gotten over him.

"You ready?"

"No!" she said, but nodded.

He chuckled. "Hang on."

Chris revved the engine and the little scooter took off down the hill, through the narrow cobbled streets of the old part of Mythelios. Naomi closed her eyes tight for a few moments as Chris drove like a maniac through the streets, but then he turned away from the clinic road onto another road. A dirt track that overlooked the sea.

"Where are we going?" she shrieked over the roar of the engine.

"Just taking the back way," he teased. "A more scenic route, since you probably haven't seen all of Mythelios yet."

"Uh, no—I really need to get back."

"Live a little, Naomi. You're always so uptight."

That was what he'd said to her when they'd first met, and look where that had gotten her. It had left her with a broken heart, an unimaginable loss and, for the first time in her life, without a clue as to how to go on.

She'd fought hard to dig herself out of that pit of heartbreak and learn to put herself first. She wasn't going to let him do that to her again.

"Chris, stop this thing *now*!"

Chris pulled over into a lay-by and stopped the scooter. Once she was off, she slipped off her shoes and began to walk barefoot down the dirt track toward the clinic.

"Naomi, I was only joking."

She spun around. "That's the thing. You're always *joking*! I have *real* work to do. I have patients to see this afternoon! I don't have time to waste driving all over the island just because I need to let loose! I've done enough of that in my life and look where it got me."

Tears were stinging her eyes—not because she was sad, but because she always cried when she got mad, and she was mad about this whole situation. How he thought things could ever be normal between them was a mystery to her.

Maybe she was cursed and maybe he had all the luck, but she worked hard for what she wanted, for what she'd achieved, and she wasn't going to let him stand in her way this time.

"Naomi!" he called out, but she ignored him, limping along the road, feeling small pebbles digging into the soles of her feet.

Chris came jogging up beside her and took her hand in his. It was so strong, so warm.

"I'm sorry, Naomi."

There was sincerity in his eyes, and a well of sadness.

"Please let me take you back to the clinic and I'll make it up to you any way that I can."

"You'll make it up to me?" she asked.

He nodded. "Of course. I was impertinent and flippant and I'll do whatever it takes to make things right. I'll do whatever it takes to make this whole thing go away so we can work together."

"Okay." She grinned suddenly. "I know *exactly* how you can make it up to me."

He cocked a wary eyebrow. "Really? That fast?"

"Yes. It's something that's put me in a bit of a predicament."

"What is it?" Chris asked hesitantly.

"*You're* going to be my feature bachelor."

His expression fell. "What?"

"At a charity auction to raise money for earthquake relief. You're going to give up your time and take the highest bidder on a romantic night out."

He wasn't quite sure that he'd heard her right.

"You want me to do *what*?" he asked in disbelief.

"Be in the bachelor auction."

"No way!" he almost shouted at her, throwing up his arms.

"You said you'd make it up to me, and being the featured

bachelor in our Hot Greek Nights bachelor auction would definitely be a highlight."

"Nope." He shook his head and crossed his arms. "I'm not a bachelor."

A strange expression crossed her face and for a fleeting moment he thought he saw that flare of jealousy again.

"You're involved with someone?" she asked slowly.

"No, but…"

She held up her hand to silence him. "Then you're doing it, pal."

"I think not. I'm a single father. I don't have time to do a charity auction."

"Even if it will help those less fortunate here in Mythelios? Those who were affected by the earthquake? Not everyone is so lucky as to have a trust fund and live like you do. There are other single parents out there seriously struggling to survive."

Dammit.

He couldn't argue with that, and if it was to help out with fund-raising, there was no way he could walk away from it. Naomi had him cornered, the minx.

"Who suggested me?" he grumbled.

"No one did. I see no wedding band. Like you said, you're a single father."

"I told you my son's mother made it clear that she did not want him and left," he snapped, surprised at how touchy he was about it.

"I'm sorry it didn't work out."

"There was nothing *to* work out. I told you it was a one-night stand. I regret sleeping with Evan's biological mother, but I don't regret having him in my life."

An unreadable expression crossed her face and he couldn't quite place it, but then it vanished again as quickly as it had appeared.

"So, will you do it?"

He ran a hand through his hair. "I guess I have no choice—because I can't have you cut your feet up walking back down to the clinic, nor have you savaged by a wandering goat." A smile tugged at the corner of his mouth when he saw her eyes widen.

"Goats?"

He laughed. "I'll do it. What do I need to do, though?"

"Just think of something romantic to do with whoever wins the date. You were always pretty good at that."

A blush rose in her cheeks and his blood heated. He loved it when she blushed, and it made him feel good that he still had some kind of effect on her after all this time.

She was the only woman he'd ever cared about. Even though he'd been completely stubborn and too pigheaded back then to see it.

And now it was too late.

Is it?

"Come on, let's get you back to the clinic," he said, heading back to the scooter.

"Before I'm savaged by a goat?" she teased.

"Yeah."

Naomi stumbled over some of the small rocks on this section of the road and without thinking he closed the distance between them and scooped her up, carrying her the short distance back to the scooter.

She was blushing again.

"This…" she whispered as he sat her down on the back of the scooter.

"What?"

"Sweep the winner off her feet. You're good at that too."

"Okay. I'll think of something." He climbed onto the scooter.

"Thank you, by the way. In case I don't say it later. You're making my life just a bit easier," she said gently.

He smiled. "You're welcome."

He fired up the scooter and made a careful turn off the winding hill road. Her arms were around him again and it felt so right. She'd told him that he was good at sweeping a woman off her feet, and perhaps he was, but there was only ever one woman whom he'd truly wanted to do that to and she was sitting behind him.

And she didn't want him anymore.

CHAPTER FOUR

"You're daydreaming again, eh?"

Chris looked up to see Ares standing over him. Ares had a mischievous glint in his dark eyes as he sat down next to Chris in the clinic's lounge.

"I wasn't daydreaming. I might've been nodding off, though. I have a young son and I don't get much sleep, so I tend to zone out."

Ares snorted. "Sure, that must be it. It has nothing to do with Dr. Hudson."

Chris straightened his spine and sat up. "What're you talking about?"

"I see the way you look at her and the way she acts around you. Is she one of your paramours from America?"

No, she was more than that. But he'd been too much of a coward back then to do anything about it.

Ares didn't need to know that.

"Something like that..." Chris stretched.

"Why didn't you tell us? If you'd told us, we could've had someone else from International Relief come in her place," Ares said.

"No, don't do that—it's not necessary." Chris sighed. "It was nothing, and we're still friends."

Ares cocked an eyebrow and Chris could tell that he didn't believe him.

"You're sure you don't want to talk about it?"

"Yes, I'm sure."

Chris didn't want to talk about Naomi with Ares, Deakin or Theo. He didn't want them to think badly of him—the way he felt about himself for walking away from her.

"I heard that you're now the lone bachelor representing us in that bachelor auction in Athens in a couple of weeks. Thanks for doing that, but I seriously doubt that you'll earn as much money as I would have."

Chris snorted. "*You* were supposed to be the feature bachelor?"

"What's with the snort of derision? Of *course*. No woman can resist me or my charms." Ares grinned and tossed his head, making those long dark curls bounce.

Chris rolled his eyes. "Don't let Erianthe hear you talking like that."

"Right," Ares said, chuckling.

"So what were you going to do?" Chris asked.

"I was going to walk across the stage in a tuxedo," Ares answered, puzzled.

Chris punched him in the arm. "No, I meant for the date. What were you going to do? What's romantic in Greece? I'm too used to sweeping a girl off her feet in Manhattan. I think I'm out of touch."

And *that* was the understatement of the year. He was definitely out of touch—and had been since the day Evan's mother had told him she was pregnant. That was when his life had come to a screeching halt.

It was also the night when he'd stopped sleeping soundly.

"Well, I was planning on hiring a yacht and taking the lucky winner out on a moonlight boat ride. Spritos isn't far, and my plan was to have a little impromptu fancy picnic set up on one of the beaches your father owns, complete with a waiter and the very best champagne. Maybe some dancing under the stars."

"You're quite the Valentino, Ares."

Ares grinned. "I know."

"Well, that might be going a bit overboard." Chris rolled his shoulders to loosen the tension knot that had formed in his back. "I'm not trying to seduce the woman. Just give her her money's worth."

"Oh, for sure—because *your* seduction technique would have her demanding a refund."

Ares got up and jogged out of the room before Chris could react.

Yeah, you'd better run!

Ares's idea wasn't half-bad, though. His father had a yacht he could use, and Chris was pretty sure that the captain who ran it would do the tour pro bono, but since his father's yacht was a bit larger than what Ares had planned, dinner on the beach was probably a bit out of reach.

What was he doing?

He should have just said no to being in the auction!

Actually, he shouldn't have done such a spur-of-the-moment thing and taken Naomi on that scooter ride at all. He didn't know what had come over him.

Exhaustion. That's what your problem is.

Or guilt. Naomi could have asked him for almost anything and he'd have given it to her.

Except marriage. You couldn't give her that.

Chris swore under his breath as he tried to forget about that. He couldn't be thinking about that now, when he had a patient to see.

Deakin poked his head into the lounge. "Stavros is here for his appointment."

He wasn't looking forward to this, but it had to be done.

"Thanks, Deakin."

"He's in exam room one." Deakin left and Chris picked up his notebook.

How did you tell someone he was dying? He'd never get used to telling patients that. In Manhattan he had all the newest equipment and the finest surgical team at his fingertips, but here in a small island clinic he was feeling distinctly uneasy.

Even if Stavros agreed to go to Athens, the neurosurgical team there wasn't *his*. They wouldn't be used to his nuances, and that upped the risk factor of this whole thing.

Chris gathered up Stavros's file and headed to exam room one. He knocked on the door and slipped in when Stavros responded.

"So the prodigal son returns to Mythelios," Stavros said brightly. "Your *yia-yia* was a regular at my *taverna*. She was a force to be reckoned with, God rest her soul."

Chris nodded. "That she was."

"You've only been to my *taverna* once, though, since you came home."

"I've been busy. And I have a young son."

"Ah, well, congratulations. I hadn't heard," Stavros said.

Only, Chris was pretty sure that Stavros had heard. Stavros knew everything, and this forgetfulness might be the tumor talking.

"Thank you."

Stavros smiled. "So I take it since they brought in such a big gun to handle my file after the headaches and the seizure, that it's something a bit more serious than epilepsy?"

Chris nodded solemnly. "I'm sorry, Stavros, but you have a grade three anaplastic oligodendroglioma. It's a fast-growing, rare and aggressive form of tumor that is growing in your temporal lobe. If left untreated, it will spread to other parts of your body."

"What're my options?" Stavros asked calmly.

"I would like to get some more scans to see if the cancer has spread anywhere else first, and then I can form a plan of attack. But ideally I would operate to remove what I can and then give you a course of chemotherapy."

"Chemotherapy?" Stavros shook his head. "But who would run my *taverna*? I can't agree to that—and I doubt I could afford it either."

"Stavros, if you refuse treatment, you'll have maybe six months to live."

"It's a risk I'm willing to take. I can't be so sick that I'm unable to work. The *taverna* is my livelihood, and without it I can't pay for the surgery."

"I'll pay for the surgery."

"With all due respect, Dr. Moustakas, I don't take charity."

"Let me at least do the scans in Athens. I'll set you up an appointment for a Sunday so that it won't affect your work. If it hasn't spread, then you won't have to have chemotherapy. I would just do the operation."

Stavros frowned. "Can I think about it?"

"Of course. I'm really sorry."

"Thank you, Dr. Moustakas. I really appreciate it."

Chris left the exam room and took the file back to the filing cabinet. Naomi was standing next to it, and she cocked one of her finely arched brows when she saw him.

"You look terrible. You okay?" she asked.

"Yeah, I just had to deliver the bad news to Stavros."

Her expression softened. "I'm sorry. How did he take it?"

"He's stubborn, but that's not surprising. He'll come around, but at the moment he's refusing any kind of charity. He wants to pay for surgery on his own—except the surgery will take everything he's saved and probably his *taverna* as well."

"It's pride. I get that. And I'm still trying to find a way to have the relief fund pay for the surgery," she said.

"I don't think he'd accept it. He doesn't want charity, but then again he may take it if it's a last resort. I'm hoping he'll at least agree to go to Athens to have a full body scan, just so I can see if the cancer has spread, because if it has spread, then all I can offer Stavros is comfort measures." He scrubbed a hand over his face. "Do you have an in with the chief of surgery at an Athens hospital?"

"I do. Why?" she asked.

"The only way I can get Stavros to agree to a scan is to have it done on a Sunday, when his *taverna* is closed."

Naomi smiled. "I'll see what I can do."

"Thank you. I appreciate it."

All he wanted to do was go home and sleep, but Naomi lingered and he had a feeling that he wasn't going home anytime soon.

"Why are you looking at me like that?"

She handed him a piece of paper. "Information about the bachelor auction in Athens that you agreed to yesterday. I've already talked to my cousin about watching your son that night."

"I know Lisa is your cousin, but you shouldn't be arranging things with my child's nanny behind my back," he said stiffly.

Even though he was grateful she'd done it, he didn't want her wiggling her way into his life. He didn't want her to get hurt when he couldn't give her what she wanted. He had to protect Evangelos. Chris didn't deserve her kindness or concern.

"I know. I'm sorry. But she was very glad to do it. I confess she's the one who suggested you when I found out that all the other doctors here in the clinic are already spoken for."

"She suggested me, eh?"

He would have to have a talk with her later, but he was

glad that Lisa was willing to work an extra night to watch Evan. Chances were that someone from outside Mythelios would win him, and he didn't want anyone to know about his son. His son wouldn't be used as a selling point in this bachelor auction.

"There will be no mention of Evangelos. You can talk about my medical career, and even who my father is, but you will *not* mention at the auction that I am a single parent."

Naomi nodded. "Of course. I understand. So who *is* your father? I always knew you were well-off, but we didn't talk much about our families."

Warmth spread through his body as he thought about what they'd done instead of talking. An image of her in his arms, naked, his hands in her hair as he kissed her over and over, flitted through his mind.

Focus.

"You ever hear of Mopaxeni Shipping?"

She raised her eyebrows. "The big shipping empire? Of course—who *hasn't* heard of it?"

"My father is one of the head figures behind that enterprise. I'm sure just a mention that I am a Mopaxeni heir will drive up the bids."

"Most certainly—but aren't you worried that some fortune-hunting heiress will get her hooks into you and sweep you off your feet?"

She'd meant it as a joke, but it hit a little too close to home and reminded him of Evangelos's mother.

"Give me a million and I'll keep the baby. You can have it, and I'll sign away my rights to it, but a million is my price. As well as an apartment in Central Park West."

"Are you serious?" Chris had shouted.

"Very," Lillian had said coolly. *"I won't have this baby for less than that."*

"What about marriage?" Though he'd cringed inwardly

even thinking about that, he'd known it was the right thing to do.

"I don't want marriage. I want money, Chris. If you won't agree to my terms, then I will get rid of this baby."

Chris had clenched his fists. What had he ever seen in her? She was cruel, vicious and greedy.

You did this to yourself, the voice in his head had told him. *You had it all with Naomi and you threw it away. This is your punishment.*

"Fine. I'll agree to your terms and you will relinquish all rights to our child. And you will agree to attending medical appointments and keeping yourself healthy. Doing nothing to jeopardize our child."

"And when will I get my payment?" Lillian had asked.

"Half now and half when the child is born."

He remembered that call to his father, when he'd had to ask for the money to buy the apartment and a check for a million. His father had scolded him about his irresponsible ways and Chris had had to agree with him on that score.

He might be a brilliant neurosurgeon, but when it came to matters of the heart, he was a bit of a fool.

"Don't worry. I won't give them too good of a time," Chris finally said, breaking the tension that had descended between him and Naomi.

"What are your big plans, then?" she asked.

"That's a secret," he replied.

The yacht idea that Ares had suggested was good, but he really didn't know much beyond that.

"I have to know beforehand. The date is sort of pitched as part of the package," she said. "I really hate doing this too, but it's a means to an end."

A smile quirked his lips. He loved it when she got all worked up and her Tennessee accent became thicker.

"I'll let you know as soon as I can."

She nodded and then glanced at her watch. "I'd better go if I'm going to catch the next ferry to Athens."

"Yes—and I should go home and relieve Lisa so she can have her dinner."

No sooner had the words come out of his mouth than there was a shout from the front of the clinic.

"Help! Please! It's my son! He was in a crash and he hit his head—he's unconscious!"

The woman was beside herself.

Chris followed the woman into the street just outside the clinic. A young man had been riding a scooter without a helmet and he'd hit a tree. And from the way he was lying on the road, with his right temple against the stone curb, Chris had no doubt the man would have a concussion.

Naomi knelt down next to him and gently began to examine the young man.

"Airway and breathing is good," she said.

"I need to get him inside," said Chris. "But first I want to assess him for any injury to his spine."

Naomi nodded. "What do you need?"

"Get a backboard and I'll examine him."

She nodded and disappeared back into the clinic as Chris made his preliminary examination. The left pupil was blown, but the right was responsive. The young man was alive, and that was all that mattered.

Naomi returned with the backboard just as Chris finished his examination. Together they gently lifted their patient on. He didn't have to bark orders to Naomi. She knew exactly what was needed, what he wanted to be done as head neurosurgeon. They had always worked well together—which was why he had been so drawn to her when he'd first met her.

There was still something there.

He wasn't blind.

Or could it be that she's also a neurosurgical fellow on top of a general surgeon?

He shook that errant thought away as they strapped the man down and together carried him into the clinic.

Right now he couldn't think about all the *what ifs* and reminisce about working with Naomi. Not now, when a man's life was hanging in the balance.

"Malakas!"

Naomi cringed as she heard Chris curse from the other room. The CT scanner was on the fritz again. She'd been told by Theo that it hadn't been working well since the earthquake, and they urgently needed a new one.

Their patient, Maximos Ponao, was still unconscious, and Chris was positive that there was a hematoma. There was a definite depressed skull fracture.

"Aha!" Chris shouted triumphantly as the scanner finally fired up. He joined her in the observation room as Maximos was scanned. "If this keeps working like this, I'm going to have Stavros scanned here. An MRI is less invasive, but a CT scan will do just as well."

"That will make Stavros happy," Naomi remarked.

They sat next to each other, waiting for the scanner to send images to the computer.

"What will you do if there is a hematoma? There is an operating room available, and we can call staff back in," she said.

But she was really hoping that Chris wouldn't attempt to evacuate the hematoma and the fracture and would just wait for the air ambulance to land. Once they had Maximos stable, she'd call for the air ambulance from Athens to come and get him.

"Unless he's at death's door, no, I don't want to do brain surgery here," Chris said. "The surgical staff are great, but they're not used to brain surgery and a depressed skull fracture requires a certain finesse. I'm not comfortable doing it here."

"Yet you are the best neurosurgeon in the United States. There's no denying it—you're at the top of the game. This young man could do worse."

Chris's jaw tightened and he didn't look at her. He kept his eyes fixed on the computer screen, but he said, "Thank you."

The images came up and Chris swore under his breath. "I'm glad you called the air ambulance. You can see he has clotted blood along the interhemispheric fissure and he's developing hydrocephalus. He needs surgery at once to relieve the pressure."

"They'll be here soon."

As if on cue they could hear the distant whir of the helicopter as it crossed the few miles between Mythelios and mainland Greece.

"I'll go let them in," Naomi said.

She ran as best as she could in the flip-flops that had replaced her broken heels and met the paramedic team as the helicopter landed on the roof. She explained what had happened, and which hospital to take the patient to.

Chris was waiting for them, and he helped the paramedics carry the stretcher up to the roof. The young man's mother followed. She would travel with the air ambulance to the mainland, since the ferry had stopped for the night.

Once Maximos was loaded, Chris put his arm around Naomi as the helicopter's blades came to life, nearly blowing her over. He led her out of their path, back into the doorway, and they watched the helicopter disappear into the inky-black night, its lights flashing as it headed swiftly back to the mainland.

"So, it looks like you lost your only ride back to the

mainland tonight," Chris remarked. "And there's already a doctor sleeping in the on-call room."

"It appears so. Well, the couch in the lounge looks comfy enough. I'm sure I'll be fine there for the night."

Though she didn't really relish the idea of trying to curl up on the couch that time had forgotten. It was fine for sitting on, or a short nap, but it really was as hard as a rock.

"Nonsense. You can spend the night with me."

Heat bloomed in her cheeks as she thought of the last time he'd asked her to spend the night with him.

"I want you to spend the night," Chris had whispered against her ear, before trailing a kiss down her neck.

"Do you think that's wise?" she'd asked breathlessly. His hands had been all over her and her body had been thrumming with pleasure.

"It's just one night. Not a lifetime."

And then he'd kissed her, before scooping her up in his arms and carrying her to bed...

She coughed nervously, trying to dispel the vivid memory. "No, I don't think that's wise."

"Of course it is. You can have my room and I'll be more than comfortable on my large sectional couch. And your cousin will be asleep in the room next to Evan tonight."

Sleeping in a bed was far more ideal than trying to cram herself onto the clinic's couch. Even if that bed belonged to the one man she'd sworn never to go to bed with again. And he'd be far away in the living room on his couch.

"Okay. Thank you."

Chris nodded. "It's the least I can do after you missed your ferry to help me."

"Well, it's my job. I *am* a surgeon too—not just a wrangler of bachelors."

He grinned at her. "True—and you're a damn fine surgeon, if my memory serves me correctly."

She blushed, heat flushing her cheeks as they closed down the clinic.

They began to walk back to his home.

"What about the scooter?" she asked.

"The headlight is burned out, and I really don't feel like riding a scooter after what happened tonight. I'll have to get a helmet before I attempt that scooter again. It's not really proper for a world-renowned neurosurgeon to be terrorizing the streets of Mythelios on a scooter without a helmet."

Naomi laughed at the image of him terrifying people on his scooter and then got an image of her *yia-yia* terrorizing people on a scooter—because she didn't know what Chris's *yia-yia* had looked like, so couldn't picture her, but assumed that she must've been a lot like her own *yia-yia*.

"You're cursed!"

She frowned, shaking her *yia-yia's* voice from her head.

"You okay?" he asked as they ambled up the hill toward his house.

"Yeah, just thinking about my late *yia-yia*. She wasn't as free-spirited as it sounds like yours was."

Chris chuckled softly. "I don't think many were—and her free spirit caused my father many gray hairs. As do I, truth be told. I have a bastard heir."

Naomi winced. "That sounds like something out of an old Victorian novel. There are a lot of unmarried parents these days. Families are no longer traditional."

"Tell that to my father. Although he never really liked having kids either. It was just what was expected of him. So he and my mother had me, and then my mother grew disenchanted, or bored—I don't know—and she left. Though as far as I know, my parents are still legally married. My father doesn't believe in divorce either."

"I'm sorry."

"And what of *your* family? I didn't know that you were half-Greek."

"Well, we didn't really ever talk about our families when we were together, did we?"

Which was true, as the time they'd spent together they had been either working in the hospital or in bed together. Maybe that was why she'd been so blindsided when Chris had upped and left her for Manhattan.

She'd been so blinded by love that she hadn't been expecting it.

Lust, not love. Remember that.

And that was what she had to keep telling herself. As she'd picked up the pieces of her heart, she'd come to realize that it hadn't been love, and that their whole relationship had been built on lust. She'd been a fool.

"So tell me about them. You know about mine—or rather the whole world seems to know about mine, since my father is one of the wealthiest men in the Aegean."

"My father was Greek, but he left Athens and went to America when he was a very young man. He met my mother in Nashville, they fell in love and here I am. My father brought me only once to Greece when I was a young girl, when I met his mother and a few of my other Greek relatives. But it didn't go all that smoothly, thanks to *Yia-yia*, and we never came back. Or at least *he* didn't come back. He passed away last year. When I saw a posting in Greece to help with the earthquake relief, I thought I'd return."

"I'm sorry to hear of your father's passing," Chris said gently, his voice somber.

"Thank you. I loved my father. We were very close—particularly after my mom died a few years ago."

"And your Greek family? Lisa is your cousin?"

Naomi smiled. "Yes. I'm glad we're getting to know each other now. All my older cousins are boys, and when

I came here, I was only about fourteen, so we didn't really have that much in common."

Chris chuckled. "No, I suppose you wouldn't."

"Do *you* have a large family?" she asked.

"No. Just my parents. My father was an only child and I'm an only child. If there are cousins on my mother's side, I don't know them. My mother left my father and me when I was quite young. She's in Corfu now. I have reached out to her over the years, but she wants nothing to do with me. I remind her of all the things she never wanted."

"I'm sorry… Did she actually *say* that to you?" Naomi asked, horrified.

He nodded. "Yes. Marrying my father was her parents' idea, and marrying him and having a child ended her medical career. So even though I became a surgeon—a world-renowned one at that—she sees it as a final betrayal. I became what she never could."

"That's really very selfish of her."

Chris chuckled again. "Yes, well, I won't deny that my parents are selfish—or that I was."

His admission of selfishness caught her off guard. She'd never thought she'd hear that coming from him. Perhaps he'd matured and grown now he was a father. Maybe he'd really changed.

Don't fall for the same trap again, Naomi.

They walked in silence the rest of the way. He unlocked the door and led her up the stairs of his late grandmother's house, which was still laid out in the traditional way of all the old houses that littered the islands of Greece and the mainland.

She laid her hand on the stone, which was cool. There was a large, modern-style kitchen at the top of the stairs. He led her out through the kitchen into a small covered courtyard that held a small table, and she heard the bubbling sounds of water from a small fountain in the middle of the courtyard.

He pointed through another set of French doors. "That's the living room, and there are stairs there that lead to Lisa's room and Evangelos's room. My room is this way."

Chris led her upstairs, higher up the cliff that this winding house had been built into. There was a solid balcony, and from there Chris took her straight into his room.

"This is a beautiful house," she said, suddenly feeling awkward as she eyed the large bed that dominated the room.

Chris nodded. "It needs some work. The bathroom is through that door, and there's another small courtyard off the bathroom, and then stairs down to the garden, where there's a small pool. From the courtyard there are more stairs down to the hallway that connects Lisa's and Evan's rooms."

"It's a maze!"

He smiled. "A bit—but this house has been in my *yia-yia's* family for a long time. They built it slowly. It does need some updating—like putting in air-conditioning—but if you leave the balcony doors open, and these windows too, you'll get a nice cross breeze this high up."

"Thank you again. I hate that I'm depriving you of your bed tonight."

"It's no bother, really. My living room is quite comfortable. Let me just grab a couple of things and I'll leave you to it."

Chris gathered some things and then headed for the balcony door, where he paused and turned around. "If you need anything, please let me know."

"I will. Thank you."

He nodded and left.

Naomi could see out of windows that faced down into the courtyard, and saw when he crossed it and headed into the living room. He closed the French doors to the living room and then the house was quiet.

She headed over to the other side of the room and opened the windows, sighing when she saw the sea and the bright moon reflected over the diamond-dappled waters. Her place in Athens didn't overlook the sea, but there was quite a nice view of the Parthenon…

She cleaned up in the bathroom and changed out of her work clothes. She wrapped one of the cotton sheets around her to sleep and settled down in the bed.

It was comfortable and it smelled like Chris. A scent she'd never forget because she often thought of being wrapped up in his arms.

He'd changed.

You don't know that.

She sighed, ignoring that niggling thought. She needed to get a good night's rest. There was a lot to do tomorrow and she planned to be up and out of here before Chris got up.

She couldn't get involved with him again. She'd promised herself that she'd keep her distance from him, but that was hard to do when she was staying in his house and sleeping in his bed.

She'd be gone before he got up and tomorrow they'd continue working together. Friendly, but that was it. That was as far as it could go.

She had to keep reminding herself of that or she'd fall into the same trap again.

A trap that would cost her her heart—and she couldn't afford to let it be broken again.

CHAPTER FIVE

WARM SUNLIGHT STREAMING through the window was what woke her up. She was disoriented, and her eyes were having a hard time adjusting to the bright light that was filtering in from the windows.

This was not her small apartment in Athens and, judging by the sounds filtering in through the open windows, it was past time that she usually got up.

Oh, no. I slept in.

Naomi groaned and glanced at the small clock next to the bed and saw that it was actually nine-thirty in the morning.

Great.

So much for her plan to slip out of the house early and avoid Chris. She got up and pulled on her clothes from the night before, cleaned herself up and made her way out to the balcony and down through the courtyard into the kitchen.

Chris was sitting at the large wooden table and in a high chair next to him was Evangelos. Chris was feeding the baby yogurt and the baby's face lit up as he eagerly opened his mouth and gulped down the yogurt while banging his little fists against the plastic table of the high chair.

She couldn't help but smile at the sight. The baby was covered in yogurt and making little noises of pleasure as Chris fed him.

It sent a pang of longing through her, which caught her

off guard. She had to get a hold of herself. She couldn't be thinking this way. She couldn't feel the pain right now and she had to keep her walls intact. That was the only way her heart would survive working with Dr. Moustakas again.

The alternative—crumbling before him and letting him see the vulnerable side to her…the side that was still mourning what she'd lost—was not an option.

"Good morning," she said, feeling completely awkward as she stepped into the kitchen and interrupted this moment between Chris and his son.

"Good morning," he said, glancing briefly over his shoulder. "You slept in. I half expected you to be gone when I got up, but Lisa checked on you before she left for the market and said you were still sound asleep."

"I'm afraid I didn't hear the alarm I set for myself."

"Ah, yeah—that clock doesn't work beyond telling the time. I usually just use my phone. Sorry, I should have told you."

"It's no problem."

"There's coffee," he said, and he got up and poured her a cup, holding it out to her.

"Thank you."

She took a sip and it hit the spot. She sat down across the table from him and his son. The baby grinned at her and then gurgled, demanding more yogurt.

"Yes, yes. So impatient." Chris beamed and spooned the last of the yogurt into the baby's mouth.

Naomi smiled. "He's adorable."

"I think so," Chris said, with pride in his voice. "Oh, Lisa left a pair of shoes in her room for you. Some ballet flats until you can get back to Athens."

"Good to know," Naomi said, relieved. "I wasn't sure how it would look, wearing flip-flops in the clinic two days in a row."

Chris chuckled. "It's not safe, that's for sure."

"Have you had any updates on Maximos?" she asked.

"Yes, as a matter of fact I have…"

Chris cleaned up Evangelos and handed the baby a toy to play with as he put the yogurt dish in the sink.

"The hospital in Athens was able to stabilize him, but he needs surgery, and their surgeons have never dealt with a depressed skull fracture of this magnitude. They want me to go and perform the surgery this evening. So I'll be heading to Athens tonight and then coming back to Mythelios in the morning."

"I'm sorry to hear that Maximos's condition is so severe. His poor mother must be beside herself."

Chris nodded. "It's hard to be so hurt and so far from home, even if Athens isn't technically that far away. I hope I can do something, but I won't know until I get in there."

"What about Evangelos?" She glanced at the baby, who was already drifting off to sleep in his high chair. His chubby cheeks were even more pronounced as he slept.

"Lisa will watch him. He'll be in good hands and I'll be back in the morning." Chris set down his coffee. "I'll just put him down, and then once Lisa gets back, we can walk to the clinic together."

"Sure."

She drank her coffee slowly as Chris picked up Evangelos, who was startled but then curled into his father's arms. It made her long once again for the baby she'd lost, and she choked back the emotion that was welling up in her.

She just couldn't help but wonder *what if?*—which was something she never let herself do. She didn't ever let herself think about what had been lost, because it had taken her so long to pull the pieces of her heart back together.

"I'm back," Lisa called out as she came up the stairs. "Good morning, sleepyhead."

"Hey—so you have shoes I can borrow?"

Lisa nodded and set the bags from the market on the table. "Yes. Come to my room and you can try them on, but I'm pretty sure they'll fit you."

Naomi set her coffee cup in the sink and followed Lisa through the courtyard and into the living room. She could see sheets at one end of the large sectional couch where Chris had obviously slept.

Warmth spread in her cheeks as she thought of him stretched out there, sleeping…

She had rolled over and looked at him. He'd been sleeping on his back, with one arm behind his head and one resting across his chest. Only a sheet had covered his hips. She'd watched him breathing in deep sleep, recalling the way his arms had held her after their lovemaking. How safe she'd felt with him.

She'd reached out and touched his chest, running her fingers over his skin.

He'd opened an eye and smiled at her.

"Good morning…"

She had to focus.

She couldn't let memories like that invade her thoughts. She had to lock all those memories away, and not *feel* when it came to Chris, so that she could protect her heart.

Up a few more steps and they were in Lisa's small but comfortable room. Lisa picked up a pair of black flats from her bed and held them out.

"These should fit you."

Naomi sat on the edge of Lisa's bed and slipped the shoes on. They were a little big, but not much.

"These are perfect. I'll bring them back to you tomorrow."

"No rush. Now, I'd better go check on Evangelos so Chris can get back to work. He's heading to Athens tonight?"

Naomi nodded. "Maximos Ponao was in an accident last night and he has a pretty significant skull fracture."

Lisa sighed. "He was one of those good-looking men from the market who were watching us the other day. That's too bad."

"He was?"

"Don't you remember? You don't see any of the men who have eyes for you, Naomi," Lisa teased as she slipped out of the room.

She hadn't given those two handsome Greek gods any thought after that day in the market when she'd had lunch with Lisa because all she could think about was Chris. When Chris was around, she didn't see any other man.

She hadn't dated after Chris and her miscarriage because even the thought of being intimate with another man made her remember what she'd lost, and she didn't ever want to be hurt like that again. It was better to focus on her work, so that she could forget the pain.

But here she couldn't hide from it.

And she hated that.

She hated the feeling that she was losing control of herself, because she'd sworn that she wouldn't make that mistake again.

"Thank you for the shoes. I'm going to head back to the clinic. Tell Chris thank you for letting me crash here for the night."

"Sure thing."

Naomi left the room, and as she glanced back into Evangelos's room, she saw Chris rocking back and forth, the baby over his shoulder.

Tears stung her eyes.

She had to get out of here before she did something she'd regret.

* * *

Naomi was avoiding him and he didn't know why.

Lisa had come in to take over the care of Evan so that he could get to the clinic, and when he'd gone to pack a bag for his overnight stay in Athens, he'd discovered that Naomi had left and gone to the clinic without him.

He'd foolishly thought that they might walk down together. He'd thought they'd gotten past the awkward stage and were becoming friends again, because that was all he really wanted.

Liar. You want a lot more than to be her friend.

He cursed himself inwardly and rubbed his eyes as he leaned back in his office chair. He was staring at the scans that the Athens hospital had sent over so he could prepare for the surgery on Maximos.

He hadn't practiced surgery since Evangelos had been born. His life had been in complete upheaval since then. Evan had been born, he'd had to pay off Evan's birth mother, Lillian, from the funds he'd had to beg from his father and then the earthquake had happened. And finally his *yia-yia* had become sick and died.

He was looking forward to getting back into the operating room, even if the team in Athens wasn't his usual team. Maximos needed surgery and he had the skill and experience to do it.

And, deep down, he was really looking forward to not being a father tonight—so he had to stop thinking about Naomi and how she was avoiding him and focus on work.

He had no time in his life for a relationship, and he would never bring a woman into his life unless he was committed to her completely. He didn't want to hurt Evan that way. He didn't want his son to feel like *he'd* felt growing up. Evan had already been abandoned by one mother, and that was one too many as far as Chris was concerned.

Focus.

He leaned over the computer again and made some notes. He could definitely use more coffee. He hadn't gotten much sleep last night. Evan had mostly slept, but the couch was not Chris's bed and he hadn't been able to stop thinking about who was in it.

She'd been so close, but so far out of his reach.

And he hadn't been able to stop thinking about all those nights they had spent together. Her in his arms, the silky feather-like touch of her hair against his cheek, the scent of jasmine and how she'd driven him wild...

If only it had been *her* who had gotten pregnant with his child. *She* would've never left their baby.

Or at least he'd like to think that. He didn't really know her, did he?

He glanced at his watch and saw that the ferry was going to leave soon. He finished making his notes and grabbed his stuff out of the staff lounge.

"Off to Athens?" Theo asked as he came out of an exam room.

"Yes. The surgery is tonight. Is Dr. Hudson still here?"

"No, she left for the ferry a few moments ago. Why?"

Chris frowned. "No reason. I left Lisa your number in case something happens with Evan..."

"No worries. She'll have it handled, I'm sure."

Chris nodded. He'd been apart from Evangelos for several hours before, but usually he stayed within a ten-mile radius of his son. This was the first time that sea would be separating them, so he couldn't get to him quickly.

It was scary, but as a parent he should think about *his* son being the one on the operating table, dependent on the surgical skills of a particular doctor. He would want the very best for Evan, so he had to do this for someone else's son.

"I'm sure too," Chris said quickly. "I'll see you all tomorrow."

He left the clinic and headed down to the docks. The ferry was boarding, and he handed in his ticket and went on board to the upper deck. As he got there, the ferry made its final preparations and was soon pulling away from Mythelios and toward the mainland.

He took a deep breath and leaned against the railing, watching the island slip into the distance, all the while trying not to worry about his baby too much. When he could no longer see the island, he turned back away from the railing—and saw that Naomi had taken a seat inside. She was reading papers from a very thick file.

Just let her be. She doesn't want to be with you.

Only, he couldn't take his own advice and he made his way to her.

"You didn't wait for me."

Naomi looked up, startled. "Chris! No, I guess I didn't. You were so absorbed with those scans from Athens that I thought I'd sneak down to the ferry and start doing my work."

"No, I mean this morning. You didn't wait for me then either," he said, taking a seat next to her.

"I have a lot of work to do."

"I thought you were running away."

A strange expression crossed her face briefly. "And what would I be running from?"

"Me?"

"I did that already," she stated firmly, and then turned back to her work.

"Would you be in the operating room with me?"

The words stunned him, but he really needed someone

he trusted in that room when he worked on Maximos. If he couldn't have his regular scrub nurse and the residents he was used to working with, he could at least have *her*.

They worked very well together. And she had been there from the start with Maximos.

She was clearly shocked. "You want *me* to be in the operating room with you?"

"You're still a neurosurgeon. Who else would I have in there with me? I don't know many of the surgeons in Athens. I haven't had a chance to get to know them. I need someone I trust. Besides, I let you sleep in my bed last night. You owe me."

She smiled at him then. "Of course I'll assist you in the surgery. I would like to see the end of that case."

Chris sat back in his chair, more at ease. "Good. I'm glad. I want us to be friends, Naomi. I know things didn't end well for us, but I want us to be friends and colleagues."

A blush bloomed in her cheeks. "I would like that too."

"Good." He leaned over and glanced at her paperwork. "Is this about the bachelor auction?"

"Yes. We have a lot of interesting bachelors. A famous Greek singer and an actor."

She held out the list and he was impressed with the names.

"We should be able to raise enough money to donate to the Mythelios Free Clinic and continue helping with the relief efforts elsewhere too."

"That's good. The earthquake was devastating on so many levels. It nearly decimated the infrastructure of Mythelios. Not only were so many injured, but the water supply was compromised and the island was without power for days. And without clean water, disease and dehydration caused a lot of the medical emergencies."

Naomi nodded. "I know. Ever since I started working

with this organization, I've seen and helped with so many disasters. I've just never had this kind of public relations nightmare shoved on me with such short notice before. I'd prefer to be helping the wounded and the sick—not doing all this fund-raising stuff. It's frustrating, but I know it's necessary, and so here I am, doing it."

"Well, put it away for now and focus on the surgery at hand. What do you know about a comminuted skull fracture affecting the parietal, sphenoid and frontal bone? As well as a depressed skull fracture of the temporal bone."

"The patient is suffering from all that?" Naomi was shocked, as a comminuted skull fracture meant that the skull had been broken into three sections. He was lucky to be alive after so much trauma to his head.

Chris nodded. "We didn't see it last night, with all the swelling, but now we have that managed there's more, and they've emailed across updated scans so I can see the work ahead of us. It will probably be a long night."

"That's okay. I want to help. I feel sorry for such a handsome young man."

Chris cocked an eyebrow. "You had time to notice if he was handsome or not?"

"No." Pink bloomed in her cheeks. "It's not that. When I was out to lunch with Lisa, she mentioned that there were two handsome young men checking us out, and she reminded me this morning that the patient was one of them. If he was, those two men were both quite striking and, yes, young."

A surge of jealousy flared in him and he was surprised by it because he had no right to feel that way. Why shouldn't Naomi date someone else? He had no claim on her. He was the one who broke it off. He was the one who had passed her over for his career.

"Well, we'll see what we can do for him," he managed to say.

"Any word about Stavros?" she asked, breaking the tension that had settled between them.

"No, he hasn't come back to me. I do hope he gives me an answer soon, because I'd like to get started on treatment as soon as possible. With that form of aggressive tumor, the best course is to start treatment quickly, but he hasn't even agreed to a full body scan yet."

"Perhaps he doesn't want to know. If it's worse than he thinks it is already, perhaps his lack of answer is an answer in itself."

"He should fight if he has a chance. He shouldn't give up. *I* wouldn't. Would you?"

"No, I suppose I wouldn't—but if there was no hope, then I wouldn't put myself through painful surgery and chemotherapy. Although I see the point you're trying to make."

After that they sat there quietly, barely talking.

The ferry docked in Athens and they disembarked.

"Do you want to split a cab to the hospital?"

"I have to go to my apartment and grab some comfortable shoes," she said. "Shoes that are suited to the operating room."

He chuckled. "I suppose so. I'll meet you in the scrub room, then."

She nodded.

Chris opened the cab door and she climbed in. It sped off through the busy streets of Athens—or rather Piraeus, as that was where the docks were. He sighed, thinking about the task at hand and hoping that he could live up to the reputation he'd thought he'd left behind in Manhattan.

CHAPTER SIX

His pulse was racing as he stood in the scrub room, watching through the window as the surgical team prepped the room and the patient. He hadn't started scrubbing in yet, but he had on his scrub cap.

You got this.

He didn't know what he was waiting for. Perhaps he was waiting for a sign.

He took a deep breath and used his foot to turn on the water, which was soon warm, and he started scrubbing with the soap. He hadn't done any surgery in over eight months. It felt good to be back, but he wasn't sure he completely deserved it.

"Just in the nick of time," Naomi said as she came into the room.

Her strawberry blond hair was braided and done up in a bun under her scrub cap. Just like she'd always had it before. And the familiar sight set his nerves at ease.

She was so good. Too good for him.

"I thought you weren't going to make it in time. I thought I'd have to do this on my own," he teased.

"Never. You are the best in the world at neurosurgery. I couldn't miss out on working with you again. Just like old times."

"Some of the best times, I hope. But I'm not a god."

"Tell that to the hospital in Manhattan," she teased. "In all seriousness, Chris, I wouldn't let you down. Maximos is my patient too."

He smiled and nodded, continuing to scrub. She never had let him down. Yet he'd let *her* down.

I don't deserve her.

"I want to do a craniotomy. Last scan shows an aneurysm, and I want to get in there and clip it before I even begin to think of how to tackle the rest of his head injuries," he said, shaking that thought out of his mind.

"He's going to need a long recovery."

Chris nodded. "It will be painful. It will really hurt when he wakes up. I don't envy him. I hope that he's a fighter."

"Look how long he's held on," Naomi remarked. "He's a fighter, I'm sure."

Chris wanted to hold on to that thought. He needed to hold on to that shred of hope so that it would wash away his nerves.

You got this.

He dried his hands, pulled up his mask and stepped through the door into the sterile environment of the operating room. The scrub nurse met him and helped him into the surgical gown and gloves. He bent down so the nurse could put on his headlight and glasses.

He rolled his shoulders to ease the mounting tension and approached the head of the table. He looked up and saw that he was operating in a room with a gallery that was packed with other physicians. All watching.

It caused his pulse to kick up a notch.

"What's going on?" he asked.

"Sorry, Dr. Moustakas. The chief of surgery would like his residents and interns to observe your surgery. You're a bit of a legend and you're in our hospital," the scrub nurse said nervously.

Just what he didn't want.

Before Evangelos, when he'd been living his life at full speed without a seat belt, he would have welcomed this. He would have eaten up the adoration. But now he felt he didn't deserve the accolades. That this was all too much.

You got this.

The operating room door opened and Naomi walked in. He let out a sigh of relief on a breath that he hadn't known he was holding as she was gloved, gowned, and then joined him at the head of the table.

"You okay?" she asked as she stood next to him.

"Perfectly. Why?"

"You seem nervous—or maybe it's just the atmosphere in the room. You have quite the audience."

"Don't remind me," he grumbled.

He closed his eyes and held out his hand.

"Scalpel."

The nurse placed the instrument in his hand and he made the first incision—and with that first cut everything came rushing back to him. All he thought about was what he was doing. Everything else faded into the background. All his fears of forgetting what he was doing disappeared, and in his mind he could see the correct way forward, what he'd done countless times before.

And working beside him, anticipating his every move, was Naomi. She knew what to do before he had to tell her. It was as if they were one surgeon, instead of two, and it made the hours of surgery fly by in an instant.

Before he knew it, they were finishing up and the patient was being closed by the resident who had been chosen to work with them.

The students in the gallery were applauding politely as he walked away from the patient to the scrub room, and it was then that the many hours of being in surgery after months of being out of practice finally hit him. He felt as if his body weighed a ton and his eyes were lined with sandpaper.

He leaned against the wall after he'd peeled off his surgical gown, gloves and mask. Then he made his way to the sink to scrub out.

Naomi joined him. "You were brilliant," she said, smiling.

Her eyes were bright and warm, making him feel he was actually wanted.

"Thank you. You were too, by the way. I don't think I would've handled it as well without you."

She blushed. "Thank you."

He loved the way she blushed. The pink in her cheeks made him think about kissing her over and over. He cleared his throat to shake the sudden inappropriate thoughts out of his mind.

"What time is it? Any chance I could catch the ferry back to Mythelios?" he asked.

"I hate to tell you, but no. You've worked all night and it's now almost noon. That was a whopper of a surgery—which took even longer because you had to clamp that aneurysm."

He swore under his breath. "I'll have to call Lisa and tell her that I won't be home until the evening ferry now. At least the hospital has on-call rooms where I can rest for a couple of hours."

"That it does—and you *should* rest," she said. "I would offer you my bed, and repay the debt, but I live in a tiny stamp-sized apartment that's only one room."

His blood heated at the thought of having to share a small apartment with her.

Focus.

"Thank you for the offer, but I told you the debt was

repaid by you assisting me on this surgery. I truly appreciate it."

"Anytime. Would you like to get something to eat after you've rested? Do your postoperative notes, catch forty winks and then come and have some lunch with me in Athens? Remember we always used to have a postsurgical celebratory dinner?"

He grinned. "And that was always followed by something else. Something more pleasant."

What are you doing?

Only, he couldn't help but flirt with her.

She blushed again. "It would only be dinner this time—in fact, it would actually be a late lunch as you need to catch the last ferry back, remember?"

"Of course. Yes, sure—I *would* like that. I have to eat, don't I?"

He was slightly disappointed that it wouldn't lead to something else, but he was mad at himself for even thinking that way about her. For wanting more when he knew perfectly well that if he had her once they would both want more—and he still couldn't give her that.

All he had left to give her was friendship.

"I better go do my postoperative notes and get my head down for a bit. Shall I meet you in the lobby of the hospital at about two?" he asked.

"That sounds good. We can have a leisurely lunch and maybe do a bit of sightseeing before you head back down to Piraeus to make the last ferry home."

She left the scrub room and he leaned against the sink, dropping his head to stare at the drain.

He knew he shouldn't go out to lunch with her, but he was a sucker for punishment. And when it came to her, he deserved every form of punishment that karma threw his way.

* * *

What am I doing? What am I doing?

She'd repeatedly asked herself that question ever since she'd invited Chris to lunch. She'd come back to her apartment to change, and something in her gut was telling her she was a making a huge mistake. She'd been overcome by his request that she assist him in surgery, and then in the operating room she'd gotten to see him in action again.

She'd forgotten how amazing it was to work with him. To have him trust her in his operating room. And she'd forgotten how they truly did work so well together.

She'd been in many operating rooms, both as the lead and the assisting surgeon, but when she was with Chris, it was like magic, and she couldn't quite put her finger on why. For one glorious moment in time she'd forgotten about their past, forgotten that he'd walked away from her, left her with a baby he knew nothing about, and forgotten how she'd suffered alone when she'd lost their child.

What harm could one little lunch do?

So much...

"Sorry I'm late," Chris called out as he crossed the busy lobby of the hospital. "After I woke up, I had to speak to Maximos's mother and it took longer than I planned. Expect the same if she ever sees you."

He grinned at her. His dark eyes were twinkling and that perfect smile made her melt. What was it about him that made her let down her guard?

"There's nothing wrong with gratitude," she said. "I'd be pleased."

He chuckled. "Well, she might not kiss you as passionately as she did me."

Naomi started laughing. She couldn't help it. "She *kissed* you?"

"It was quite a good kiss—but she's not a single lady." Chris winked. "Where shall we go?"

"There's a lovely *taverna* down on Pritaniou, and then maybe we could take a stroll around the Acropolis and Parthenon. I have yet to see them."

He cocked an eyebrow. "You've never seen them?"

"I've seen them from a distance, but I haven't actually *seen* them. When I was fourteen, I didn't have much of a chance because my grandmother was dying, and since I've been here this time, I've just been so busy…"

"*Everyone* should have a chance to go to the Parthenon and the Acropolis."

"Well, now I can—and *you* can tell me all about them. I'm relying on you for authenticity," she teased.

"That's putting a lot of pressure on me."

"Good," she said pertly, and she took his arm as they walked out into the bright sun of Athens in the afternoon.

The streets around the hospital were buzzing with traffic, but Chris led her through the hustle and bustle, and they managed to find a cab to take them to the part of the city near the Parthenon and the Acropolis.

An open-air *taverna* sat just below the hill. And even though it was sweltering, the *taverna* was in the shade of some olive trees and had a nice cross breeze.

Chris pulled out a chair for her to sit down and he sat next to her.

A waiter came over and greeted them. "*Yassou*, what can I start you with?" he asked.

"Coffee," Chris said.

The waiter looked at her.

"Water, please," she said.

The waiter nodded and left.

"You're having *coffee* in this heat?" she asked incredulously.

"You forget I don't get much sleep at home with an infant. I'm sure there are bags under my eyes."

"Not too many." She grinned.

The waiter returned with their drinks and they ordered a light lunch of fish and salad.

Chris took a sip of his coffee. "That hits the spot," he said, and leaned back. "I hope the heat breaks before next week, when I have to go up on stage in a tuxedo and be bid on."

"Thank you for doing that. The other doctors in the clinic were all going to step up, but…"

"Yeah, they're all conveniently taken," he grumbled, but then he smiled. "I don't mind. Though I don't know what a single father can offer…"

"You have a lot to offer. You're a doctor, and being such a caring father is very attractive to most women."

"Is it?"

"Oh, yes."

"And how about you? Is it attractive to *you*?"

Affection glowed in his eyes and it made her catch her breath. She could feel warmth flooding her cheeks. Before she could answer the question, the waiter returned with their fish and salad.

They continued chatting about the surgery, and mundane things about the clinic and the hospital. When they were finished, and the waiter had taken everything away, he caught her off guard again.

"Are you going to be bidding on anyone at the auction?" he asked.

"What?" she asked, almost choking on her water.

"I asked if you will be bidding. You organized it, but surely you can bid too—and if so what kind of date are you looking for?"

"I don't think we should be talking about this," she said quickly, looking away.

"Why? Are we not friends? You said so yourself."

"Of course we're friends." She sighed. "Okay...no, I will not be bidding on anyone because I will be hosting the event. I'll be doing the auctioning, so I can't really bid on one of the lots, can I?"

"That's disappointing, but I get it."

She opened her purse and paid for her half of the bill. "I have so much on my plate I can't even *think* about dating anyone—even for charity. I'm way too busy."

And that was the way she liked it. Being busy meant she didn't have time to think about the pain, or the way her heart ached when she thought about what might have been.

He tossed down the rest of the amount owed and then pulled out her chair before they left the *taverna* and headed out onto the street, up the hill toward the Parthenon.

"Well, at least the line is short today," Chris said as they took their spot in line to pay for admission. "And this is my treat. You've never been, and I've been way too many times."

"Thank you," she said. "I'm looking forward to it."

"There's not much left of it, but the views of the city are worth the price."

He paid for their tickets and they were ushered through the gate and were soon wandering through stones and crumbling ruins.

As they moved away from the regular tourists, Chris put a hand on the small of her back, and her body came alive with just that simple touch from him.

"See—look at the views over the city. Can you imagine what this must have been like when it was all brand-new?" he said wistfully.

"You mean when Zeus ruled all?" she teased.

A smile quirked at the corner of his lips. "You mean Athena, don't you?"

"That *does* make more sense. Why did they name the city after her?"

"Because she gave its citizens the gift of the olive. It was food, its branches would burn in their hearths and its oil would light their lamps."

"And was there a rival for the citizens' affections?" she asked.

"Poseidon. He struck the ground and gave them a salt-water well—but what could the people do with a saltwater well? They couldn't drink it. Whereas Athena gave them the olive and so Athens was born."

He smiled at her, and that dimple in his cheek made her blood heat, and in that moment, with the loud rush of the city below them and tourists all around them, she saw only him. Heard only him. Drowned everything else out.

Naomi could feel herself melting for him.

Get a grip on yourself.

"Poseidon must've been mad," she said huskily.

"Yes, he caused a flood and drowned a bunch of people—but I won't say a bad word about the god of the sea…not when I need calm seas tonight to get home to my son."

And he moved away from her then, breaking the spell that had been woven around them.

They finished walking around the Parthenon and the Acropolis and then headed back down the hill, to take a cab to the docks at Piraeus.

"When will you be coming back to Mythelios?" he asked after he'd bought his ticket.

"Tomorrow morning."

He nodded. "I'll pray for calm seas then too."

"I would appreciate it." She tucked a loose strand of hair

behind her ear nervously. "I'll check on Maximos tonight. I have a round I need to complete there anyways."

"Thank you. I appreciate it. And I'll feel better leaving him now that I know you'll be there."

The ferry horn sounded and Chris glanced back over his shoulder.

"You'd better go," she said. "You can't leave Evangelos for another night."

"No. I can't." He leaned over and kissed her cheek. "Thank you for helping me with the surgery. It was good having you there beside me again. I'd forgotten what it was like."

"You're welcome. Now, go."

He nodded and walked through the gate toward the ferry.

She sighed and stayed there even though she couldn't see him get on. She watched as the ferry pushed away from port, and continued to watch as it faded into a dot on the horizon, heading off toward Mythelios.

What are you doing?

She wasn't sure what she was doing, to be honest. She was setting herself up for more heartache if she even *thought* about this—but she missed him. Being with him reminded her of how much she'd enjoyed being in his company and how much brighter her life had been in his presence.

But they could be friends and nothing more.

That was the least she could do for her heart.

CHAPTER SEVEN

NAOMI KNOCKED ON the door of one of the exam rooms in the clinic. She'd quickly fallen back into her routine of working at both the clinic and the hospital in Athens. It had been a few days since she'd said goodbye to Chris at the ferry and made that vow to herself that she wasn't going to allow anything to happen between them except friendship.

Friendship she would gladly handle. It would mean a more pleasant work environment.

And so far it had been working well. Although actually she hadn't seen him since they said goodbye in Piraeus, because Evangelos had gotten a bad cold and Chris had been devoting all his time to his son. A baby with a cold wasn't a pleasant thing, and it had taken all her willpower not to run up to his house and check on the both of them.

But she knew she would just be getting in the way if she did that. Lisa was working at his house, and she didn't want to interfere with her cousin's job either.

"Come in."

Naomi opened the door and saw one of her younger patients who'd had his spleen removed a couple of weeks ago was waiting for her.

"How are you feeling today, Giorgos?" she asked.

"Better," Giorgos answered. "But I'll feel fabulous when I can get the all clear. Will that be soon?"

"You ruptured your spleen. You lost an organ. That's not great. You have to recover from major abdominal surgery and your body has to adjust."

Giorgos's mother put her hand on her son. "Dr. Hudson, do we need to pay anything toward the surgery? Giorgos wants to work. He's of age, and his father…"

"I understand, Mrs. Veritas, but he can't work. Not yet. He needs to rest. He's only two weeks post-op from his splenectomy. But the loss of his spleen was as a result of an unstable structure in the aftermath of the earthquake, so whatever the Greek national health care system can't pick up will be paid for by International Relief."

Mrs. Veritas let out a sigh of relief. "Oh, thank goodness. I was trying to work it all out in my head."

"It's okay. It's taken care of. He would've died had he not been flown to Athens and had the spleen removed."

Giorgos didn't look too pleased, but she couldn't blame the boy. He was seventeen, and he wanted to get back to the things that he liked, which included sports. And he'd lost his father in the earthquake. The boy was now head of the household.

Giorgos wanted to work. He wanted to fill his father's shoes. Except losing a major organ was putting a crimp in his plans.

"After we take the stitches out, you will have to go on some medication, which will also be covered by International Relief. I'm sorry, Giorgos, but I think you're on bedrest for a while yet. Your white count is elevated, which suggests that your body is fighting an infection, and you're not healing as fast as I would like."

"Malakas!" Giorgos cursed.

His mother gasped. "Such language in front of the doctor!" Mrs. Veritas screeched.

"Sorry, Dr. Hudson," Giorgos said contritely. "That earthquake caused more trouble than good."

"Don't they always?" Naomi asked. "But you're alive. If you rest now, then you can help out your family when you're as good as new."

Giorgos frowned anxiously. "When will that be?"

"Six more weeks," Naomi said. "I'll call you in to clear you in six weeks—but that's only if you rest so your body can heal. If you have any issues, like fever, which is a sign of a postoperative infection, come to the clinic right away. Don't worry about the cost."

"Thank you, Dr. Hudson," Mrs. Veritas said, and she and her son left the clinic.

Naomi sighed and made a note in her chart. There was a knock on the door and she looked up to see Chris hovering in the doorway. There were dark circles under his eyes, worse than usual, and she felt bad for him.

"Hey," she said. "How is Evan?"

"Better, thank God. That was *brutal*. He was so congested—and I won't explain to you the horrors of trying to relieve a baby of nasal congestion."

Naomi laughed. "I already know, but thanks for that mental picture."

Chris slipped into the room and shut the door. "I need your help."

"Sure—with a case?"

"No. My father."

"What about your father?" she asked.

"He's coming to visit me tonight."

"Oh?"

Chris nodded. "I need you to come over for dinner. I tried to get Ares, Theo and Deakin to come over with their significant others, but apparently they're all too busy. I don't believe it for one second. They just don't want to see my father. Not that I blame them—I don't want to see my father either."

"So I get that honor instead?" she asked, arching a brow.

"You *have* to help me. If you're there, maybe he'll ease up on me, and we can steer the conversation away from how I wasted my money on the clinic, and how terrible a son I am for not following in his footsteps. Maybe he won't point out so many of my faults if there's a pretty woman dining with us tonight."

"If you think it will help, then sure. Does he know about the upcoming bachelor auction?"

"I hope not—but probably." Chris rolled his eyes. "You're really doing me a solid favor here. I owe you one. He's a bit of a bully. I hope you won't get upset if he acts like a jerk toward you."

"It's no problem—and bullies I can handle. I didn't get where I am in my career by bowing down to pompous, arrogant people."

He smiled, relief washing over his face. "Thank you. So—come to my place around seven. He'll be arriving about eight."

"Sounds good—but I'm warning you already that I'm going to call in my favor later this week."

He cocked an eyebrow. "Oh…?"

She handed him Giorgos's chart. "Splenic rupture. It's a seventeen-year-old boy and I really would like someone else to be familiar with his case should he come in while I'm not here. He was injured when an unstable building that had actually been cleared by engineers came crashing down on him about two weeks ago. He'd been working in construction since his father died in the earthquake back in May."

Chris pulled out a pair of glasses and read the chart she'd handed to him. She was surprised to see him wearing glasses. He'd never worn them before. But they didn't detract from the overall sexy, godlike appeal of him. They enhanced it even more and her heart skipped a beat.

"That's bad. Poor kid." He took off the glasses and slipped them back into the breast pocket of his lab coat. Then he looked at her, realizing she was staring at him. "What?"

"Since when did you start wearing glasses?"

"A year ago. I only need them if I've been staring at a computer screen too long, or when I have to focus hard on small details on things like X-rays. I'm not getting any younger."

"You're aging well. Like a fine wine."

Heat bloomed in her cheeks as she realized she'd let that thought slip from her lips instead of keeping it firmly inside her head, where it belonged.

A strange expression crossed his face and a smile quirked his lips as he crossed his arms. "Is that so…?"

She cleared her throat. "Would you get out of here? *You* have to prepare for your father's arrival and *I* have things to do!"

He ran a hand through his hair, making it stand up on end. "Right. Thanks again."

Chris left the exam room and Naomi let out the breath she hadn't realized she was holding. She was going to have to get better control over herself. He was just a friend. A work colleague. Nothing more.

He couldn't be anything else.

Why did you ask her over to dinner?

Chris wasn't sure what he was thinking. All he knew was that he'd missed Naomi these last few days. Leaving her behind at the docks in Piraeus had been harder than he'd imagined. Even though he'd known he would see her the next day, that ferry ride home had been lonely.

But then when he'd gotten home, he'd been overwhelmed with a sick child, a sick nanny and the news that his father was going to be paying him a visit shortly.

Maybe the seas had been calm, but Poseidon was punishing him in other ways for talking up Athena.

He smiled to himself at that thought, but just remembering that time in the Parthenon brought the images of that afternoon with her back into sharp focus.

Being so close to her had reminded him of a simpler time in his life. When he'd been happy. But then he'd remembered how much of a fool he'd been and what a mistake he'd made in walking away from her. Not that he'd had any choice in the matter.

Now she wanted to be his friend, and he wanted that too. He wanted her in the operating room beside him, working with him. He'd forgotten how much he relied on her.

"Dr. Moustakas—Stavros is here to see you," a nurse said, coming up the hallway.

"He is? He doesn't have an appointment, does he?"

"No, but he's hoping you'll see him. He had some time…"

"Of course. Send him into a free exam room and I'll be with him momentarily."

The nurse nodded and headed back to the waiting area of the clinic. Chris ducked into the room where the files were kept and grabbed Stavros's notes. By that time Stavros was already in an exam room, waiting for him.

Chris entered the room to see Stavros pacing up and down. "You wanted to see me?" he asked.

"Yes." Stavros held up his hand and it shook. "It's getting worse and I'm forgetting things. I'm concerned."

"Do you want to have the scan now?" Chris asked. "Have you eaten or drunk anything yet today?"

"No, I didn't feel like it. I *would* like to do it now, if that's possible, Dr. Moustakas. I have time today because I've closed the *taverna*… I'm not saying that I'll agree to you cutting open my head, but I would like to know what I'm dealing with."

"That's wise. I'll have a nurse prep you for a CT scan. Do you have someone in the waiting room?"

"Yes, my wife came with me."

"Good, because you might not be feeling too well after the dyes and the stuff we make you drink."

Stavros wrinkled his nose. "I suppose this is all worth it?"

Chris clapped him on the shoulder. "It is, Stavros. I promise you. Once I get a clear picture of everything that's going on, we can decide what the next step should be."

Stavros nodded. "Thank you, Dr. Moustakas."

"I'll send a nurse in."

Chris left the room and sent a nurse to prep Stavros for the CT scan.

It took a couple of hours for the prep and the dyes to take effect, but soon Stavros was lying down on the bed of the CT scanner and Chris was in the other room, watching for the scans to come up.

He put on his glasses and watched as the images came up on the screen. As he went through each image, he could get a better look at the anaplastic oligodendroglioma that was growing in his temporal lobe, and he was relieved to see that it hadn't spread anywhere else in Stavros's body.

"Are those Stavros' scans?" Naomi asked, leaning over him.

Being this close to her, he could smell her perfume— and it made him think of things he shouldn't.

Focus.

"It is. The cancer hasn't spread. Which is good news. It means he might actually go through with the surgery—but just look at this," Chris said, clicking on one of the scans of the man's head. "This is a monster. It's a complicated and aggressive anaplastic oligodendroglioma."

"It certainly is—and if he doesn't get it out, he'll have a slow, painful death."

Chris nodded. "I know. Hopefully that will further my cause and get him to go to Athens and have it taken care of. Is there any word about the funding?"

Naomi sighed. "They won't cover it. It's not related to the earthquake, and if he can't wait for a place on the national health care list to come up, he'll have to cover what his private medical insurance won't."

"His medical insurance won't even cover the entirety of my fees," Chris stated. "So I guess I'd better do it pro bono, just to make sure."

Naomi smiled warmly at him. "I *knew* you had a good heart."

"The problem is getting the hospital to agree to the rest… It will be an expensive surgery. Hopefully whoever is assisting me will also offer up *her* services pro bono?"

Naomi made a funny face. "Of course. What a silly man you are."

Chris grinned. "I can be."

"I'll work on the board at the hospital in Athens. We'll get it taken care of. Convince Stavros of that—and also try to convince him it's not charity. I know he's a proud man."

"I'll take care of it," Chris said. "Don't worry."

"So, this dinner tonight… I don't want to presume, but will I be able to crash at your place afterward, since I'll be missing the last ferry back to Athens?"

His pulse kicked up a notch at the thought of her staying another night. He hadn't even thought of that when he'd asked her to dinner.

"Of course. I'm sorry—I forgot."

"When I agreed to it, I forgot too, to be honest. I'm sorry that I won't be able to dress up for your father. All I have is my business stuff."

"That's fine—that's actually the way he prefers things."

"Good." She got up. "I'll leave you to break the news to Stavros and I'll see you tonight."

"I look forward to it."

Naomi left and Chris let out a breath he hadn't even been aware that he was holding. How could he have been so foolish?

It's because you want her to stay overnight.

Of course, his father would have his boat, so maybe he could take Naomi back to Athens. If Chris put him on the spot, his father wouldn't say no. Naomi might not appreciate it, but it would be better for both of them if she didn't stay the night.

Wouldn't it?

CHAPTER EIGHT

THE BELL RANG at seven.

"Don't worry, Lisa, I got it!" Chris called out as he ran down the steps to the front door.

Naomi was waiting on the front step, holding a bottle of ouzo.

She held it up. "I thought this might make things easier."

He took the bottle from her as she came inside and he shut the door. "This is strong stuff. Yeah, it might help if I can get my father to take enough shots, but he grew up drinking this stuff like water."

Naomi laughed. "It's like my grandpa and his bourbon—or moonshine. That stuff is *horrible*. It'll knock you flat on your butt if you get it from the right place."

Chris chuckled. "Well, we'll take it easy—but thank you for this."

"Where's Lisa?" Naomi asked, following him up the stairs to the kitchen.

"She's in her room. Evan is asleep and she's resting. She's still getting over a cold too. She'll bring the baby out later, after dinner. She's had the pleasure of meeting my father before and says she'd rather keep to her room."

Naomi's eyes widened. "Oh, good Lord, what am I in for?"

"Hold on to your hat," Chris teased.

Naomi wandered out to the terrace. "We're dining al fresco tonight?"

"It's cooler out here."

"I'm going to quickly say hello to Lisa."

Chris nodded. "Good idea."

Naomi slipped in through the living room doors and Chris tried to calm the erratic beating of his heart. His father coming over had him on edge, and the idea of Naomi spending another night under his roof wasn't helping. He seemed to be digging this deep hole for himself—and he wasn't sure how he was going to get out of it.

Naomi returned a couple minutes later. "She was sleeping, so I didn't bother her. Can I help you with anything?"

"No, I have dinner mostly taken care of. Would you like a shot of ouzo?"

"Sure—why not? I can hold my moonshine."

He grinned and poured them two shots. He held it up. *"Yamas."*

"Yamas," she replied, and then downed it. "That's strong, all right."

He laughed and took back the shot glass. "I told you."

"So, how did Stavros take the news? Is he going to go through with the surgery?"

"He'll let me know—but he's having increasingly worse symptoms of anaplastic oligodendroglioma and he really doesn't like it. He has all the facts now, and I'll prepare a battle plan on how to take it out without too much damage to the nerves."

"It'll be good to prepare. Speaking of preparing—is there any topic of conversation I should steer clear of when your father is here?"

"You mean like how we dated a few years ago?"

"Did he know about me then?"

"No," he said. "My father and I aren't close, and I didn't

ever tell him about the women I was dating. He knows that I was a bit of a playboy—he read the gossip papers that were floating around—and he knows about Evan's mother because I had to go to him to ask for the money."

"The money?" she said blankly.

"The money his mother demanded from me to keep the child. She was going to get rid of my baby unless I paid her a huge sum of money."

The color drained from Naomi's cheeks and a strange, sad expression crossed her face. "That's horrible!"

"What? That I paid her?"

"No, that she blackmailed you. I thought that you never wanted children."

"I didn't," he admitted. "But I wouldn't want to lose one of my children once I knew they existed."

She looked away and then headed out onto the terrace, as if she was upset. He was confused by her behavior and followed her outside.

"Naomi, are you okay?"

"I'm fine," she said, but her voice shook. "I guess I'm just horrified by the greed of some people."

"Then you'll be horrified all over again when you meet my father. He can be pretty greedy too."

The bell rang again.

Speak of the devil.

"You got this," she said. "You're a brilliant surgeon and a good father. It's his problem if he can't see that."

Chris nodded and then touched her hand. It sent a jolt of electricity through him. Just a simple touch of her skin did serious things to him. He was doomed.

"Thanks for being here."

"That's what friends are for."

She smiled at him, but the smile didn't quite reach her eyes. He could still see sadness in their depths.

He would try to find out more about that later, but right now he had to steel himself against his father. Against the constant disapproval and disappointment his father smothered him with.

He ran down the stairs and opened the door. *"Yassou, Pateras,"* he said formally.

"Yassou," his father responded in clipped tones as he stepped inside his childhood home and began scanning the walls, looking for faults. "There's some cracks in the plaster there."

"From the quake. The house is under renovation, *Pateras*. It takes time."

His father made a *tsk*ing noise under his breath. "You should hire men from Athens to deal with it. They'd get it done. Modernize this house and sell it."

"Why would I sell it?" Chris asked disapprovingly.

"You're not seriously going to *stay* here, are you?"

"Why not?"

"And give up your neurosurgery practice in Manhattan?" his father asked in disbelief.

"You never wanted me to be a surgeon," Chris snapped. "Now suddenly you care about whether I'm giving it up or not?"

"Only if you mean to give up a lucrative business just to grub around in that nothing of a…"

His father trailed off and his eyes widened as Naomi came down the stairs. She was a beautiful woman, and his father did have a soft spot for beautiful women.

Of course, once she started exuding her sparky personality, his father wouldn't be as gracious. His father was too old-fashioned to appreciate an outspoken woman.

"Pateras, let me introduce you to Dr. Naomi Hudson. She works with International Relief, the aid agency that is helping us after the earthquake."

His father nodded. "It's a pleasure. I am Nikos Moustakas."

"The pleasure is all mine," Naomi said graciously.

"Come up, *Pateras*. I know you have to get back to Athens tonight and dinner is ready."

Chris shot Naomi a look, which made her chuckle a bit under her breath as she led them up the stairs.

His father glanced around the kitchen. "Well, this is more like it. Very modern."

It would be the closest he'd get to a compliment all night from his father.

"Naomi, why don't you and my father head outside and I'll start serving the food?"

"Sure."

Naomi and his father wandered outside. Chris watched his father as he held out a chair for Naomi and sat next to her.

He took a deep breath. He could get through this.

Although it might take a bit more ouzo than the one bottle Naomi had brought.

Naomi could tell that Chris was uncomfortable in his father's presence. She had never seen him like this, and it almost made him seem a bit more human. In fact, she liked this more mature version of Dr. Christos Moustakas much better than the man she'd originally fallen in love with.

The man who had broken her heart.

Be careful.

She did understand why Chris didn't like his father. Nikos Moustakas was cold, and appeared uncaring, but Naomi couldn't help but wonder if there was a caring father buried deep inside him somewhere. Nikos had obviously been hurt when Chris's mother had left him, and he had built up strong walls to keep everyone out—including his son.

Chris and his father were so alike they'd probably always butt heads, and both of them were so stubborn they couldn't see beyond the end of their noses.

"Where is my grandson?" Nikos asked when they'd finished their dessert and were having a drink of wine.

"He's sleeping. He was ill earlier this week," Chris said.

"If the boy is sleeping, then let him sleep. I will see him next time."

"Oh? And when will *that* be?" Chris snapped.

Nikos shot his son a warning look before he turned to her. "So, Dr. Hudson, tell me—what kind of charity events is your relief agency holding to raise money for the earthquake victims?"

"I'm running a bachelor auction, but charity is not my primary focus. I'm a surgeon first and foremost."

Nikos looked slightly horrified and ignored her latter statement as he turned to Chris. "And you have single men here *agreeing* to take part in this auction?"

"*Pateras*, it's not as bad as it sounds. Women bid for a date. That's all. And it's usually something over the top—like a helicopter ride or… Well, I'm planning a night cruise and dinner on one of your yachts, if you'd be kind enough to donate it for a night."

Nikos looked even more horrified by this. "*You're* one of the bachelors?"

"He is," Naomi said, interrupting. "And his date for the auction is definitely generating the most buzz."

"I don't like it," Nikos stated. "Christos, do you think it's *wise* to be doing this when your track record with women hasn't been the best?"

Chris's back stiffened, and she saw him glare through the dim light of the terrace at his father.

"This is just for charity—and I don't date anymore. I have a son to think about now."

"Exactly," Nikos growled. "You have a son to think about. And what would he think about his father *selling* himself, even if it's for charity?"

"I'll pay to rent someone else's yacht, since you disapprove so much."

Nikos rolled his eyes. "And how would *that* look? I'm a shipping magnate and my son has to *hire out* a yacht for a charity event? I don't think so."

"It's an event you don't approve of, but I think it will bring in lots of money and help raise funds for people in need as well as for the clinic. So, yes, if I have to hire a yacht, I will," Chris snapped.

"I will lend you a yacht, Christos. All this fuss for something that I think will bring you nothing but trouble in the end. Need I remind you of—"

Nikos stopped and eyed her.

"I have to be going. Dr. Hudson—it was a pleasure meeting you. Can I escort you home? It is late…"

"My apartment is in Athens and I've missed the last ferry. I'll stay here."

Nikos frowned. "I can take you to Athens in my boat. You don't need to stay here."

Naomi blushed and glanced over at Chris, who was scowling at his father.

"Chris…?"

"Go with him," Chris said curtly.

Naomi felt as if she was stuck between a rock and hard place. She wouldn't mind sleeping in her own bed tonight, but she didn't want to make Chris mad at her for taking off with his father. Both of them were so stubborn. Exactly the same. Why couldn't they see that?

Nikos didn't wait for her on the terrace but headed through the kitchen and down the stairs.

Chris scrubbed a hand over his face. "I'm sorry you had to see that," he said. "My father is…"

"Don't worry. He's not that bad," she said gently. "If you want me to stay, I can."

"No," he said quickly. "It would be foolish of you not to take the ride. Besides, if you refuse, it'll just make matters worse and then he'll start shouting. Everyone does what he says."

"Except you?"

That made him smile. "I suppose so. Which is why he doesn't like me very much."

"I think you're wrong about that."

Chris snorted in disbelief. "Go. Don't keep him waiting. I'll see you tomorrow."

Without thinking, she leaned over and kissed him on the cheek. "Good night."

His eyebrows arched in surprise and she blushed.

She didn't stick around to gauge his response further or discuss what had happened. Suddenly she was glad she was going to be riding back to Athens with Chris's father.

It would be a good thing to get some distance from Chris right now. She had to remember he was just a friend. A work colleague and nothing more.

There was a luxury sedan with a driver waiting outside, and Nikos opened the door for her. He was quite charming, like his son. The only difference was that he was cold, whereas Chris was warm, but they both kept people at a distance in their own way.

Nikos climbed in beside her and the driver drove away as Nikos pulled the door closed.

"I'm sorry for my son's behavior. He really doesn't think sometimes."

"I think he *does* think. He's very careful about his decisions in the operating room, which is why he's one of the best neurosurgeons in the world."

Nikos grunted in response. "If he's one of the best, why is he here, instead of back in America? And he piddled away good money on that clinic."

"'That clinic' saved so many lives when the earthquake happened, Mr. Moustakas."

"Nikos, please."

"Nikos, then," Naomi said gently. "Your son is a good man, and in my opinion you two are very much alike."

"We are *not*! I would never have had a string of affairs just because my heart was broken over some woman. He gave up a good woman, from my understanding. Ah, well, he's paid the price for *that* mistake."

Nikos turned away and was quiet.

Naomi was stunned.

He'd had all those affairs after he left her because he regretted his mistake in giving her up? It seemed unlikely, and she didn't know how to process the information. If it was true, then karma certainly was biting Chris in the butt.

Still, she thought Nikos was being too hard on his son. Chris was doing right by both baby Evan *and* the clinic. Deep down, regardless of all the mistakes Chris had made, he had a good heart. She could see that. He'd changed.

Still, there was a part of her that was still deeply hurt. That remembered all too vividly how he'd thrown her over for a job. How he'd told her that he never wanted to settle down and have a family.

He'd been so sure, and she was having a hard time trusting him again—trusting that he'd really changed when there were still glimpses of his old self simmering just below the surface. She really didn't want to get hurt by him again.

But then there was that other part of herself. The old part of herself, of who she'd been when she'd first met Chris—

the part of her that had believed in love and happily-ever-after and wanted to try again.

They pulled up at the docks and Nikos helped her out of the sedan like a gentleman. They boarded the yacht and the captain waited for instructions.

Nikos turned to her. "I have some business to attend to, but please make yourself at home, Dr. Hudson. I have to arrange a yacht for my son to wine and dine some woman with apparently more money than sense."

"International Relief really appreciates that you're donating the use of one of your yachts for this. The money will help so many that were affected by the earthquake."

Nikos softened. "You're welcome. When we dock, my chauffeur in Athens will take you back to your apartment."

"You're too kind…"

Nikos nodded and disappeared below decks.

Naomi stayed outside. The night air was cool and the sea was calm and there were so many stars glittering in the sky. It was a perfect night.

Too bad she was alone—but that was her choice. It was for the best.

As the yacht pulled away from Mythelios and the island grew smaller, she began to long for something different. For a second chance and a life there with Chris. But Chris had just come here to say goodbye to his grandmother and deal with her affairs after she'd passed. His time on the island might not be permanent.

Chris would most likely return to Manhattan, or even go on somewhere else. And she had a great job and didn't want to give it up to follow a man who probably didn't really want her—not after what had happened between them before.

Even if his father *had* said Chris's string of affairs had been an attempt to get over losing her…

She needed to hear those words from Chris, and he

hadn't been very forthcoming about it. She wasn't sure that she could put her whole life on the line again. She'd be a fool if she did—but that old part of her wanted her to take a chance, nonetheless.

"You're cursed, Naomi. Cursed."

She shook her crazy *yia-yia's* words from her head. She had to stop thinking about this. There was so much to do this week. The bachelor auction was coming up fast, and she'd promised to help Chris with Stavros's surgery. Then there was Giorgos, who still needed careful monitoring, and Chris had agreed to help her with that.

She had to focus on her career. That was all she had time for. Because the alternative—love, happiness—had brought about a world of hurt the last time she'd experienced it, and she wasn't willing to put herself through that kind of pain again.

CHAPTER NINE

CHRIS WAS UNUSUALLY quiet the next morning, when they met at the clinic to do an emergency surgery on a patient who was having a gallbladder attack. Not that Naomi could blame him. Things had not gone well with his father the night before.

This was the Chris she remembered from when things had ended between them in Nashville, just before he'd left for Manhattan and hadn't looked back. This quiet, brooding, cold man who had broken her heart. The man she'd almost thrown it all away for.

Although according to Nikos Moustakas, Chris had looked back and regretted it...

Still, Chris hadn't ever said the words, and she wasn't going to pursue it. What was the point? It was ancient history now.

They stood in the small scrub room side by side as their patient was taken away to the post-anesthesia care unit.

"You did good in there," Chris remarked. "I haven't seen a gallstone that big in so long—although, granted, it's been a while since I've assisted in a cholecystectomy. I'm not usually called on to assist a general surgeon."

"Thank you," she said. "I'm glad I was able to help. It just sucks that the patient was so close to rupture. She'd probably been feeling ill for months. She said something